"The past has us terrified to reach for anything in the future…"

"What is it about you, Margo Ballad?" Gideon asked huskily.

"You ask me that like I know." Margo answered honestly. "I'm just me. I guess folks aren't accustomed to people wearing their hearts on their sleeve anymore. Everyone is so hidden, afraid of being who they really are or being hurt by it."

"Aren't you?"

"I am. Terrified, actually, but I don't know how to be any other way."

"And that's what makes you special."

"Ready to head back?" Margo asked, not sure what to say to his compliment. "If we take this path, we'll end up back in the movie theater parking lot."

"I love Charlotte for this," Gideon said as they began walking again. "Each road leads back to home."

"And do you think of Charlotte…as home?"

Gideon glanced at her. "Yeah…yeah, I do. It feels good here. Claire is happy, and I am too."

She could see Gideon and Claire's future easily. Could see him and his daughter being happy in Charlotte, but where did she fit in?

That was the big questio

Dear Reader,

As a military wife, a devoted member of the United Service Organizations (USO) and deeply connected to the Wounded Warrior community due to my husband's service, I have borne witness to the incredible challenges faced by our brave soldiers and their loved ones. I've seen friends and my husband's fellow warriors navigate the treacherous terrain of deployments, love and loss. In my heart, I've always held a fervent wish: that every hero and heroine of our armed forces could return home to a life brimming with joy and family. This is precisely why I am so passionate about crafting stories that depict military men and women finding their own happily-ever-afters within the pages of my books.

My pride in my husband's service knows no bounds. Despite enduring the harrowing experience of three separate explosions, he defied the odds and returned home to us, whereas others were not as fortunate. In *A Home for the Marine*, Margo and Gideon show courage as they confront some of these same issues. It is also a testament to the unbreakable bonds of the Ballad family. I hope that you will find immense joy in embarking on this journey alongside Margo, Gideon and the entire Ballad clan.

Kellie

HEARTWARMING

A Home for the Marine

—

Kellie A. King

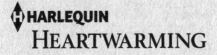

HARLEQUIN®
HEARTWARMING™

Recycling programs
for this product may
not exist in your area.

ISBN-13: 978-1-335-47584-8

A Home for the Marine

Harlequin Enterprises ULC
22 Adelaide St. West, 41st Floor
Toronto, Ontario M5H 4E3, Canada
www.Harlequin.com

Printed in U.S.A.

Kellie A. King is the *USA TODAY* bestselling author with a hint of Caribbean spice. Born and raised in Barbados, she now lives in Charlotte, North Carolina, with her large family. Kellie is married to her longtime love—her "Sarge" is always with her for every adventure. As an author of color, Kellie features strong heroines with a proud cultural heritage. Writing is her passion, and she hopes to inspire your imagination within the pages of her books.

Books by Kellie A. King

Harlequin Heartwarming

A Home for the Doctor

Visit the Author Profile page
at Harlequin.com.

To Nurse Margo

If anyone needs to see a warrior and a hero
with a heart of gold, it would be you. You're a
rock star in my world and I'm blessed to know you.
Thank you for our grandson, Griffyn.

CHAPTER ONE

ANOTHER SPRING AT Ballad Inn and life had evolved tremendously. In nearby Crawford's pasture new houses were being built. Margo Ballad's sister Mia and her husband Ryan were already living in their own home and ground had been broken for homes for the rest of the family. Ballad Inn, the business the three sisters had created, was flourishing. They were booked solid from July through October, with July having two weddings on the property.

Margo was now a private home health nurse to various clients. It was easier to go to their homes and give them more personal care. The agency she worked for made patient care a wonderful priority. The policies at the rest home didn't favor the seniors she was responsible for and with no changes being made Margo knew she had to leave. The new job also gave her more time at home at the inn, and to be in the kitchen, where creating her dishes calmed her.

It was also a time of change because sister number three had fallen off the roof and broken her wrist. Margo shook her head recalling the sound of tumbling, a falling scream, then a cry of "Ballad Girl down!" She'd been working the front desk. She and Mia ran out the front door to see Micki lying close to the bush that her body had bounced off. It was the only thing that'd kept her from being injured worse. As it was, Micki was holding her injured hand and when Margo looked at it, it was easy to tell that she'd broken her wrist.

"I'm putting my foot down, Micki," Mia told their sister at the hospital that night. "No more crazy handyman stuff. I'm hiring an on-site maintenance person and contractor. We make enough."

"Where are they gonna live?" Micki shot back.

"We have the little apartment above the garage that we only use for storage. If we clean it out, it could work," Mia replied seamlessly. "Until then, whoever we hire can live in one of the guest rooms."

"But…"

Mia raised her hand. "No buts, Michelle."

"You used my full name!" Micki hissed. "How dare you, ma'am! You affront my sensibilities with your insult!"

"What?" Mia said in confusion.

"It's probably the pain medication they gave her while the doctor set her arm," Margo told her sister, amused.

"Either way—*Micki*—" Mia emphasized the word. "No more handyman stuff, you should be concentrating on other things."

"Yeah, I know. I was waiting to tell you I'm starting law school in the fall, so we'll need to hire someone anyway." Micki sighed.

"Micki!" Mia fanned her face as tears formed in her eyes.

"You didn't tell us!" Margo gasped happily and hugged her.

"I didn't want to say anything until I got the acceptance letter," Micki grumbled. "That and you guys act like this. I started some of the pre-law classes online and found I had a knack for it. I took the LSAT and smashed it. My teacher was impressed and wrote a recommendation letter for Carolina Shores University, Charlotte Campus, and I got in."

"Our baby is growing up." Mia's laugh was full of emotion.

Micki pointed at her with her good hand. "I'm going to be on this new guy twenty-four seven. There's a certain care needed for Ballad Inn, she's finicky."

"Huh." Margo mused. "I never thought of the inn as a woman."

"Created by women, run by women—it's like the obvious choice," Micki pointed out.

That was a week ago and Margo was impressed that Mia had already found a replacement. They wanted someone diligent, someone they could trust. Plus, they wanted to give a veteran the opportunity to have a full-time job. They placed the notice on all online employment sites listing that veterans would be given preference, with background checks and the right references. A new hire was made in days, and Margo would be the one to get him all settled when he arrived. Mia had an appointment and Ryan went with her, something was going on with those two, but Margo couldn't quite put her fingers on it. Her sister and brother-in-law would share when they were ready. She sent up a prayer that all was okay.

A noise from the porch caught her attention. It was more like a combination of noises. Curiosity was about to drive her from behind the reception desk when the front door was thrown open and a large man filled the entrance way. The pink-and-gray strap of a baby bag was around his neck, under his arms was a folded-up something, possibly a booster seat, which he attempted to lean against the wall. All the while a set of chubby legs kicked. The cutest baby girl had her head thrown back laughing. She grabbed her father's face trying to give him a kiss.

"Claire—okay. I love you too, sweetie pie, but let Daddy…"

His voice faded away as he began to lose his

grip on the squirming body of the toddler he held. There was no other option than to put her down. The baby girl he called Claire dashed away like she had the wings of Hermes on her feet. That was when Margo moved. Before the baby could round the corner and head to the hallway that led to the kitchen, she picked Claire up and brought her back to her father.

"Hold on there, Speedy," Margo said with a laugh. Her heart melted when the baby girl smiled back. "Hello."

"Lo-lo," a tiny voice answered and began to tell Margo something in baby gibberish.

"Sorry about that." He finally set everything down and took his daughter from Margo's arms.

"Not a problem. She's cute and apparently has a lot to say." Margo laughed. "Now, how can I help you? Did you have a reservation?"

He frowned. "I'm Gideon Holder, the new on-site maintenance man."

"Oh— Oh!" Margo exclaimed. "We're expecting you, but I didn't know you had a family."

"Only my daughter," he answered simply.

Margo smiled. "That's still a family. Well, the room that we were giving you until the apartment over the garage is finished definitely won't do. That little one will need her own space too. Let me go see what I can do about that."

"You don't have to go to any trouble." Gideon

played with his daughter's hand while Margo went behind the desk. "I have her pack and play. That can do for a few months until we have a place to set up her crib."

"It's no trouble at all." Margo lifted her head and smiled. Each time the baby smiled at her, she felt a fist squeeze sweetly around her heart.

She focused on the computer screen, tapping lightly at the keyboard and talked to herself. "There it is. Yep, I can switch this here and give them this room... Perfect."

"I take it you have good news?" Gideon's voice held amusement.

She laughed self-consciously. "Sorry, I tend to talk to myself."

"That's fine. We all do it. Sometimes we are the best conversation around," he teased.

"I agree." Margo reached into a drawer for a key. "Well, I call it creativity because sometimes the only one who can answer the question is me."

"Touché." His voice was an appealing deep baritone. "So where are we heading?"

"We're heading up to the second floor." Margo came around the desk again. "I'll help you get this stuff to your room."

"You don't have to," Gideon said quickly.

"It's absolutely okay. I want to." Margo bent over to pick up the bag and what she assumed was the pack and play. "If she has a stroller we can store that in the hall closet so you don't have to lug it up and down the stairs anytime you need to use it."

"You sure?" Gideon followed behind her.

"Yep, its only paper towels and stuff like that on the shelves in there. Plenty of room." Margo trudged up the stairs to the second floor speaking as she walked. "We don't have an elevator. Sorry, but we kept the house as true to its original build as possible."

"As you should. It's a great historic Queen Anne–style house with a wraparound verandah no less," Gideon remarked. "Has the house been designated as a historical landmark?"

Margo frowned. "I think Mia said something about having the certificates done after it was toured by the society three years ago. We're one of the first houses built in this area. I can't remember what year Mia said. You'll meet her and she can tell you what you need to know."

"Great. I want to ensure if I fix anything it stays true to the design," he said.

Margo got to the room and unlocked it before handing him the key. "We don't use key cards—again part of the historic value of the house. We didn't want to ruin the doors with those metal slot thingies."

They stepped inside and put down his things before she showed him around the rooms.

"This suite has its own bathroom and a small bedroom, while the main room has a pullout love seat," Margo explained. "There's plenty of space if you want to get her crib and a few of her things to make it more comfortable for Claire?"

She let the words hang in the air until he answered.

"Sound great. Thanks," Gideon replied. "This little Claire Bear is two."

"Two? Aren't you a big girl," Margo crooned.

"Two!" Claire said the word distinctly. "Heyyyy Dad-deee, ba-ba-ba."

She went off on a string of garbled baby speak and Gideon nodded sagely like he understood every word.

"Care to enlighten those of us who don't speak baby?" Margo asked with a grin.

"She wants her milk and a nap." Gideon chuckled. "We stayed in a motel in South Carolina last night and had a decent breakfast before we left. So, it's time for her lunch plus milk, and an afternoon nap."

Claire was a mass of reddish-brown curls and wide hazel eyes set in plump rosy cheeks. A little pink bow sat crooked in her hair. Margo could only guess that trying to get an energetic baby girl dressed and organized was an effort. She smiled at the little girl but stepped away. That sweet ache was becoming something more, and the memories of the past would buckle her if she didn't leave.

"I'll let you guys get settled so Claire Bear can have her nap," Margo said softly. "We eat a family style meal around six in the evening. If you have a high chair…"

"I have one," he answered.

Margo ran her hand against the smooth door frame that led from one room to the other. "Great, and there's the light switch… Well, you can see it for yourself. Dinner at six."

"Thank you," Gideon called after her.

She raised her hand in a wave and left the room, closing the door as quietly behind her as she could. Heading back downstairs she thought about Gideon and his hazel eyes that matched his daughter's. He was tall compared to her own average height, and the military haircut accentuated his rugged jawline. He didn't raise his voice; it was right in the middle of a baritone. She could just tell that Claire fell asleep listening to him read a story in that calming cadence.

Margo's caring personality told her that he had been through a lot, but it was his story to tell. She also knew that she could find herself caring too much and ending up with hurt feelings, especially to do with Claire. They were a sad reminder of a long-ago time in her life. One she never truly got over.

Margo went back to the front desk and focused on the to-do list that Mia had left. Her very particular sister's detailed bullet points included her preferred method of how to change the plastic jug in the water cooler.

"Mia, you are a giant pain in my neck," Margo murmured, but she would have her sister no other way.

Mia, trailed by Micki and Ryan came through the door thirty minutes later. She'd just checked out their last guest. June would be stock car racing season and they never took guests during that month after the last debacle of bad customers, bad weather and just a general badness all round from previous enthusiasts who'd stayed at the inn. Instead, it would be a time for renovations and prep for the first wedding right after the Fourth of July.

Their schedule was booked well into next year. After a family meeting they'd decided that June would be the one month they closed for vacation. New staff would be coming on to be trained to help with events, so Mia had two employee workshops for new hires in their vacation month as well.

"Hey, family, where did you find our bird with the broken wing?" Margo teased—meaning her younger sister, Micki.

"We saw the poor thing outside under a tree

and decided to save it," Mia replied. "Ryan coaxed it with some sugary water and then it came home with us willingly."

"Ha-ha." Mick rolled her eyes.

"Look, Micki, cotton candy." Ryan pulled a bag of blue and pink sugary strands from his knapsack.

"Ooh gimme." She snatched the parcel and held it against her body with her casted hand and tried to open it with the other. When that didn't work, she used her teeth.

"See, sugary," Ryan remarked as Micki shoved a piece of the sweet treat in her mouth.

Micki leaned against the reception desk. "First of all, I don't care what y'all say. Secondly, for some reason the hospital has the best cotton candy. It's like how? Why?"

"I think they get it delivered from Carowinds or something. Who knows?" Ryan replied.

"How did everything go?" Margo asked her sister and brother-in-law.

She saw the look that passed between them. The sadness that crossed over Mia's face was fleeting before she put on a bright smile. "Fine. It was all good."

"We'd probably believe that if we knew what it was," Micki pointed out.

"Tax stuff." Mia lied. They knew it, but they let it go.

"The new handyman, contractor, maintenance guru, whatever title you decided on is here," Margo said. "Gideon Holder and his daughter are now in residence."

"Whoa, daughter?" Micki looked at Mia. "You didn't tell us he had a kid."

Mia sighed. "Shoot, it slipped my mind. Sorry, guys."

Margo smiled. "It's not a problem. Claire is a two-year-old cutie."

"A baby I can spoil." Micki clapped her hands. "I wonder if she would like Monty."

"She's a toddler," Ryan said drolly. "Just keep her from trying to taste him."

"Ewww, no!" Margo shook her head. She would have to tell Gideon about her menagerie of pets. It wouldn't be wise to pet them without her or a family member around.

"Well, I can't wait to meet my replacement." Micki popped another piece of cotton candy in her mouth.

"You better be nice, Micki." Margo snagged the bag of cotton candy from her hand. "You can have the rest of this after dinner. Mia, the desk is yours. I'm going to my domain."

"I'm a grown woman," Micki called out behind her.

"Yep, you are a grown woman who will ruin her dinner."

Margo entered the kitchen grinning and surveyed the wide room. Two baker's racks stood along the far wall, they'd chosen an open cupboard design for her spices, and the copper pans hung over the stone hearth. They didn't use the fireplace anymore, but it made the room feel more homey and comfortable. She sighed at the sense of peace that overcame her.

She pulled out ingredients for that evening's dinner and dessert, and put on the radio to her favorite station—humming along lightly as she worked. Gideon and Claire filtered through her mind, and she smiled for just a moment. *Stay away, don't get attached*, because Margo knew she would. Nothing could replace what she'd lost.

THE EVENING CAME but daylight savings time in Charlotte meant the sun didn't go down until after seven. Sometimes you could sit on the verandah and watch the oranges and yellows of the sunset blend with the Carolina blue sky. The sun was still up when Margo and Enid got the food on the table. The family came in first, and finally Gideon came downstairs with his daughter, Claire.

"Um, hi?" Gideon said from the doorway.

"Hi, hi, hi," Claire sang out and waved a small hand.

"Hey, guys." Margo looked away and pasted a

bright smile on her face. "Let me introduce you to the rest of the gang."

"I can intro myself," Micki said, and stuck out her hand. "I'm Micki Ballad. Just call me Micki. You're filling my shoes, buddy."

Micki shook his hand and Margo saw she was trying to squeeze his fingers firmly—a sign of superiority. She almost laughed when Gideon didn't even flinch.

"Nice to meet you," Gideon replied with a grin.

Micki stopped for a second or two before she laughed out loud. "I like you. Plus, you have a baby and that's my kryptonite."

"This is Claire," Gideon introduced his daughter.

"Hey, little girl," Micki crooned. "Will she let me hold her?"

"Go for it," Gideon answered. "If she doesn't want to be held, she'll be very vocal about it."

"Ah, my kind of girl." Micki held out her hands and Claire reached out to be held, making Micki beam. "Look, she likes me! I got to hold her first."

"Actually, I held her first." Margo claimed her victory. "Anyway, this is Mia, the oldest of the trio and her husband Dr. Ryan Cassidy."

"Nice to meet you." Mia also shook his hand. "Your daughter has enthralled us all, I think."

Ryan was next. "Luckily you have an on-site

pediatrician and nurse available in case she ever needs us."

"You're a pediatrician?" Gideon asked.

Ryan nodded. "Indeed, and Margo is a registered nurse with a Master's of Science in Nursing."

Gideon turned to her. "You didn't tell me that."

"We didn't have much of a conversation," Margo said and changed the subject quickly. "And this is our Enid. She's the foundation of this house and everyone in it."

"Nice to meet you, Mrs. Ballad," Gideon said politely.

Enid laughed. "Oh no. I only helped raise these girls. Their parents travel frequently. I'm the chief cook and housekeeper."

Gideon nodded. "I'm sorry I presumed."

Enid patted his shoulder. "It's not a problem. You brought a baby I can spoil."

Micki danced around with the baby. "Besides she was practically our mother."

"Let's eat before this all gets cold," Margo said. "Gideon, I set up the high chair you brought next to your chair."

"Great. Thank you." Gideon held out his hands for his daughter. "Time for nom-noms, Claire Bear."

Claire kicked her little feet as he tried to put her into the chair. "Nom-nom-nom-nom."

They all laughed, as they sat around the large mahogany table, and started to pass the serving dishes. Margo took in account their new tiny guest, and made mashed potatoes and soft peas, while the others also had roasted chicken and its natural gravy, biscuits, salad. For dessert she made pineapple upside-down cake with fresh whipped cream. Gideon made sure the baby's plate was made and her cup with water was close by. He fastened a plastic bib around her neck before pressing a kiss in her hair.

"Eat up, little girl," he said gently.

The conversation went back and forth as they ate, more from them than Gideon, so she tried to make him comfortable.

"So, you were in the military?" Margo asked casually.

Gideon nodded. "Marine. I did a few tours and became a full-time dad when I came home."

"No mother?" Enid asked bluntly.

"Enid, no…" Mia said.

Gideon held up his hand. "No, it's fine. Claire's mother passed away soon after I returned from my last deployment. Then it was just me and her. This job gives us a fresh start away from old memories."

"Well, we're sorry for your loss." Margo shot a glare toward Enid who glared back in return.

"You drove cross-country with Claire?" Micki asked. "That's quite a journey."

"We drove all the way here from Tacoma and saw the sights as we went along." He spoke after a mouthful of food. "By myself it would take about forty-eight hours. With my precious cargo, it took around four days. I stopped when she was tired, of course, and got a hotel room for the night."

"I want to do that on a motorcycle one day— drive cross-country," Micki said with a wistful sigh.

"But she won't because she doesn't want me to die of a heart attack," Enid said sweetly.

Micki rolled her eyes. "Of course, I won't."

"I saw that look, little miss thang," Enid scolded. "Don't make me put you on KP duty the rest of the week."

"Yes, ma'am."

Margo glanced at Gideon who grinned in her direction, making her smile in response. While they chatted, Claire tore into her food. The potatoes disappeared in no time, followed by the peas. Once that was gone, she gobbled up dessert.

"She eats like a linebacker," Margo said in approval. "My kinda girl."

"Wait till you see her eat oatmeal and fruit in the mornings," Gideon said, amused.

"I look forward to that." Margo chose to ignore the teasing looks that passed between her family.

"Is it okay if I put her in the stroller and tour the grounds tomorrow?" Gideon asked. "I'd like to check out the property and buildings, see my workspace and all that."

"Please, go ahead. Margo can show you around," Mia offered up with a wide smile.

"I'd love to," Margo said warmly. She pinned Mia with a quick look.

"Great, well this has been the best meal I've had in a long time—well, we've had. I'm sure Claire was sick of my cooking," Gideon said with genuine warmth in his voice.

Margo could tell he was relaxing in this new environment already. The wariness in his eyes had faded but the exhaustion remained.

"I'm going to go get this messy one in the tub. She'll be ready for a bottle of warm milk and then she'll be out for the night." Gideon cleaned his daughter up as best he could and tried to also tidy up the high chair.

"Don't worry, we can get that," Margo told him. "Go on up with her."

"I left her stuff, like her milk and juice cups, in the kitchen, if that's okay," Gideon said hesitantly.

"No worries at all." Enid got up and began to bustle around with the leftovers of the meal.

"Our home is your home until the apartment is ready. I'll clear some space in the mudroom for any of her things that don't fit upstairs."

"Thank you, everyone, for everything." Gideon hesitated. "I think this will be a good fit for us."

Mia's tone was confident when she spoke. "I think we made the right choice."

"Well, good night, all, and thanks again," Gideon told them. "Say nighty night, Claire Bear."

"Nite-nite." Claire waved over his shoulder.

They echoed their good-nights and watched as he climbed the stairs with the baby still happily waving her tiny arm. Margo waited until he was out of sight before looking at Mia.

"What the heckity-heck was that?" Margo exclaimed. "Why did you just offer me up on a silver platter."

"Margo, I offered for you to show him around the property, not to be the entrée in a luau." Mia laughed. "Besides, it was cute, how you guys kept glancing at each other when you thought the other wasn't looking."

"We were not!" Her faced warmed. "I just don't think it's my place."

"It won't take long, sis." Micki laughed now. "And this way you can make goo-goo eyes at him with no one looking."

"Ryan, help," Margo pleaded.

He looked immediately at the open doorway. "What's that? I'm needed in the kitchen. On my way."

"Ryan, there is no one in the kitchen," Margo said dryly.

"Yeah, but it's an escape. I know better than to get in the middle of the notorious Ballad girls." Ryan grinned.

"I don't want you hanging with Mr. Bolton or Marley anymore." Mia ruffled her husband's hair and kissed him. "They teach you bad things."

Margo pointed at each of them. "All you people are too much."

"Oh, honey, you are one of us." Mia stood and came over to hug her shoulders. "Now, help clean up, so I can go home and water my garden."

"Never thought I'd hear her say that about cleaning." Micki grabbed a chafing dish.

Margo shook her head in amusement. Love. This was her unique family and she loved them, even though they were exasperating. Now she had to figure out how to keep a safe distance from Gideon and his daughter while maintaining a professional and polite business relationship. *That girl was a cute little Claire Bear to a very handsome father*, she thought to herself. She ducked her head so her braids would cover her face while she helped her sisters clear the table. It seemed they could always tell exactly what she was thinking.

CHAPTER TWO

GIDEON HAD BEEN looking out at the property while Claire slept in the pack and play after dinner. Eventually, he'd fallen asleep too. When he woke, he got up and put her into her bed. Now he was wide-awake and sitting on the balcony right outside his room. The second-floor balcony wrapped around the building and each room had an entrance. Gideon sat listening to the night sounds of the new place that he would call home. The moon was high in the sky casting an almost ethereal hue over the tress and landscaped acres of Ballad Inn. It felt good here. He hadn't expected it to, but his shoulders relaxed from the release of the heavy weight of stress. It was the first time in a very long while that he wasn't worried about a work schedule or who would look after Claire if he was forced to do overtime.

This job had good hours with great pay, plus a lovely place where he and Claire would be living. It also got him away from Tacoma. There were too many memories and old hurts there.

Charlotte, North Carolina offered him and Claire a new start, and amazing weather. Washington State was known for its rainfall. Here it was sunshine and blue skies more often than not.

His mind turned to the family of Ballad Inn—the three sisters that ran it, and their personalities. Margo seemed the quietest with shy smiles and a sweet disposition. Claire had immediately taken to her—well, all of them—which surprised him because his daughter was very hesitant around new people. Yet she let each of the sisters play with her and both Margo and Micki held her without the usual sirens of unhappy screams.

Margo had kind brown eyes and braids she kept tied back neatly at her nape. Her skin was the color of a dark sable brown, and she had an easy smile. He could see a spark in her though and wondered if she was maybe more of a spitfire than people realized. *This will be a good fit*, Gideon thought to himself knowing it was the right decision to move.

He had a few days before he started his new job. He would use that time to explore the area and their surroundings. It would also give him a chance to get Claire registered into the daycare Mia recommended after he got the job. He wanted to visit first before he committed to his daughter being placed there, but it was close enough to the inn that he could put her in her stroller and walk there. He'd be able to have leisurely mornings with his daughter before he kissed her goodbye until four in the afternoon. He couldn't find that in Tacoma and Gideon was looking forward to it now.

With his penchant for sweets, he was invited to raid the fridge or kitchen anytime he wanted. Maybe there was ice cream in the fridge, or pie. The thought made him give the stars one last glance before leaving the balcony to check on Claire, then grab the baby monitor and head downstairs. It was a good way to start their new life, with dessert, a tall glass of cold milk and sitting on the balcony watching the night sky. He found the kitchen easily enough, before flicking on the light switch. When he opened the fridge, the first thing Gideon saw was an already sliced layered chocolate cake.

"Oh, I'm going to need to take up running or something to burn off these calories."

Gideon grinned as he took the cake from the shelf and grabbed the milk before finding a glass, plate, and knife. Not that he was really worried, he worked with his hands, and would be all over the grounds doing his job. It was pretty much a certainty he would get more than enough exercise daily.

The light flicked on just as he got the thick

slice on a plate and was licking the chocolate ganache off his fingers. Margo stood at the door wearing red pajamas with happy faces and holding a baseball bat.

"Running away to become a baseball player for the…" Gideon stopped. "Does Charlotte have a baseball team?"

"Minor league, they're called the Charlotte Knights." Margo lowered the bat from over her head. "You're lucky I didn't bean you."

"Bean me?" Gideon repeated the words amused.

"Yeah." Margo made a motion with the bat. "You know like upside the head."

"You'd have a time trying to reach me." Gideon chuckled.

"Ha-ha. I've heard all the short aka pixie-sized jokes there are." She leaned the bat by the door. "I thought we were being robbed."

"Of chocolate cake?" He held up the plate. "You said eat what I like so…"

"You went for a sugar rush?" Margo said amused. "Have whatever you like, but that's sure to give you nightmares."

Gideon shrugged. "I don't dream. Well, not anymore, so I'm good."

"You don't dream?" Margo went around the counter to the fridge and pulled out a bottle of juice.

"I was in the military. After seeing what I

have—being able to sleep without them is a blessing," he explained.

"I can only imagine." Her voice was filled with sympathy. "I hope you get to have good dreams when they return. Is Claire Bear asleep?"

Gideon was pleased she used Claire's pet name. "Deeply, the trip and then that amazing dinner took her out."

"I'm sure she's going to be running around this place in no time," Margo said. "Which reminds me, in the upstairs family room, we have another family member. Monty is my bearded dragon who lives in his aquarium next to the window. Claire is welcome to meet him, just don't let her be too rough and make sure she washes her hands afterwards."

"You have a lizard named Monty?" His lips twitched.

She nodded. "Yep, there's also Blizzard and Snow-cone the rabbits in our backyard. But they are not my fault. Ryan is an amateur magician, and he had them in a hat to entertain the kids at the hospital. I liberated them."

"Ah, so you like to take care of things—animals and people," Gideon said knowingly.

Margo shrugged. "Sometimes it's necessary. Everyone needs a little extra care sometimes. There's also Doodle, our neighbor Walter's cat. He's Monty's nemesis, or they have some weird love story, we're unsure. But he sneaks into the house to get at Monty, so if you see that bright orange menace, put him outside."

"Oh, this is great," Gideon said, grinning. "You guys have some unique scenarios going on here."

Margo laughed. "It is a little bit out of control, isn't it?"

"In a good way," he replied. "I should get back upstairs and check on my little one. So tomorrow, the tour, right?"

"Yes!" Margo said brightly. "Mia also told me Claire is going to Tiny Tots Academy down the street. My friend Ellen runs the program, and I can take you to meet her as well."

"Sure. I was going to call and ask for an in-person meeting before registering her," Gideon said gratefully. "This kills two birds with one stone."

Margo grimaced. "I don't like that saying. I'm always, like, poor birds."

"You're a kind soul. It's easy to see why it would bother you," he said gently. "Anyway, see you tomorrow?"

"You will." Margo shrugged. "Can't help it around Ballad Inn."

Gideon took his milk and chocolate cake, with a quick nod and a smile, he headed back upstairs to his room. After checking on Claire, Gideon went back outside to enjoy the night, and put a big mouthful of the chocolate cake into his mouth. He closed his eyes at the decadent sweet taste and then took a gulp of the cold milk. Whoever made the cake knew how to hit his weak spot, and he was okay with it. Gideon grinned as he looked out into the night. Yep, he'd made a great choice taking this job.

WAKING UP LATE with the birds singing outside and a light breeze coming through an open window was something new for both Gideon and Claire. Usually they were up by six, out of the house by seven thirty, and he was dropping her off at her babysitter's. He worked long hours in construction and hated the fact that she spent more time in the care of others instead of being with him.

Today, his eyes opened slowly to a room filled with sunlight instead of catching a glimpse of cloudy skies and rain. Claire had woken up in the middle of the night and fretted, not wanting to go back to sleep without him. He ended up tucking her close to him with her favorite blanket, and they drifted off to sleep together. Now, she rolled over and looked at Gideon, smiling around her pacifier, and his heart almost burst with love.

"Hey, sweet girl," he said, his voice still scratchy with sleep.

"Daadee." Claire laid her head on his chest and patted his stomach. "Nom-nom-nom."

Gideon chuckled and sat up. "Okay, you little cookie monster. I get it. Time for breakfast."

He got her cleaned up first, dressing her in a mint-green T-shirt and little yellow overalls. Her sneakers had tiny flowers and when she knocked them together, they lit up and jingled. Gideon put her in the playpen and made quick work of his own morning routine. He lifted her into his arms and off they went to see what they could find for breakfast in their new home.

Gideon stepped into the kitchen that smelled of fresh baked cinnamon rolls and bacon. The sweet and savory aromas made his stomach growl. Enid was there, and Margo too, dressed in light blue scrubs with her hair pulled back.

"Morning," Gideon said politely.

"Heyyy." Claire lifted her hand in a little wave.

"Isn't she the sweetest?" Enid rushed over to take her. "Oh, look at you. So pretty this morning. Do you want something to eat?"

Claire gave a cute head nod and Enid walked off with the baby to show her all the yummy things for breakfast.

"I'd like to eat too." Gideon raised his hand.

Margo laughed. "Give up and fend for yourself. She can no longer hear your pleas of hunger over the happy baby endorphins now coursing through her brain. Coffee is over there." She pointed to the counter.

"Did you have guests this morning?" Gideon asked. "There's a whole lot of food here."

"No, we don't have any reservations until the end of the month. Enid just doesn't know how to make a small breakfast," Margo said in an overly loud voice.

"I'd hear you, even if you whispered, little girl," Enid replied. "Ryan and Mia will stop in and eat it. Or Hunter, that's our landscaper, if he drops by. Don't make me warn you off again for being lippy."

"How was I being lippy?" Margo asked in fake surprise, giving Gideon a wink.

"You know." Enid passed behind her and nudged her with her shoulder. "Don't make me."

"Yes, ma'am."

Gideon smiled at the interaction as he made his coffee and a plate to eat. The Ballads were close-knit, he could tell, and that kind of family unity wasn't something he'd ever seen or experienced. It was nice seeing how they embraced him and Claire so easily. They hadn't been there for a good twenty-four hours yet and it already felt comfortable.

"Working?" Gideon asked.

"Yes, for a few hours. I'll be back by two,

and then I can show you around," Margo said brightly.

"You're not a hospital nurse?" he asked.

"No, I used to be, but I left that job. I didn't like how they valued money over patient care," she explained. "I have regular patients I see through the service I work for. I'm able to treat them at their homes however many times a week they need me."

"How many patients do you have?" Gideon asked.

Margo packed a small cooler while she spoke. "Eight right now. Some days it varies."

"I'm not being nosy, I promise, but how does your job work exactly?" Gideon asked.

"No worries, I have people ask me that all the time." Margo went through her bag, and he watched her make sure her tablet and other supplies were there. "Rather than being in assisted living facilities or rest homes, some people can opt to stay at home. Many times, this is something patients or their families set up years in advance and organized their retirement plans to pay for it. I do home visits to make sure patients are maintaining the baseline for any medical issues they may have. I'm always in contact with their doctors about medications, and if anything needs to be changed in their care plan."

"Sounds like a service for the wealthy," Gideon surmised.

Margo's lips formed a firm line. "Money isn't associated with patient care at the agency I work for. We have seniors from all income brackets and even help families find financial assistance if they need it."

Gideon could tell his words had offended her. "I'm sorry, I didn't mean any offense by it."

Margo sighed. "It's not you, it's me. I'm all prickly when it comes to this subject. I've seen too many people struggle and sort of waste away. Families absent or uncaring. Everyone should be offered the dignity to age with grace, not just be dumped or ignored when being old or diagnosed with something makes it more difficult. That's why I picked this area of the nursing profession. Everyone wanted to work with babies, and I chose the elderly because that part of life is just as important."

"You're right," Gideon agreed. "I'm one that wishes I still had my parents around."

"Ours are, they just travel a lot." Margo grabbed her things. "I need to get going, but I'll be back around two, maybe two thirty. Is that okay?"

He nodded. "Works perfect. Claire Bear will have had some lunch and a nap. She'll be at her best."

"Okay. See you then."

Claire waved a hand at Margo. "Byeee!"

He watched emotion cross over her face. Was it sadness? It was so quick before she fixed a mask firmly in place.

"Bye-bye, Claire Bear." Margo smiled but her eyes were still sad. Gideon wondered what she had faced in her life that brought back unhappy memories.

Too early for you to be digging into these ladies' business, he told himself. He sat down at the farm-style kitchen table to eat with his daughter.

AFTER THE MEAL, he found Mia in the inn's office and, while bouncing Claire on his knee, he tried to complete his employment forms and discuss the specifics of his job requirements. Claire saw things she could touch and tried to wriggle out of his arms.

"Claire, please," he begged.

Mia laughed gently. "Here let me take her so you can actually write legibly."

"Thanks," Gideon said gratefully as Mia took her. "She turned two a month before we moved here, and it's like the terrible twos kicked in the exact same day."

"Tell your daddy you're a smart girl, and that means you need to explore," Mia said, bouncing Claire in her arms. "Between the three of us and

Enid, I hope you know, Gideon, she's going to be spoiled rotten."

"Enid started this morning. Claire had the biggest breakfast Enid could make," he said. "Speaking of which, our food cost. I'm good with you deducting it from my pay until the apartment is done."

"We won't be doing that." Mia smiled. "Anyone who works here, including our landscaper, Hunter, is welcome to join in for meals. Enid would never forgive me if I took anything from your check for food."

"Ah, well, we don't want that to happen." Gideon finished Mia's employment packet. "Can I at least help work on the house that's being built? I know you have a crew on it but I can lend a hand. It could be finished at less cost."

"Are you sure?" Mia asked doubtfully.

Gideon smiled. "Yeah, that's what I was hired for—to build, renovate and fix stuff."

"Then go for it. I'll let the crew know, so they don't think some stranger has just happened along to help them," Mia replied, grinning. She focused on Claire who smiled wide and patted her face. "You are such a doll. I could sniff your hair forever."

"That baby smell is addictive," he teased. "Be careful or you and Ryan might catch baby fever."

"We already have." Mia sighed wistfully.

"Well, time to get back to it. You guys are welcome anywhere in and out of the house. Margo's showing you around later, but that doesn't mean you can't explore on your own for a while."

"That's true, but I should go get the crib and a few other things from the storage place." Gideon stood and took Claire. "Do you think Enid would be okay watching her for a little bit? The place is right down seventy-four. I'm guessing that's close by."

"Enid will snatch your child as soon as you say can you watch her." Mia laughed. "Yep, for seventy-four, turn the opposite direction from how you came in and it's pretty easy to find after that."

Gideon hesitated at the door. "Great. Thank you again for everything, the job, the welcome, all of it. We needed this, and you can be assured that I'll give you and the inn my best."

"Of that we have no doubt." Mia gathered the papers he'd signed. "See you both later."

The trip took an hour each way, and by the time he came back, Gideon had her crib and other paraphernalia in the rear of his truck. The powerful four door truck was his other baby. The one thing he'd bought as soon as he'd returned from deployment. Claire's car seat and all her necessities fit wonderfully in the spacious back seat.

Upstairs in the inn, Claire played in their

room, while he set up her crib and added the sheets and her stuffed rabbit, plus her blanket.

"All done." He looked down at her. "Your castle is ready."

She held up her hands and he put her in her crib that was much better than the pack and play she'd slept in the night before. Claire promptly pulled her blanket up and found her pacifier. She rubbed the fuzzy ear of her bunny and went to sleep for her nap. With a sigh, Gideon walked back into the living room and sat on the small sofa before taking his phone in his hand. There was a call to make, and while it always tied his stomach in knots, Gideon knew it had to be done. He waited for the familiar voice to answer.

"Hello."

The soft voice of an older woman came across the line. Claire's grandmother from her mother's side. Since his wife's death, her parents had been hard to deal with. He understood they were hurting, but so was he, and Claire Bear.

"Hey, it's Gideon," he said. "I wanted you to know that we made it okay, and we're settling in just fine."

"I can't believe you did it. You took her so far away from us," Denise said angrily.

"I didn't take her away from you," Gideon said in a tired voice. "We just need to make a life of our own, away from…"

"From us. That's what you mean," she cut him off.

He pinched the bridge of his nose. "Can we not do this? I wanted you both to know we're okay. I'm not trying to exclude you. You can visit. Give me that much. Can't you see I'm trying to be cordial here?"

"Cordial! Like we're strangers," she gave a short laugh.

"Okay, I won't do this—not again," Gideon said. "We're fine. I'll talk to you another time."

Gideon disconnected the call and tipped his head back to rest on the sofa. Even this they wouldn't let be easy, but he'd made the hard choice for the life he and Claire deserved. He wasn't going back, and Gideon vowed to look toward a bright future with his daughter. One not steeped in broken dreams. He heard a small meow and looked out to the balcony to see the largest orange tabby cat he'd ever seen.

"Good grief!" He sat up, startled, and by the time he turned to the window again the animal was gone. "How did it move so quick?"

Time also moved quickly. When Margo got home, closer to two thirty, Claire Bear was up, and fed. Gideon stood on the porch, and his daughter stopped right against his leg. He was excited to see the area, and Margo's warm smile only made it better.

"Hey, look at you two enjoying the sunshine."
Margo closed the door to her own truck.

"Trust me, we needed this," Gideon replied.

"I guess I'd better get changed."

"Take your time. Claire can chase a ball
around on the lawn."

"I'm okay, just let me get into some clean
clothes." She ran up the steps quickly. "I won't
be long!"

Gideon watched her braids bounce, and then,
before the door closed, he heard her yell "Micki!
Don't you dare! Ack!"

He was almost tempted to go inside and see
what shenanigans the younger sister was up to.
Margo came out about ten minutes later with the
stroller from the hall closet.

"Alright let's hop to it," she said brightly.

Gideon clipped Claire into the stroller and she
kicked her legs happily. "Daycare first? I wanted
to get to them before they closed for the day."

"I was thinking the same thing."

He was instantly impressed with the small
but efficient daycare that was set up like a mini
classroom. There were nine children, and Claire
would make the tenth. Gideon liked the fact that
with three teachers the kids had personal attention. By the end of the visit, he knew Claire
would be starting on Monday, just like he'd be
at his new job. From there, the three of them

took a detour to walk around the Sardis Woods neighborhood.

Margo showed him the ice cream parlor, the hardware store and the place with the best burgers and fries.

"Just remember if you eat there, sneak it in, or bury the bag in the trash outside," Margo warned him. "Enid has a vendetta against any fast-food restaurants taking away from a home-cooked meal."

"I'll remember that," Gideon said solemnly. "I don't want to offend the person who makes all the desserts. That chocolate cake was divine."

"I'll have you know I made that cake." Margo took over pushing the stroller. "I just didn't want to toot my own horn in the kitchen last night."

"Ah, so you'll be the one to feed my sugar addiction." Gideon lifted his head and took a deep breath of the fresh air.

"We both will." Margo nudged him with her shoulder. "Be nice to us, or you'll be eating cauliflower bites for dessert."

Gideon shuddered. "Please don't destroy the sanctity of dessert."

They turned into the cul-de-sac and made their way toward the inn. Before getting there, they stopped in front of a house across the street.

"Hey, Mr. Marley, Mr. Bolton, this is our new on-site contractor, Gideon Holder," Margo called to the men who sat with a chessboard in front of them. "This is his daughter, Claire."

"Nice to meet you both." Gideon raised his hand in greeting.

"Does that mean Micki won't be bashing things and falling off ladders anymore?" the man wearing the fishing hat asked. "I'm Mr. Bolton by the way."

"She will not." Margo pointed at Gideon. "Fixing, replacing, upgrading, that's all up to him now."

Mr. Marley was wearing a veteran's hat and he looked over to Gideon. "You a serviceman, young fella?"

"Twelve years in the Marine Corp," Gideon replied.

Mr. Marley grinned and nodded. "I know a Devil Dog when I see one. Semper Fi!"

"Semper Fi and thank you for your service, sir," Gideon replied politely.

Mr. Bolton snorted. "He hasn't seen a military base in a while, son."

"Once a marine, always a marine." Gideon grinned. "It was nice to meet you both."

"A baby and those Ballad sisters," Mr. Bolton murmured and shook his head. "Things are about to get crazy."

"Have a good evening, you two," Margo said dryly.

Moving over to the Ballad property, Margo showed Gideon the workshop that would be his domain. Plenty of tools and supplies for whatever jobs he'd be starting with around the house and the grounds.

In the connecting shed, she showed Claire the rabbits, and Gideon watched as she taught Claire how to pet them gently. The Ballad property was a fantastic place—lots of room for the sisters to expand as families or growth of the business made it necessary. He was looking forward to starting his job, and the first thing on the list was the roof of the inn, the same one that Micki fell from.

By dinnertime, Gideon had the lay of the land and over dinner, he felt more inclined to talk and be less reserved. Ryan did magic tricks to entertain Claire, making her laugh, while the conversation was light and flittered from one thing to the next.

"So, Margo showed you around huh?" Ryan asked. "How did that go?"

"It went great. I love the area, oh, and I think I saw the orange cat this afternoon." Gideon chuckled. "I might be mistaken, because that cat moves pretty quick for his size."

"No, that was him," Mia said amused. "For such a large feline he's like a ninja."

"I guess I'll have to keep an eye out just in case." Gideon glanced at Margo, who met his gaze, and gave her a wink. "We've got Monty to protect."

"Thank you," Margo said. "Maybe we should have a mediation between the two. See if we can settle this."

"Interspecies mediation? I love this family." Ryan laughed. "Do you think it's a good fit for you, Gideon, or are we about to scare you away?"

Gideon glanced at Margo and their gazes connected. "Oh, I think I like what I've seen so far."

Margo looked away quickly and a slow smile crossed over Micki's face.

The rest of the meal was pleasant but uneventful. Later, everyone trailed away and like the night before, the baby went to bed easily and was asleep within minutes.

On impulse, he went downstairs again to feed his sweet tooth. *Maybe Margo would be there, and then another conversation would happen*, he mused with a smile. He opened the fridge, and this time found the half-eaten lemon meringue pie from dinner.

"I love everyone here," Gideon said as he took out the pie. "And I love you, you gloriously put together pie…"

The kitchen light flickered on, and Margo stood at the door. "Did you just compliment the pie?"

"Yes." Gideon felt no shame at his affection for dessert.

"Do you want me to turn off the light so you and the pie can be alone?"

"Nah, you can stay." He took the pie to the large island. "Our love is revealed."

Margo laughed. "You're a funny guy."

"I aim to please." He reached to grab a plate. "Do you want another slice?"

"No, I just came for a bottle of water. If I eat that now, that pie will have legs and haunt my nightmares. I'll grab my water and go."

"No, stay," Gideon said quickly. "I have the baby monitor. Stay, and we can talk."

"Okay," she said in a shy voice. She sat on one of the stools at the granite island. "So, Washington State, huh?"

"Born and raised. I guess I can say that." Gideon wrapped the pie with cellophane before putting it back in the fridge. "I was a military brat, so we moved around a lot, at least until my dad left the service. Still, I always felt unsettled, like I never really had an actual home."

"That's rough," Margo said, gently twisting the cap off the water bottle.

"I adapted, like I always do," he said, and cut into the thick slice of pie. "Kind of par for the course when it comes to my life lately."

"Is this why the big move?" she asked after a sip of water. Margo's eyes held sympathy.

"Me and Claire Bear only have each other. I need to give her a place where she can be happy and secure," Gideon explained. "This job allows me to have more time with her, and I can really watch her grow up."

"I guess you'll be frequenting all the activities for the kiddos with her." She smiled.

"I don't know the area. You'll have to show us around some more," Gideon hinted.

Margo nodded. "I'll free up some time in my schedule."

"I'd like that. I mean both me and Claire would like that."

"Well, it's back to bed for me. I'll be gone by the time you guys wake up. It's my early start tomorrow." She got up and took her bottle with her. "Good night, Gideon."

"G'night, Margo," he called after her.

He watched the door close, and this time finished his dessert in the dim light of the kitchen. The silence that surrounded him was comforting. It was like a security blanket, and Gideon felt a sense a peace. One that had been absent from his world for a very long while.

CHAPTER THREE

THE NEW WEEK passed and Margo saw Gideon quickly become more comfortable at the inn. Each morning he was up at eight to get Claire breakfast and then out the door to the daycare center. After that, he walked back and went directly to the workshop and started tasks for the day.

One of the first things that needed to be done was the area of fencing that separated their house from that of Mr. Webber. It needed to be replaced. Thereby improving Monty's odds of survival. However, the main concern about the job was, of course, how the older man would be able to keep Doodle out of Gideon's way. The three sisters and Gideon had convened outside to discuss the matter with their neighbor.

"Can't you crate him for a few days?" Micki asked.

Mr. Webber looked at her skeptically. "Have you ever tried to put a cat in a crate, let alone

one this large with claws. I'd like my arms not to be shredded like ribbons thank you very much."

"How is the cat…" Gideon began.

"Doodle." Mr. Webber corrected him.

"Doodle." Gideon held back a smile as he spoke. "How is he, or she, getting out?"

Today Gideon wore a plaid shirt rolled up to the elbows and faded jeans. His tool belt was hooked around his waist, and the dusty boots on his feet were well-worn. Margo had to admit he was handsome in a blue-collar, down-home kind of way. As if he felt her staring, Gideon looked in her direction. Margo averted her gaze quickly hoping that he didn't catch her assessing him. Her faced warmed when he went back to the conversation at hand, but this time a small smile was on his face. *Oh, shoot, he caught me*, she thought feeling embarrassed.

"He's a nefarious feline stealth assassin," Margo announced. "He's had a vendetta against poor Monty for years now."

Gideon held up his hands. "Whoa, I thought they were in interspecies love or whatever?"

"That's Ryan's theory," Mia explained, since she ran the inn, he wanted to first show her his plans for replacing the fencing. "We, on the other hand, think Doodle wants to make our lizard his supper."

"Seems more likely. Cats do eat lizards—even

though Monty would be a real mouthful," Gideon commented.

"I think we're missing the overall problem here," Margo said and pointed to Doodle watching them from Mr. Webber's porch. "How to keep the menace out of the house."

"How about I fix Mr. Webber's doors and window screens?" Gideon suggested.

"Been there, done that," Micki drawled. "I even replaced both doors."

"Catnip?" Margo suggested.

Mr. Webber shook his head. "No, he hates the smell of it."

They all looked at him in shocked silence.

"So, your cat doesn't like the thing that is named after him?" Mia asked.

"Go figure." Mr. Webber shrugged.

Gideon couldn't hold back his laughter. "This is the best conversation I've ever had in my life."

"I'm glad Monty's impending doom amuses you," Margo said with an offended sniff.

"I'm so sorry. I'll do my best to keep him safe," Gideon promised.

In the end, it was decided that until the fence was completed, the door to the family room would be closed at all times. Mr. Webber vowed to do his part to keep a more watchful eye on Doodle. The cost of the fence was being covered by the inn, so that alone made Mr. Webber grateful and more conciliatory. Gideon went back to work, and soon the sound of a table saw filled the air.

A little while later, Margo was at the kitchen sink when he passed by the window. The grin he flashed her made Margo's heart skip more than a few beats.

"If you stare at him any harder your eyes will fall out of your head," Micki said from behind her.

A small squeak of surprise escaped her.

"Are you trying to kill me?" Margo asked, scowling.

"You'd hear me coming if you weren't mooning over our handsome new contractor." Micki snatched an apple from the bowl and took a bite. "You should ask him out."

Margo stared at her aghast. "When in my existence have I ever approached a guy, let alone asked him out on a date? No! I'm not asking him out. He's here to start a new life, and he has a baby to care for."

"Um, single dads need love too, and you love kids more than you love animals," her sister pointed out.

Margo couldn't even tell her sister about all the turmoil going on in her head at those words. It would be so easy for her to give in and fall for Gideon's little Claire Bear, but things like marriage and children had to go on the back burner for her own peace of mind. To protect her heart from shattering once again.

"Hey." Micki put her arm around Margo's shoulders. "It's scary, after all you've been through. I know, but you've got to step back into the dating pool at some point."

If the family only knew how much I've lost. Margo pushed the unhappy thoughts from her mind.

"I'm fine, Michelle." Margo turned and hugged her sister tight.

Micki hissed. "You always use my full name when you want me to get off your case. I don't appreciate it."

"Love you, little sister," Margo called to Micki's retreating form.

The response she got was another hiss, making Margo laugh as she went back to her task of washing strawberries for that night's dessert. She'd caught on easily enough to Gideon's sweet tooth and was now making desserts she knew would get him into the kitchen for a late-night snack. Plus, their nightly conversations felt nice. Margo had to admit that she didn't come down only for a bottle of water before bed, it was to see him and talk.

Micki stuck her head around the kitchen door.

"Hey, Margo, Gideon needs a favor and I have to get going."

"Where're you off to? I thought you had zero plans today." Margo wiped her hands.

Micki grinned wickedly. "Things change, you know me. Always doin' something."

Margo narrowed her eyes at Micki. "Yeah, sure."

Out on the porch, she spotted Gideon opening the stroller.

"Hey," she said pleasantly.

Gideon glanced up and straightened to his full height. "I forgot Ellen said that the daycare has half day today, and I wanted to start getting the fence poles up this afternoon. Can you watch Claire for a few hours? I wouldn't ask if I didn't have to. I don't want Mia to think she hired the wrong guy for the job."

"Mia wouldn't think that at all," Margo protested. "But I don't mind. She and I can play on the grass and watch you work."

Gideon looked relieved. "Thanks a bunch. I'll have something else in place for any other short days in her schedule."

Margo said gently. "You're a part of our world now, our lives. If you need help, all you have to do is ask."

Gideon shoved his hands in his pockets. "I guess I need to get accustomed to that. In Washington State asking for help came with a whole set of strings I wanted no part of."

"Anytime you want to share, I have broad shoulders you can lean on," Margo offered.

"As long as I can do the same for you," Gideon replied. "Sharing is caring."

Margo laughed. "I'll remember that."

"Be back soon."

Margo watched him jog down the driveway and round the corner. Micki appeared at her side and also watched him go.

"Glad you're here, little sister. I need to get the tarts in the oven, so you can watch the baby until I get them done," Margo said. "Luckily I made the shells yesterday."

"But I have to go…"

Margo glared at her. "Remember what they say about liars and pants on fire?"

"Okay, jeez. I was trying to play matchmaker here." Micki shrugged.

"Well, don't do that," Margo said in a soft but firm voice. "I'm not looking for love right now."

"Maybe you should, then you wouldn't be so mean to me!" Micki yelled.

"No tart for you!"

Margo got the tarts on the rack to cool and set. Before dinner she would add the Chantilly cream and a little crème brûlée topping for even more added sweetness. Claire was on the porch rolling a big red ball with Micki. Margo came out with a mango fruit Popsicle for the toddler, and one for Micki because she was just as bad as any kid sometimes.

"Oh, Popsicles! Mango?" her sister asked eagerly.

"As if you let us buy any other kind for you," Margo said dryly. "Hey, Claire Bear, I have one for you too."

Claire toddled over and held out her hand. "Mmm, yay, pretty mummy."

Micki gasped. "Did she just call you mummy?"

Margo's heart lurched, ached sweetly, and she instantly wanted to cry. "No, she likes the word nom-noms or nommy. She's a two-year-old. Her letters are all in toddler speak."

"Mmm, hot nommies." Claire shivered.

"Cold, sweetie," Margo corrected her and then spoke to Micki again. "See, all catawampus."

"I hate that Enid has cloned you into saying her weird Southern words." Micki grimaced. "You're two steps away from saying bless your heart."

"Get me a wet washcloth, will you?" Margo ignored her and focused on Claire who was now a sticky mess of melted mango sorbet. "Before she becomes a bee's delight."

"On it." Micki ran into the house.

The rest of the afternoon Margo was in bliss.

She played ball with Claire and then they ran around on the lawn in between the sprinklers set on low. Micki found pinwheels that caught the wind, and the three of them sat on the front steps with their faces leaned back into the sun watching the colorful petals twirl. More than once Gideon passed by with poles and other parts for the fence. He grinned and let Claire run over and give him a quick peck on his sweaty cheeks.

"Are you having fun in the sunshine, pretty girl?" Gideon asked. "You smell like fruit."

"Mango," Margo supplied. She came down the steps to where Gideon stood and bent down to Claire. "Look, I found some little sunglasses so we can all match."

She slipped them on the toddler's face. "Ooh you are styling and profiling."

"You're the coolest Claire Bear on the block," Gideon said to his daughter. "Now I've got to get back to work while you guys have all the fun."

"We're just two girls living our best life." Margo lifted Claire in her arms. Micki had retreated to her room to study. "It's almost five, you should call it quits soon that way you can get cleaned up for dinner."

Gideon wiped the sweat from his brow. "I'm going to get these last posts in and call it a day. I think I should do the fence around the entire property with this new design and layout. These posts stand up better in high winds, and North Carolina does have to deal with hurricane season."

"Discuss it with Mia, but I bet she'll see it as a good expenditure," she replied. "That's why she wanted the roof updated before we deal with high winds and old shingles."

"I'll ask her about it tomorrow. It wouldn't be much of an expenditure if she adds it into the cost of the construction of the other houses," Gideon replied. "Let me get this done and I'll grab little miss so we can get cleaned up before dinner."

"Sounds good." She turned away and led Claire back up the porch steps.

Somewhere, Micki found an Aquadoodle—a mat that used water markers to make colorful patterns without the mess of fingerpaints—that kept Claire and Margo both entertained until Gideon took his tools to the shed and joined them on the porch.

"Thanks for watching her," Gideon said in appreciation.

Margo tweaked the baby's nose. "It was a fun day for both of us, but I'm guessing she'll have an early night tonight. Her usual schedule's all messed up."

"I think she will too." Gideon kissed Claire's

temple. "It's good for both of us. I'm feeling the soreness of construction work."

"Bad or good soreness?"

Gideon's eyes were lit with happiness when he looked at her. "Good. I haven't felt this good in years. I'll see you guys at dinner after we clean up, thanks again."

"Don't thank me. I was happy to do it." She opened the door for him and Claire to enter, a cool waft of air hit them from the air-conditioned home.

That night after dinner, Margo assumed Gideon was upstairs with Claire. But when she passed by the front door on her way to the shed to feed her animals, she heard him outside talking to his daughter and listening to her happy chatter in response. Leaving them to their bonding time, she continued through the kitchen and out to the backyard. Margo made sure her little friends were all warm, clean and fed. Monty already had his food, and she had cleaned his terrarium earlier that morning.

Now walking back to her room, Margo realized Gideon was no longer talking to Claire. Instead, his deep baritone voice was singing. She laughed huskily when she heard it wasn't a traditional lullaby. Unable to resist, Margo stepped out onto the patio where the amber light cast a soft hue. Claire lay in his arms, holding on to her bottle as he sat in the bench swing, rocking them with his foot. Gone were his work boots in favor of simple white sneakers.

"Rather than goodnight sweetheart, we go for light rock?" Margo teased.

Gideon chuckled. "The girl knows her classic rock. Come sit with us."

"I don't want to invade your nighttime routine." She hesitated.

"Come sit down." His voice was gentle and welcoming.

Margo sat and her foot in moved in tandem with his to rock the swing. Claire held out one hand and tugged one of her braids gently before trying to scoot over into her arms.

"Ah, Daddy isn't good enough anymore?" Gideon teased.

"Do you want me to go?" Margo said, a little alarmed.

Gideon took her hand and squeezed it. "I'm kidding, she wants to go to you. Take her."

She lifted the little girl into her arms. Claire smelled clean and sweet, and Margo recognized lavender too. Gideon had taken the clips out of her hair and combed her damp curls.

Claire looked up and smiled around the teat of her bottle. Her milky drool running down her cheek, which Gideon caught with one of her pink washcloths. Was this how it felt to be a mother?

A sense of comfort and contentment as a child looked up at you with such trust and love that it stole your breath away.

Her heart ached for what she had lost in the past and something she craved for her future. A family of her own was one of her dreams, something she longed for and had almost had in her grasp. Almost, because dreams were like fleeting wisps of wind that floated away as soon as you opened your eyes.

"Are you okay?" Gideon asked clearly concerned. "You closed your eyes and I felt like you just needed to be held."

"I'm fine." Margo cleared the hoarse emotion that clogged her throat. "Memories, that's all."

"Sometimes those are the hardest," he said gently. "Anytime you need to talk—broad shoulders."

She nudged him with her shoulder. "Look at you, using my own words against me."

The bottle fell limply on her chest making Margo look down. "It looks like your Claire Bear has gone down for the night."

"With her fingers wrapped in your hair." Gideon leaned over and gently unraveled the braid from between Claire's small fingers.

He got her braids free and looked up, their faces inches apart. Time seemed to slip away as she drowned in his hazel gaze. Gideon took her lips in a soft kiss. Margo's eyes fluttered closed. The sweet sensation of his lips against hers caused butterflies to take flight in her stomach.

Margo moved away with a soft sigh. "Maybe you shouldn't have done that."

"Or maybe it was meant to happen," Gideon replied huskily. He took Claire from her. "I'll get this little Miss to bed. Good night, Margo Ballad."

A smiled pulled at her lips. "Good night, Gideon Holder."

The door closed behind him with a soft click, and she sat outside as the cicadas sang out and fireflies danced through the trees. His kiss was still on her lips and her mind full of thoughts of him and Claire. The pair were winding their way around her heart, and she was surely unable to resist. Trepidation made her restless, and she got up to go do what always calmed her nerves—bake. Gideon didn't come down later that night. In a way, Margo was disappointed, but she also understood why he might stay away. The kiss might have affected him just as much as it did her. Maybe they were both afraid of what it might bring.

WITH NO GUESTS about until next month, the house was quiet except for everyone following their usual routine. Margo would be with her patients later, but until then, she'd catch up on a nursing newsletter she liked to read. Gideon was busy, but had come inside for a cool drink in the kitchen, where she'd been reading. Her favorite spot in the place would be mostly empty once she and her sisters all had their own homes. Their small staff would be on-site for guests.

They had already decided that no matter what, evening meals would be in the dining room with the guests. Dinner was one of the things their visitors loved and raved about in reviews. That sense of togetherness was important to Margo. For her, family was everything. Even if they lived apart in their own homes, being with each other around the dinner table in the house where they were raised would be the thing that kept their bond strong. Even so, coming downstairs before to the hollow emptiness made her a bit sad.

She closed her eyes. She remembered how Micki would come through the front door like a whirlwind, or Mia and her skateboard adventures. Both would make Enid fuss about scraping the hardwood floors or making mess. Now, everything was pristine with the scent of lemon pine wood polish in the air.

The telephone rang, bringing Margo out of her pensive thoughts. She hustled over to the reservation desk in the foyer to answer the main line of the inn.

"Good afternoon, Ballad Inn. How can I help you?" Margo asked politely.

"I'd like to speak to one of the owners—the sisters," a female voice said in a clipped tone.

Margo frowned. "This is Margo Ballad, who am I speaking to?"

"This is the grandmother of Claire Holder," she answered. "Sans the formalities, I want you to fire Gideon Holder."

A short laugh of amazement escaped Margo. "You are presuming a lot, ma'am, to tell us how to run our business."

"Gideon Holder is a veteran with PTSD. He's unstable and he has taken our granddaughter across the country so we can't see her." The woman's frustration and ire came through loud and clear. "He's not a good father and needs our help. He caused our daughter's death and never took responsibility."

"I'm sorry, but it's not my place to get into any family dispute. You'll have to take this up with Gideon," Margo replied. "I hope you have a nice day."

"You'll do as I request or—"

"Let me stop your right there." Margo's tone lost its pleasantness. "You will never presume to speak to me, or anyone at the Ballad Inn, in such a manner again. We do not know you, and during his time here, Gideon has been nothing more than a doting father. As I suggested, please contact him. Goodbye."

"Now, wait—"

Margo hung up, astonished. "The nerve of that woman."

Still, she knew this was an issue that could develop into something further and might cause trouble for not only the business, but herself and her sisters. Margo called them. Micki was on her way home from orientation for her return to college, and Mia was nearby, checking on construction.

It wasn't long before they met up in the office, where she explained to them about the call from Claire's grandmother. Her claims and demands.

"Sounds like a controlling woman Gideon was trying to get away from," Micki commented.

Margo nodded. "Gideon said that asking for help always came with strings. I'm thinking it was from her."

"No doubt." Mia tapped her chin musingly. "Still, we need to talk to Gideon about this and cover our bases if we need to."

"I'll go grab him. I saw him measuring distances along the new fence line near the back of Mr. Webber's house." Micki was up and running before either Margo or Mia could say a word.

"One ounce of her energy and I could work back-to-back shifts for three days nonstop," Margo murmured.

"I wouldn't need to inhale coffee in the morning." Mia chuckled.

"I told you that coffee isn't good for you," Margo complained. "Drink the naked juices I buy you."

Mia wrinkled her nose. "They taste like lawn clippings and dirt."

"Wheat grass, honey, energy boost pomegranate shots…" Margo listed ingredients.

Mia grimaced. "Doesn't make it any more appealing."

"Okay, how about we buy some sweet mangos, and you can blend that into it?" Margo suggested. "If you make the switch, you'll be less jittery, and your evening crash will be a thing of the past."

"Fine," Mia grumbled. "Ryan bought one of those Vitamix blenders anyway. He's impressed the engine could power a boat or something like that."

"Just to let you know, I'll be at your house using that." Margo rubbed her hands together. "I've wanted to buy one of those forever."

"Found him!" Micki said brightly as she stepped into the room.

Gideon followed, his eyes wandering to each of them. "Am I getting fired?"

"Far from it," Mia said. "Sit down, we've had a call."

Micki sat on the far side of the desk between her sisters.

Margo spoke next. "Claire's grandmother called. I can only assume to cause trouble. She wants us to fire you and made claims that you're responsible for their daughter's death. She said you're a bad father and you took Claire to spite them."

"Do you believe any of that?" Gideon directed his question to Margo.

"Of course not," Margo answered quickly. That was the truth. Her heart and her instincts never failed her. She could tell Gideon was a good man and father.

"We just want to protect ourselves and the inn, Gideon," Mia said gently. "Do we have any legal trouble or liability coming our way, or do you?"

"No." Gideon shook his head. "I have full legal custody of Claire, and their visitation was by my decision and not the court's. They lost Trudy, and their world stopped. Then they tried to replace her with Claire, but she's my daughter—not a replica of the one they lost. Our marriage was in trouble. My deployments, coming home and me not being able to cope with the losses we faced when we were in Afghanistan made it hard for me and Trudy to connect. The one saving grace was Claire. I went to my VA appointments, did what I needed to do to get myself to a point of being a husband and father that Trudy and Claire could be proud of."

"That sounds like hard work. And the help you got… You should be proud of that," Margo said gently.

Gideon sighed and ran his hands over his head. "Trudy's parents are well established. Her father is a judge and thinks he can control the situation. Her mother thinks that tears, threats and passive-aggressive behavior will work. I ask for help babysitting so I can work, they say I can't care for her. I don't ask, and they say I'm being selfish and keeping Claire from them. I was in a no-win situation, in a place that brought us no joy or happiness. This is why I applied for the job at the inn and here we are. That's it. Cards are on the table. No trouble other than they won't see past their own selfish needs at this point."

"That's a total rock meet hard place situation for you," Micki said sympathetically.

"I'm sorry you're going through this." Margo leaned over to take his hand. Gideon held on tight.

He turned to address her sister. "Mia, I can understand if you don't want the trouble and would like us to leave."

"Hush up," Mia said firmly. "We just needed

to know where we stood, and now we know. You have our support Gideon. We like you, and love Claire."

Gideon give them a boyish grin. "Gee, thanks. Claire gets the winning ticket, huh?"

"Always." Micki grinned and jumped off the desk. "If that's settled, I need a snack and I know banana bread is in the kitchen."

"That's it from me," Mia said. "I can get to some work before dinner."

"It's my day to make dinner, so I'm going to do that." Margo stood. "I'm glad you're here, Gideon. Please don't ever feel like you can't come to us if you need us. You have people in your corner now that care."

Gideon nodded. "Thanks. I'm going to follow Micki for a slice of that banana bread and then get back to that fence."

"Dude, a glass of cold milk will help with that too." Micki clapped him on his back.

"Are you following me at night?" Gideon asked.

She looked at him curiously. "No, why?"

"It's like you know me," he replied.

Margo watched him and Micki leave the office before turning to Mia who had a knowing look on her face.

"What?" Margo asked.

Mia smiled. "He fits in, doesn't he?"

"Yeah, he does," she replied.

"He held on to your hand a little tight there, lady," her sister pointed out. "Ask him out already."

"Don't you start too." Margo waved to her sister and stepped out of the office.

Margo thought back to how he held her hand. Maybe her sisters were right, and she should ask Gideon out. It would take time for her to build up the courage to do so, until then, a meal had to be made.

As she washed potatoes for baking, he passed by the window and gave her an unforgettable smile. Margo dropped the potato she was holding, splashing water in her face.

"Get a grip," Margo muttered to herself.

Yet thinking about him while she chopped and peeled brought a smile to her lips that wouldn't go away.

CHAPTER FOUR

"WHY DID I kiss her?" Gideon wondered out loud and then answered himself. "Because she's beautiful, down-to-earth and Claire adores her already."

If he set criteria to assess people, it was best to use Claire as a gauge. If she didn't like a person, he knew they didn't need to be in his life. Children and dogs were great judges of character. It's like they could sense an underlying issue in a personality, and instantly get wary and uncomfortable. Claire was automatically drawn to Margo, and so was he.

He also saw a wariness in Margo's eyes, as if she was unsure about letting them into her life. Then there was the sadness that came across sometimes when she held or cuddled his daughter. A moment in the past had hurt her badly, but like him, maybe she wasn't ready to share that secret yet. He couldn't fault her for that. If Denise, Claire's grandmother hadn't called, he would probably be keeping that part of his life secret. Margo Ballad was special, he could see that.

June in the Sardis neighborhood also meant the Spring Fling. It was the only time their streets were barred from cars being able to use them as a shortcut to get into the Matthews area. Their neighborhood became festive. Streamers hung from houses, and colorful flags crisscrossed above the roads, courtesy of Hunter and his landscaping crew. There was cotton candy, popcorn, music, games for the kids and adults, a square-dancing group that Mr. Bolton and Enid were a part of. It was a fun day in the area. Everyone in the inn was looking forward to it.

Gideon got Claire's shoes on in the dining room while her stroller sat open to one side. They were invited by Margo to spend the day with her at the festival.

"Since she invited us, can I consider this a first date?" Gideon asked his daughter dressed in pink sundress and white capri tights.

"Nope you can't. If you want a first date pretty much sure you need to ask the lady politely," Ryan said, grinning from the door.

Gideon didn't even hear Ryan come in and wondered why. Especially since he was dressed like a magician down to the shiny black shoes on his feet and the satin black top hat.

"Is there any type of animal in that hat?" Gideon asked with a grin while Claire clapped her hands happily. "And how did I not hear you come in with those tap shoes on?"

"Nope. Margo steals any and all furry creatures," Ryan answered and waved his hands before pulling fake flowers from his jacket. "And I'm magic."

"Uh-huh," Gideon said dryly.

Claire squealed in delight when Ryan gave her the flowers.

"Don't you need that, magic man?" Gideon asked.

"I've got tons of those." He laughed. "Anyway, where are you going to take Margo?"

"Got any ideas?"

Ryan thought for a moment. "Movie and Bistro on Monroe Road. She's always complaining she hasn't been to a movie in forever. That's a good starting point. The new romantic comedy might be a solid way to go."

"I'll get online and see what's playing," Gideon said. "Thanks for the suggestion."

"You're welcome. There's an app—download it later." Ryan turned toward the door, stopped and faced Gideon. "Also, make sure your intentions are good. Those three can come together and form one super sister that is a force to be reckoned with. Add the parents and Enid… Full-on Ballad family hurricane."

Gideon laughed. "You went from a robot superhero reference to weatherman."

"Just how it is, my man," Ryan called over his shoulder. "You've only had a small taste of the chaos here."

Gideon shook his head while getting Claire into the stroller. "These nice folks might be a bit eccentric, but they're good people."

"Daadee, kiss!" Claire grabbed his cheeks, and he pressed a kiss on her forehead.

"You don't care. You like them, and you're the best at figuring people out, Claire Bear," he told her gently. "That's why you're my entire world."

Claire was chattering away while he waited for Margo to come downstairs. The sound of music, and a faint smell of popcorn and cotton candy, was in the air. Gideon felt the excitement of being a kid again. The few times he got to go to amusement parks or fairgrounds were some of the most fun he'd ever had. He opened the door to see outside and almost jumped back with a screech. The large orange cat from next door was standing there, looking at him, and then at Claire.

"Whoa..." Gideon pulled the stroller back warily, not knowing if the animal Margo called a feline menace would try to scratch his daughter.

"Kitty!" Claire said happily. She made grabby hands and began to sing. "Meow, meow, meow, meow."

Gideon watched while Doodle, the cat, slowly extended his front paws up to lean on the stroller so that Claire could pet him. He purred when she patted his head and cooed at him. That's how Margo found them a few moments later when she ran downstairs. Gideon noted that she wore white capris and a yellow blouse. White sneakers featured laces the color of her top, while her hair was in a high ponytail. Margo skidded to a stop when she saw the cat, and Claire's open affection.

"What in the orange demon cat hellscape is going on?" Margo asked.

Gideon shrugged. "He was waiting politely at the door, and then the lovefest began."

"Weird." Margo took out her phone and snapped a picture. "There needs to be proof of this scene playing out before me."

Doodle finally put his paws on the ground and gave them both a look. With a swish of his tail, he sauntered back outside to the tree that bordered the two houses. He was up and over in seconds and disappeared into Mr. Webber's yard.

"That wasn't creepy at all," Gideon said.

"Welcome to my world," Margo quipped, then added brightly, "Ready to go?"

"As I'll ever be." Gideon let go of the stroller as Margo took over. "I smell cotton candy, and if I'm lucky there'll be funnel cake."

"You're worse than Ryan, and he lives for summer. Last year I thought he hit every fair between here and South Carolina for funnel cake." Margo laughed.

Gideon chuckled. "I'm not that bad. Why would I be when I can just raid the fridge every night. Your desserts are much better."

She flushed beneath her chestnut-brown skin. "Thank you."

They didn't have to walk far to find the Spring Fling was going strong. Everyone was out of their homes visiting booths and with each other. Barbecues were going full-tilt, and Margo explained how neighbors who participated had individual tents and offered their signature dishes. Vendors also came in with food. Ballad Inn had a large tent with a team Mia hired to serve Enid and Margo's specialties. From slow cooked ribs to their famous potato salad, coleslaw, mac and cheese and more. That was their first stop, and under the shade of a wide apple tree on benches, he, Margo, and Claire Bear ate.

He got them all cool bottles of juice and water from the storage area under the stroller. Grateful and happy, they took long sips.

Most of the time he ended up pushing Claire Bear's little scoot-scoot, aka her stroller, which was slowly being filled with tinkers, basically crafts that Margo bought for Claire. Otherwise,

Margo walked with his daughter, holding her hand, stopping at intervals to feed her ice cream from a small cup. As a trio they were having a great time. Margo was made to be a mother. He was seeing in real time how his daughter bloomed under her attention and affection.

He sat on a bench, pulling apart a warm funnel cake covered in powdered sugar and strawberry preserves, and watched as Margo held Claire while two artists painted their faces. Their backs were to him, but he could see that Margo was talking, and that she bounced her knees anytime Claire seemed to impatiently fidget. Finally, they were done, and Margo shifted his daughter in her arms before they turned to walk back to him. Seeing their faces, Gideon's laughter rang out. This time he pulled out his phone with sticky fingers and snapped a photo.

Margo and his daughter had one side of their faces painted as tigers and it was the most adorable thing he'd ever seen. Memories darkened his thoughts for a moment. There wasn't one time when he and Trudy, and Claire, were this happy together. Not once where the three of them had gone out to enjoy the day and interacted so easily.

But here his Claire Bear was beaming and Margo seemed genuinely joyful as well.

"You both look ferocious." Gideon grinned.

Margo made a fierce face. "Better be nice to us."

"I shall," Gideon replied. "I've been noticing that no one has sat in the dunk tank all day. Is it just for show?"

Margo glanced across the grass. "Oh, yeah, it works, but who wants to risk getting dunked? Few dare to try it."

Gideon snorted. "I remain undefeated when it comes to dunk tanks. Never been in the water yet… I psyche out my opponents."

"Well, that's good and all, but everyone here knows not to go up against The Fastball Queen," Margo answered mildly. "That record of yours would be gone for sure."

Gideon's competitive side reared its head. "Doubtful. Even some of the biggest marines couldn't get me in the water."

"You should hop up there, then," Margo encouraged. "I'll tell them to announce a dunk tank contestant."

How easy could it be? Gideon rubbed his hands together. "Let's do this thing."

"Strap Claire in and I'll get them to set up." Margo flashed him a smile and ran off.

"Did she seem a bit too excited to you?" Gideon asked his daughter as he got her secured into the stroller.

"Hi. Hi-ho. We've got a volunteer for the dunk tank!" The words came across the loudspeaker.

"Gideon Holder from the Ballad Inn is the victim... Oh, I mean volunteer."

"Victim?" Gideon said dubiously.

Micki came running up. "Dude, how brave of you!"

"Who is this mysterious perfect-throw person?" Gideon asked, then it dawned on him. "It's Margo, isn't it?"

"Well." Micki drew the word out.

"It's all three of them. They were on a female softball team that went to nationals about five years ago," said Mr. Marley who was standing next to him. "Let's go get you ready, son."

"Why does it sound like you're leading me to my doom?" Gideon asked, hesitantly falling into step with the older man.

Mr. Marley shrugged. "Just remember to close your mouth when you fall in."

Soon, Gideon was barefoot, dressed only in his shorts, and sitting on the wooden bench in the dunk tank. More people than he expected crowded around, including Enid who now had Claire's stroller. Ryan was grinning and making prayer hand signals at him, and the sisters were in various stages of stretching their arms. It was then Gideon knew he'd been conned into a sucker's bet. Especially when Margo gave him a wicked smile and wink.

"Let's get this over with so he can get past the

drowning part quickly," Mr. Bolton called out. "Which sister goes first?"

"Margo should have the honor. She got the body into the seat for us," Mia said with a smile.

"The body?" Gideon called.

"I accept the honor, my dear sisters." Margo handed Mr. Bolton five dollars for three tennis balls.

"It's like a pride of lionesses, Gideon. You were being hunted and didn't even know it." Ryan was standing close by and shook his head, a look of sadness on his face.

"Why didn't you warn me?" Gideon asked helplessly.

"Better you than me. I was working off a theory of self-preservation," Ryan said solemnly. "Besides, Claire's going to love seeing her daddy underwater like a merman."

"Uh-huh."

Margo took one of her three balls. "Ready up there?"

"No, because you snowed me. I thought you were supposed to like me," Gideon said.

Margo tsked and shook her head. "I do, but all's fair in love and dunking."

"That's not how that saying go…"

Margo threw the ball with precision and Gideon went under before he could finish his sentence. Water filled his ears and through the glass he could see the sisters giving each other high fives. Claire was clapping happily. *They've pulled her into the fold, she's part of the female consortium at Ballad Inn now*, Gideon thought. Twice more he climbed back up and Margo took him down with the remaining two balls just as easily.

As he wiped the water away from his face, the next sister stepped up. The look in her eyes made Gideon wary.

"Micki, me and you, we're dedicated to our craft and wood is our medium," Gideon implored as he got on the seat again.

Micki nodded and gave him a Cheshire grin. "We are, but I can't pass this up, buddy. Sorry in advance."

"Micki, argh!"

He was splashing in the water again. Three different times. He wondered if he should stay down there. Claire waved at him through the glass and Margo's eyes were alight with merriment—and what Gideon hoped was affection toward him. So, he climbed back up in the seat and waited for Mia to take her turn. The usual calm professional expression she wore was now a wide goofy grin while she warmed up her arm.

"I thought at least you would be the voice of reason." Gideon tried to be somber, but amusement was evident in his voice.

"I am the voice of reason," Mia replied, and her tone became downright devilish. "The reason you're going to be underwater."

This was his third strike, so to speak, and yes, he was out, because like the sister before her, Mia sent him into the depths of the water. The muffled sound of people cheering could be heard. Margo met his gaze when he finally surged out of the water and his heart soared for a minute.

He knew it was the first pangs of attraction and longing for a new relationship, where boy meets girl, and everything is so heightened.

But he couldn't go by his instincts or wants alone. He had Claire to think about as part of the package. He'd thought Trudy was the one, and that turned out worse than he could've possibly imagined. He wanted to explore the feelings within him when it came to Margo, but it was also a path that had to be trod carefully.

He finally escaped the dunk tank and went to the house to change his clothes. There was no way to brood with someone like Margo around. Her good spirits were infectious and there was just a feeling of comfort and home around her. To him, Margo radiated beauty both inside and out.

Gideon had to admit that after the kiss they shared, he couldn't stop thinking about her. It seemed like it would be easy to fall in love with someone like her. Being gun-shy after Trudy couldn't be helped. Their relationship had been tumultuous, and that was just one layer. Weighing the merits of asking Margo on a date filtered through his mind. If they connected and then it didn't work out Gideon knew he'd be looking for a new job, for one. Margo's laughter brought him back to the present as evening set in at the fair and they sat together on hay bales watching Ryan's magic show.

"Are you having fun, hmm?" Margo bounced Claire as she spoke to the little girl. "Was it fun watching Daddy go splash?"

"It wasn't Daddy's intent to be half drowned," Gideon mused. "Also, darling daughter, Daddy was led into a trap."

Margo chuckled. "Oh no, your boastfulness got you in that mess. Writing checks your tush can't cash."

Gideon shook his head, amused. "Okay I give you that. Between you and your sisters, I was thoroughly humbled."

"I guess I should ask you if you're having fun?" Margo nudged him with her shoulder gently.

"I actually am," he admitted.

Gideon turned to face her, and for a moment he forgot to take a breath. The setting sun cast an amber glow across her ebony skin. Her eyes were alight with happiness, and their gazes met, held and the wide smile on her face grew softer.

"What?" Margo asked.

"Has anyone ever told you how beautiful you truly are?" he asked gently.

"Stop it," she murmured and lifted her lemonade cup to take a sip.

Gideon cupped her cheek. "I won't—can't. Go on a date with me?"

Margo started to cough. The liquid must have gone down the wrong way.

"What?" she croaked.

Gideon patted her back like he would Claire's. His daughter was standing in Margo's lap, trying to help with tiny hands patting her back as well.

"Okay— Okay?" Claire asked worriedly.

Margo smiled at her and cleared her throat. "I'm okay, Claire Bear. Thank you for helping me."

Claire beamed.

"What did you say?" Margo asked Gideon in a low voice, looking around.

"I was asking you out, not slipping you CIA ops information." Gideon grinned. "Why are you whispering?"

"Because if anyone hears you asking me out it will be all over this neighborhood before the lights go off for the Spring Fling," she explained.

Gideon rubbed his chin, feeling the stubble there before speaking. "Would it be so bad if they knew I asked you out?"

"No, but something this new," she paused. "I'd

want to have it to myself first," Margo replied, holding Claire's hand as she wiggled down to the grass to stand. "Trust me when I say even the cashier at the supermarket will ask, 'How are you and Gideon doing?' each time I step in there. And that's just one example."

"I get it." Gideon looked down at his daughter as she toddled over to hold on to his leg. He leaned closer to Margo, and, whispering loudly, asked, "So, wanna go on a date?"

A laugh escaped her. "I would, very much. Thank you for asking."

"Wednesday next week?" he said hopefully. "A movie and bistro night?"

Margo nodded. "I'd like that. Micki would have no problem babysitting."

"I'll get the tickets." Gideon kept his voice smooth even though excitement made his heart race a bit faster. This was a big step for him, and he wanted it to be right.

Claire started to yawn and fret by seven thirty, which meant it was time for bed. Margo left with him and waited on the patio while he got Claire down for the night. Her sleep pattern had changed completely since the move. She went down easier without fussing. Before, it was chaos, which ended sometimes with him watching TV with her in his arms because she cried every time when he got up to put her in the crib.

Margo looked up at him when he stepped out onto the porch.

"She's asleep already?" she asked.

"Out like a light," Gideon answered and held up the baby monitor as he claimed the seat beside her on the porch swing. "I'm not complaining. Bedtime was once a nighttime ritual of her stubbornness and mine, but now it's smooth and easy."

"The warmth and fresh air of the South does that to you." Margo handed him a plate. "Enid's red velvet cheesecake with a crème brûlée topping and a scoop of fresh Chantilly cream."

"Bless you." Gideon breathed out.

"Your reverence at dessert amuses and worries me." Margo laughed. "Your sweet tooth is out of control."

"I blame you and Enid." He cut into the cake eagerly. "I had it under control until I got here."

"Lies." She called him out for his statement.

"Okay I lied, but store-bought pies and cake don't do justice to what you guys create," he replied.

"Because those are premade and from a box," Margo explained. "I'm so sorry you had to eat that. I bought a pie once and Enid wouldn't let me forget it for two months. She was right, I could make better. But it had been a long day and I'd needed a quick boost."

"I don't know how you do your job. It takes

a wonderful caring heart to do what you do," Gideon complimented her. "I saw scary, tragic things each time I was deployed, and there're days I can still playback every minute. The hurt's never lessened. You, Margo, get up and face it daily without letting it mar your soul."

Margo shrugged. "I know sadness and death are a part of life, but I also believe no one should be alone in their later years, especially people who have cared so well and so long for others. I saw too many in the rest home fade away, lonely, when I was in school. I think I mentioned I was going to be a pediatric nurse, but after my rotation with seniors, I went to my adviser and told her I wanted to train in geriatrics instead. I wanted to be the one who held their hand and reminded them they're not alone or forgotten."

"Do you know how rare you are?" Gideon was floored by her commitment.

"There are tons of nurses that do exactly what I do." She looked away shyly.

"I'm sure there are." Gideon turned her head to face him with a soft touch on her chin. "But they're not you, and you should be proud of your beliefs."

"I am," she replied huskily.

"May I kiss you, Margo Ballad?" Gideon asked.

A slow smile crept to her lips. "Yes, you may, Gideon Holder."

A soft sigh escaped her just before his lips touched hers gently. Gideon laced his fingers with hers while they shared the sweet romantic moment. Their hands stayed together when he broke the kiss.

"You make me feels things I thought I'd forgotten," Gideon admitted, his tone a deep timbre from all the emotion he felt in his heart.

"It's the same for me," Margo admitted. "It scares me more than a little."

"Me too." Gideon lifted their connected hands and placed a kissed on her fingers. "Should we follow how we feel and see where it goes?"

Margo nodded. "I think we should. It would be foolish not to."

Gideon wrapped his arm around her and kissed her temple. "Never let it be said that I was foolish."

He felt her shoulders shake as a laugh escaped her.

Margo held up two fingers. "Maybe a little bit."

"Oh, you're teasing me. Bold, after you coerced me into a dunk tank," Gideon teased.

"Me, coerce? Never."

"You keep thinking that."

Gideon went back to his dessert and from where they sat, they could see the square dancing begin. He slowly pushed the bench swing with his foot while they watched. First, the big group dance, and then individual performances of various genres of music.

"Enid and Mr. Bolton can sure cut a rug," Gideon said. "Look at them go! Did you see how he flipped her over his back for 'The Boogie Woogie' thing? They've got more energy than I do."

"Tomorrow she'll be complaining about how stiff she is," Margo commented. "You can't tell from the way they're moving now though. They can jump, jive and shake. Oh, to be that filled with life when I get to that age."

"I can drink to that."

Gideon picked up his glass of sweet tea and clinked it against Margo's. As they watched the dancers and talked from one subject to the next, Gideon couldn't stop watching Enid and Mr. Bolton. In his mind's eye, he could see himself and Margo being on that stage years from now and enjoying life together. *Don't let me mess this up*, he thought as images of his rocky life with Trudy filtered through his head. He was a good man, but maybe he ruined anything he touched when it came to romance. He was still learning how not to let the guilt of his past cast a shadow on his life now and beyond. Gideon glanced at Margo and hoped that she was a part of that future as well.

CHAPTER FIVE

"Why did I agree to this?" Margo moaned as she carefully applied her makeup in the bathroom mirror.

"Because you and Gideon seem to have a connection and you want to see where it goes," Micki said. "Want me to give you the smoky eye look with the eye shadow?"

"What's a smoky eye?" Margo asked.

"This." Mia held up her phone. "I don't think it goes well with your jeans and sweater. It's a late-night dinner slash party kind of look."

"I say she can pull it off," Micki said stubbornly. "That jade green sweater with the good earrings and her gold necklace and pendant will knock this ensemble out of the park."

Margo glanced at the picture and then looked at herself in the mirror. "That's not me. I'll look like a raccoon. And I'm pretty much nervous as is without blinking at him from behind a ton of dark makeup."

"I don't know why you're all jittery. You and

Gideon are so seamless around each other."
Micki sat on the closed toilet. "Here, wear these
sandals."

"Nope. The cute half-cut boots. It's cold in the
movie, my toes will freeze before I get my food,"
Margo protested.

"Beauty is pain," Micki chastised.

"Micki, hush, beauty is not painful, and she
shouldn't need to get frostbite on her feet to look
cute." Mia stood behind Margo and helped her
tame her braids. "When I pin your hair, I wish I
hadn't cut mine. I cannot believe that your hair
is this long and gorgeous."

"You can always start going with me to my
braiders. She uses these oils and shea butter in
my hair each time she braids it." Margo focused
on that conversation instead of the butterflies.

"Now, why are you so nervous about going to
the movies with Gideon?" Micki asked, derailing
Margo's plans.

Mia sighed. "Michelle, we're not like you—a
serial dater."

"I mean it's not like I form relationships with
all of them and even if we don't click, I've gained
a friend." Micki defended.

"I haven't gone on a date since…" Margo hesitated and firmed her shoulders. "Since I lost
Scott."

Mia squeezed her shoulder. "Slow and steady

wins the race. If it's taken until now for you to feel ready, it's okay."

"Gideon has some baggage too with Claire's grandparents." Margo sighed. "I'm so afraid of caring for him and Claire, and then something happens. I don't have good luck in this area at all."

Micki stood and hugged her. "You have the best luck. What happened had nothing to do with you. You're so caring and you have a good soul. I know putting yourself out there can hurt, but it will hurt even more if you don't try."

"Look at you, being the voice of wisdom," Margo teased with a watery laugh and kissed Micki's forehead. "I love that you guys are my sisters and best friends."

"The Ballad sisters for the win," Mia said. "We'll let you finish getting ready. We're going downstairs to snag Claire and enjoy her baby smell."

"It's so addictive." Micki followed Mia to the door. "I see why Mom always talks about baby toes being the best part. Oh no, am I turning into Mom?"

"One of us had to," Mia said sagely. "It would be you."

"Seriously, do you think I'm becoming Mom?" Micki demanded, and Margo smiled, listening to their conversation fade away.

"You got this, it's just dinner and a movie," Margo told herself.

She got her shoes on, sprayed on a little of her signature fragrance, and with one last look in the mirror, she left her bedroom and headed downstairs. She heard the squeals of happiness and voices coming from the family room and followed the sound. Her sisters were playing with Claire and Gideon was standing, watching them with a grin on his face. When he turned it was like time stood still. Margo couldn't look away from his face and the soft smile on his lips.

She loved that there weren't any airs he put on about his life. Not about being a decorated soldier and veteran, or the fact that he worked with his hands to build and create. That evening, he wore a simple white plaid shirt over a dark blue T-shirt, and his version of dress pants—dark jeans. His boots were still the scuffed pair he used for work and Margo would have it no other way.

"You look amazing." His voice was husky.

Margo looked down at her clothes with a tiny laugh. "It's just a sweater and some jeans."

"Same for me," he teased.

"Hi… Hi!"

Claire left Mia's arms and ran over to Margo. She was already in her princess pajamas and socks, ready for bed, when she wrapped her arms around one of Margo's legs.

She looked up at Margo. "Up!"

Unable to resist, she lifted the little girl into her arms and as the baby lay her head on Margo's shoulder, she fell more in love.

"Sleepy, night night," Claire patted her shoulder.

"Not tonight, sweet pea," Micki plucked Claire from her sister's arms. Margo was unwilling to let her go for an instant. "You play with me tonight and we can eat cake."

"Cake!"

"Not too much," Gideon pleaded. "Then her warm milk and bed."

Mia steered them both to the door. "Go have fun. I promise we won't spoil her. Too much."

"That's highly doubtful." Margo slipped her hand through the crook of Gideon's arm and her gaze caught his. "I'm kidding. Enid will keep them in line. She will be the gatekeeper of the cake."

"Does she monitor my sweets intake?" Gideon asked as they stepped outside and headed to his truck.

"I don't know, but if she sits you down for a talking-to then your sugar intake might be out of control," she teased.

Gideon helped her into the truck, and she glanced at Claire's car seat in the back. He slid behind the wheel. The engine of the truck purred as he turned it on, pulled from the parking spot and made his way down the driveway of the inn. The movie and bistro were on Monroe Road, and his truck ate up the short distance between their Sardis neighborhood to the theater. When he parked, Margo waited patiently for him to come around to her door before hopping out of the cab of the truck herself.

"I would've helped you down," Gideon said with a grin.

She gave him a teasing glance. "How do you think I get out of my own truck?"

Gideon took her hand. "Any particular reason you drive such a large truck…"

"I call mine The Rocket." Margo enjoyed the sensation of his hand holding hers.

"I'll keep that in mind," he chuckled, as they walked toward the ticket booth. "It reminds me of a major who could drive an amphibious vehicle like a bat out of hell when we were on training missions. She was something else."

"I think maybe it's the fact that I want to feel safe," Margo admitted. "I feel safer driving my truck. Especially with the boom in our population of folks from bigger cities and the rise in road rage incidents."

"If you ever don't feel safe, you call me and I'll come get you," Gideon said firmly.

"I'll be fine." Margo laughed.

Gideon kissed her hand. "You call me, promise."

Margo looked at him and her breath caught in her throat. "Okay, I promise."

Gideon bought them both tickets for a new movie she wanted to see. After their tickets were scanned, they got in line for food. He chose pulled pork nachos, and Margo went with a bacon chicken ranch flat bread pizza. They both chose large cherry ices, and a popcorn to share, and took the little buzzer with them to their seats in the number seven theater.

"I've never been to a movie like this before," Gideon admitted. "So, they just bring us our food and drinks?"

"Yep, and watch this." Margo sat down and he did as well. "Press the buttons on the side."

"Recliner seat?" Gideon asked, impressed. "And heat! I may never leave."

"This is why sometimes when I'm working, I'm technically not working," she admitted. "I take in a good movie matinee in the quiet of an empty theater."

"Hey, invite a guy along next time." He took her hand and played with her fingertips.

She leaned into his side conspiratorially. "Only if you enjoy a good action movie, or scary movie. It's my secret pleasure."

"I won't say a word," he promised.

The movie started just as the food was brought to their seats, and they munched while they enjoyed the previews. Together they made note of coming-soon shows they wanted to see together, or kid's movies they could bring Claire to. The feature started and soon they were engrossed in the scenes that played out on the wide screen. Margo was keenly aware of the man sitting next to her.

Not just because he was handsome, but because they seemed to mesh so well. She felt comfortable around him while the butterflies of new attraction, and the possibility of love, were still there. They finished their dinner and worked on the popcorn, exchanging shy smiles like teenagers when their hands touched, grabbing the puffed kernels. It was a pleasant two and a half hours. After they filed out of the movie, they agreed it was still too early to call it a night.

"Ice cream?" Margo suggested. "Carolina Creamery makes a wonderful banana split."

"I'm in." Gideon took her hand. "To the truck."

Margo laughed. "It's right over there, and we can sit on one of the outdoor benches or walk the trails in the park."

"Let's walk, I should burn off some of the calories I ate today." Gideon chuckled.

"Really?" she asked dryly.

"Nah, it just makes it sound like I'm a responsible adult," he answered.

Margo loved the casual stride he took that ensured she could keep up with him. "You do that fine, raising a daughter on your own."

Other movie patrons had the same idea about the ice cream. There was a line at the counter, and other people were already sitting at many of the picnic-style benches. When it was their turn to order, both Margo and Gideon stepped up to the counter.

"Hey, Margo!" Paige greeted. Paige and her husband, Robbie, owned the creamery and lived in the neighborhood with their teenage children, Robbie Jr and Sally.

"Hey, Paige," Margo said with a warm smile. "Looks like a busy night. Where are the kids?"

"Out living their best lives." Paige laughed. "Hey, Gideon, met you briefly when you were being dunked by the sisters. I handed you the towel after."

"Huh, I don't remember," Gideon said. "In my defense, I was trying to recover from being half-drowned."

"No worries. In my defense, I was laughing so hard you probably didn't notice me from all the others doing the same," Paige teased. "What can I get you both?"

"You know me, the chocolate chip mint gelato," Margo answered. "What about you, Gideon?"

"Margo tried to sell me on the banana split. I

think it was to detract from the chocolate chip mint so she could have it to herself," Gideon mused. "I'll have that in a waffle cup please."

Paige nodded sagely. "Good man, thwart her nefarious intentions."

"Hey!" Margo said good-naturedly. "And to think I was going to invite you to my birthday party."

"You'll still let me in since I'll have an ice cream cake," Paige replied as she made their order.

"She better let you in or I'll meet you on the porch." Gideon took his waffle cup and Margo took her cone. "How much do I owe you?"

"On the house if you promise to make an honest woman out of this one." Paige gave him a wink.

"I'll keep you updated."

Margo felt her heart tumble at his words. Was that where they were heading—to something permanent? She didn't overthink it, not at this point, with only a kiss or two, and an actual first date, there was a long way to go. They fell into step and followed the sidewalk to the park close by, and the trail where joggers ran, a number of couples walked, and families enjoyed the warm evening.

"Tell me about life in Tacoma," Margo said lightly.

"It rains a lot," Gideon answered automatically. "I was born there. First time I saw anything else was when I joined the Marines. Then I never wanted to go back there, but by the time I made that choice it wasn't on the table anymore."

"Trudy?" Margo didn't want to pry but after the conversation with Claire's grandmother, she was curious why the relationship was so caustic.

"Yes, she got pregnant, so we married. We thought we would grow to love each other, but that didn't happen," Gideon told her.

Margo was silent as he took a bite of his ice cream before speaking again.

"Trudy's parents were…are very strict. When I was deployed each time, she went home, and they took control. When I came home, they thought I would just fall in line. I'd married her, Claire was my child. I had the Marines giving me rules, I didn't need it from them in my home life as well."

"That would be difficult." Margo licked at her cone before the sweet treat could melt onto her fingers. "I'm sure they had the best intentions."

Gideon shrugged but his tone was stiff. "Maybe."

She nodded. "We don't have to talk about this. I know things from the past are hard. I've been there and done that."

"Yeah." Gideon took a deep breath. "This is a

little heavy for a first date. I don't want to scare you away."

"I doubt that would happen," Margo answered with amusement in her voice. "You can ask me something about me to make it even."

"Hmm, let's see, tell me about your parents."

"Oh, that's easy."

Margo finished the rest of her cone before wiping her hands with the napkins and tossing them in the trash. Gideon did the same with his waffle cup. As they continued to walk, she slipped her arm through the crook of his.

"My parents are travelers extraordinaire, we called them Carlo and Carmen Santiago for the longest time," Margo told him. "They were never really around when we were growing up. Mia was more mom and sister, and Enid filled in the rest of the gaps. Even though a few people in the neighborhood might take exception to that and insist we were wild."

"Like Mr. Bolton and Marley?" Gideon chuckled.

"Add Mr. Webber and we have the perfect trio." Margo laughed. "Last year after a small blowup with Mia, we found out they traveled to find better treatment for my mother's illness. She has lupus. They had kids young, and then it turned into something more. They were here for Mia and Ryan's wedding and have been coming home frequently. We're forming a new type of bond besides them buying trinkets for my sisters and I, and occasional drive-by check-ins."

"A person like me wished I had a real home to come back to," Gideon said. "My dad was career Army, we moved around a lot, base housing to base housing, but never what felt like a home. It always made it hard to fit in—new schools, new kids."

"I get that," she took his hand. "It's always hard to find a place to fit in as a child, especially if you're on the move constantly."

"When I lost them, I think I felt like I lost any chance at figuring out the foundation of a family. Maybe that's why things were so difficult for me and Trudy. But when Claire came around, the both of us tried our very best to give her what she needed."

Margo sighed. "I like home. I like cooking and family meals. I always thought I'd have a family of my own by now, but…"

"But?"

It was her turn to shrug. "Fate had other plans for me, I guess."

"There's a story there," he commented.

Margo lifted her face to look at him. "One I'll share at some point."

Gideon stopped and caressed her cheek. "Aren't

we a pair? The past has us terrified to reach for anything in the future."

"I think that might be changing," Margo said, offering a small smile.

He nodded. "Definitely."

Gideon lowered his head and their lips touched. She hadn't felt this way about anyone in a very long time. It was like standing on a diving board staring into crystal-blue waters. Your heart raced with excitement, but you're also so very afraid. That was Margo right now. Excited at the possibilities, and terrified at the thought of the fall. Gideon paused and his gaze seemed to bore into her being to see every secret and fear, yet Margo couldn't look away.

"What is it about you, Margo Ballad?" he whispered.

"You ask me that like I would know," Margo answered honestly. "I'm just me. I guess, people aren't accustomed to people wearing their hearts on their sleeve anymore. Everyone is so hidden, afraid of being who they really are, or being hurt by it."

"Aren't you?"

"I am. Terrified, actually, but I don't know how to be any other way."

Gideon kissed the tip of her nose. "And that's what makes you special."

"Ready to head back?" Margo asked, not sure what to say to his compliment.

"I love Charlotte," Gideon said as they began walking. "Each road leads back to home."

"And do you think of Charlotte...as home?" Margo watched their feet as they walked, his and her strides matching in step.

Gideon glanced at her. "Yeah...yeah, I do. It feels good here. Claire is happy, and I am too."

"That's nice to hear."

Margo released a slow breath as if his answer would make or break whatever was happening for them. The short drive home together was pleasant. They talked about what their upcoming week looked like—repairing an upstairs window for him, meeting a new patient for her. It didn't take long to arrive at Ballad Inn. They walked up the steps to the front door together and hesitated.

"Should I kiss you now and not in front of your sisters?" he teased.

Margo laughed softly. "That would be best. Those two are incorrigible."

Gideon leaned in for the kiss and when he stepped back, Margo noticed her sisters standing at the window, grinning like loons.

She sighed and leaned her head on his chest. "The peanut gallery is watching."

He turned and a rich laugh escaped him. It made her feel light, and her heart filled with joy.

"The joys of siblings," he finally said. "You guys are great."

"I'm glad you think so," she said and opened the door so they could step inside. She saw her sisters and pointed. "You two are the worst."

"Whatever do you mean?" Mia asked innocently.

Margo shook her head. "And you're the oldest. She learned this behavior from you." She nodded at her other sister.

"Hey, I'm a grown adult, you know," Micki said.

Gideon, getting in on the fun, joked, "But are you really?"

Micki rolled her eyes. "Great funny, man. I should've filled your baby up with sugar."

"Speaking of which, after a rousing game of hide-and-seek, which a two-year-old plays very badly, she went down easily." Mia laughed.

"Played badly?" Margo was curious.

Gideon answered. "Oh, she hides in plain sight, and you must pretend you don't see her. All the while she is laughing so loud, she can hardly keep still and when you say, gotcha… You know what, I'll save that for when you get to play with her."

"Now I'm excited," Margo said.

"Want to come up and check on her with me?" Gideon asked.

His offer stunned her, and her sisters glanced at each other with a sweet smile.

"Sure, I'd like that."

Together they went to his room and to the little nursery nook he'd set up for his baby girl. The white crib was against the wall with a pink flower light suspended high enough that Claire couldn't reach. He'd hung a tapestry of the Alice in Wonderland tea party and a small set of white drawers had stuffed animals decorating the surface. A play mat with a colorful alphabet sat on the floor, and an assortment of toys were in the corner. It was the quintessential girl's room and Margo could almost see how it would evolve as Claire grew older.

From cute flower lights to regular twinkle lights and a canopy bed. The stuffed animals would stay, but a white desk with a diary would be added. It would drive her dad crazy, and Gideon would start to go gray at the temple.

Margo looked down at the sleeping baby with her tiny hands tucked together and Gideon's larger hand covering hers. She could see Gideon and Claire's future easily. Could see them being happy in Charlotte, but where did she fit it? That was the big question. What role would she play in their lives? She thought about that after she left his room with a soft goodbye. When

Margo lay in her bed and closed her eyes, in her dreams, she was happy with them.

IT BECAME NORMAL for Margo to pick up Claire from daycare once or twice a week if Gideon was busy. There were tons of projects to get done before the July rush at the inn started, and Mia's list kept getting longer. Gideon didn't seem to mind in the least. He looked happy in the evenings and after dinner, the sounds of his laughter combined with Claire's filled the house with joy that crept into every hollow.

She and Gideon grew closer as well. In the evenings, she sat with him outside on the porch swing while Claire drank her milk. In these moments, they spoke quietly about movies, books, and the things he saw while deployed. It was hard to hear how much suffering and loss a soldier could face in their career.

Many times, while they talked, Margo ended up holding Claire, patting her back gently while she fell asleep. As much as she tried to keep her heart shackled and locked away, it opened and flourished with Gideon and Claire in her life.

Margo greeted the daycare teacher and signed Claire out before strapping her into the stroller.

"Let's go play for a little bit before we go home," Margo said to the toddler.

"Yay!"

Claire's bright voice and hand clapping made Margo smile. The little girl liked to kick her feet while being pushed and as usual Margo stopped to slip her tiny pink Croc back on when it slipped off her foot. Margo recalled being in the mall with Gideon when he tried the shoes on Claire's feet.

"What do you think?" he'd asked while kneeling in front of his daughter.

"That's very—pink," Margo replied dubiously. "Neon Pink."

He nodded and grinned. "Exactly, they'll be easy to find, and we can add some of those shoe charms to them."

"Okay, I guess." Margo looked in the basket nearby. Plastic charms that fit in the holes of the plastic shoes. Lots. "There're flowers, rainbows and unicorns."

"Get two of each please." He got Claire's shoes back on. "What kind of charms do you like?"

"Hmm." Margo investigated the basket further. "There's a smiley face one. Oh, and a butterfly, and look, there's a turtle and a bunny. OMG there's a lizard!"

"Those sound cool, what size shoe do you wear?"

"Eight and a half," she said. "Why?"

She turned and he held up an exact pair to match Claire's.

Margo shook her head slowly. "That's so nice, but you don't have to."

"Don't you want to match this little sweetheart?" Gideon crouched down next to the stroller and looked up at her with puppy dog eyes.

Margo was unable to resist the power of that kind of cuteness.

"Fine." She sighed. "You found my kryptonite. Cute babies, and a handsome dad who's caring and kind. Use this knowledge sparingly."

Gideon stood and nodded somberly. "I will only use my powers for good…and for sweets, but mostly good."

"You're so weird it's cute." Margo laughed.

He kissed her cheek with a loud smack. "Thanks, babe."

The endearment warmed her, and they'd walked out of the shop together. This was why as she pushed Claire to the park, they wore matching pink Crocs with charms. As soon as she opened the clasp to the stroller, Claire took off like she had wings on her feet and Margo gave chase. That was how the afternoon was spent, down the slide, on the swings, and lots of running. *Good grief how much energy does one little girl have?* Margo sat on the bench and coerced Claire to sit and to take a cool drink from her kiddie thermos.

"They're a handful, aren't they?" a woman sitting close by, asked in an amused voice. "Trevor, do not hang upside down on the monkey bars. You might fall!"

Margo glanced over at the woman who was patting a baby resting over her shoulder, and then to the four-year-old now taking off his shoes in the sandpit.

"I just need a few shots of their energy," Margo replied. "I'm going to sleep good tonight."

"Are you…her nanny?" the woman asked and then blushed down to her brunette roots. "I apologize but…"

"I get it. She's white and I'm black," Margo said. "I'm not offended. She's the daughter of a friend of mine, and I picked her up from daycare. I'm watching her for a while."

"Would you consider being my friend?" she asked with a laugh. "Because Momma needs a Sunday brunch with actual adults."

Margo joined in on the laughter. "I think I can be coerced into that kind of afternoon. I'm Margo Ballad."

"Dawn Rush," the brunette held out her hand. "You're one of the sisters that own the cool inn?"

"Yep. I'm the middle sister. Are you guys new to our neighborhood?" Margo spoke warmly.

Dawn nodded. "You have that right. We moved from Chicago late last year and then I had the baby, so I'm still trying to learn my way around.

My husband's name is Phillip, and he works the short new rail line."

"Oh, I've always wanted to take a ride on that. I was waiting for a client to be over that way."

"What do you do?" Dawn asked.

"I'm a registered nurse, what about you?"

"I work from home. I'm an artist."

Margo gasped. "Oh, wow, we have a great group of artists and craftspeople here. You'll fit right in."

"Awesome." Dawn grinned. "Phillip is going to be thrilled that I made a friend!"

"Stick with me, kid, and I'll show you around. A lot of your neighbors have been here most their lives, including me and my sisters," Margo explained. "You guys are going to love it. It's a tight community…fun fairs and Roller Derby nights. The Sardis committee plans stuff throughout the year."

"Sounds terrific. This is nothing like our old neighborhood that's for sure, and I love our house," Dawn said happily. "I'd like to talk more, but I have to get these two kiddos home. Hopefully, during the walk, Trevor loses all the sand in his clothes."

"I should do the same before her father comes looking for her. Call the inn sometime and we'll set up a Sunday brunch date under the gazebo." Margo stood.

"That sounds wonderful. It was lovely to meet you," Dawn said genially.

"Same here." Margo got Claire strapped into her stroller. "See you around, new friend."

"Bye." Dawn waved as she went toward the sandbox.

Claire wasn't kicking her legs anymore. *She'd probably tired herself out*, Margo thought as she pushed the stroller. When she and the baby got to the inn and upstairs, Claire was fussy. She tried to get her cleaned up, and finally Margo just sat in the white rocking chair with yellow cushions and rocked the baby until she settled down. Her pacifier soothed her.

"Claire Bear, are you over tired?" Margo crooned. "It's okay, when I'm tired, I get cranky, and when I'm hungry and tired I get hangry, but you'll learn about that later."

Claire reached up and patted Margo's cheek. "Mama."

Margo stilled when she heard the word, and then Claire said it again, *Mama*. Something inside Margo broke free, and the first few tears slipped down her cheek. That one word felled her. It was something she never thought she would hear after that fateful night. Margo brushed the tears aside quickly and looked down. Claire had fallen asleep in her arms. Pressing a soft kiss on the little girl's forehead, she lifted the baby gently and laid her in her bed, covering her lower half with her soft blanket. Margo rushed out of the bedroom barreling right into Gideon's broad chest.

"Whoa, there." Gideon steadied her by the shoulders.

"Hey." Margo kept her voice light. "Claire tuckered herself out, and she was fussy so she's down for a nap."

"She's usually a one nap kind of girl. Did you let her run the entire property?" Gideon asked with a grin.

"No, the park, but she's down. You may want to give her like an hour before you wake her up." Margo tried to step around him.

"Hey, are you okay?" Gideon's tone held concern.

Margo was barely holding it together and wanted to escape to her room. But she pasted a bright smile on her face and hoped he couldn't see she had been crying.

"Oh, I'm fine," Margo lied. "You chase around a two-year-old in the park. I think I'm more exhausted than she is."

Gideon nodded. "Go lie down and get off your feet. Thank you for picking her up for me. I'll see you at dinner?"

"I may be skipping dinner tonight. I have a migraine brewing. Enid and my sisters know how they affect me, so they'll make me a plate later if I'm up to eating."

"I'm sorry. Is there anything I can do?" Gideon asked.

"No, I'm going to go lie down in a very dark room," Margo replied. "I'll see you tomorrow."

"Feel better and sleep well."

Margo fake-smiled and went to her room where she silently screamed the truth. *No. I'm not okay. Don't make me care for you and Claire!* But it was the way the little girl looked up at Margo with love and trust in her eyes that Margo knew she was sunk.

Margo took a shower and put on a T-shirt and shorts before getting into bed. She knew that when her sisters heard migraine, they would come up to check on her. She wanted them to think she was asleep.

With the blanket up to her chest, the first sob escaped and then another until her body was wracked with them. She curled into a ball as if she wanted to fold into herself. It wasn't possible, so Margo wrapped her arms around her core. She sobbed for all she'd lost, what she could gain, and the ache that had filled her being when Claire had called her...mother. It was all she'd ever wanted. She silently begged for mercy from the pain, and to have all those things she craved.

CHAPTER SIX

CONFUSION DIDN'T EVEN begin to cover what Gideon was feeling. He honestly thought that he and Margo had made a connection, but now she'd pulled away and was keeping him at arm's length. Well, not only him, but Claire too. While Margo was still affectionate to his daughter, after that night when they collided in his room, things had been different. Was Claire too much of a handful and Margo realized it after spending the afternoon with the baby? Or did she now know that a man and a baby might not be what she wanted in her life?

Gideon was a straightforward man by nature. He never said a thing he didn't mean and was honest to a fault, even if it hurt. Maybe that was what was wrong with the relationship formed with Trudy. She wanted to be taken care of, whereas he always thought partners take care of each other. She avoided independent decisions, instead she was accustomed to her parents deciding for her. He wanted her to be a mother to their child and make choices for herself to benefit them as a family. That's what he tried to do. If Margo was rethinking how she felt about them, he wished she would just come out and say it because now he didn't know where he stood.

He hardly saw Margo that week. The evening routine of sitting outside on the swing was nonexistent, and Claire was already asleep by the time she came home. One such night, instead of going inside, he waited on the verandah, listening to the cicadas sing, holding his little girl in his arms. It was yet another occasion when Margo had missed dinner, which, from her family's view, was absolutely not her normal routine.

"Hey, stranger." Gideon kept his tone neutral and friendly when she came up the porch steps.

"Oh, hi." Margo was dressed in her scrubs and shifted her bag to her other shoulder. "You're out here late."

Gideon hesitated. "I wanted to see you. I feel like I did something wrong, and you won't tell me."

"What? No!" Margo said instantly, yet she looked away before speaking again. "It's been a busy week for me, that's all."

"Something is wrong Margo. I can feel it. Just tell me what it is," Gideon implored. "This isn't easy for me, putting myself out there, and now I feel like I don't know where we stand."

Margo sat on the swing next to him. She caressed Claire's soft curls and pressed a kiss on her forehead.

"She smells like milk, baby and love," Margo said in a soft voice.

He smiled. "That's a sweet way to describe it."

"But an apt choice of words." Margo sighed wistfully. "Gideon, I'm trying to work through some things, and it has nothing to do with you or Claire and how I feel about the both of you. It's scary for me, all of this—these feelings."

"For me, as well, but I'm not pushing you away," he pointed out.

"I know," she whispered.

"Tell me what it is, and we can work through it together," Gideon offered gently.

Margo lifted her gaze to his face, and he could see the turmoil in her eyes.

"I will, one day soon, I promise. But I can't even voice it yet."

He nodded. "Okay, but don't keep us too far away, okay? She doesn't understand it, and I'm trying to."

"I get that, but I also need time," Margo pleaded. "Slowing down a bit won't hurt any of us if it's right."

He leaned his forehead against hers for an instant. "Roger that, ma'am."

Soon after that, he'd taken Claire inside. He

was feeling a bit better, but also worried if he'd made a big mistake letting Margo get so deep into their lives. It was not only him that he had to worry about, but Claire. He didn't want her to ever feel rejection.

His daughter was too young to remember what Trudy was like as a mother. Gideon knew that she loved Claire with all her heart, but because of her upbringing she was unable to show an open, generous type of affection. He tried as best he could to make it work with Trudy, but whatever he did was never enough for her, and she was never willing to accept she needed to meet him halfway.

Meanwhile, to her parents, everything was perfect, no matter how much he and Trudy were honest with them. In the end the demise of the marriage was, of course, everyone else's fault except Trudy's and theirs. Going over the past only opened old wounds.

He had to focus on the right now and what he wanted in life.

And what he wanted at the moment was for Claire to eat. After waking from her nap, his little girl was in a mood. Claire was fussy all through dinner. She hadn't even wanted her milk that night, only juice and cold lime Jell-O.

Things didn't improve later on outside. "She must be teething," Gideon said as he walked

Claire up and down the verandah, patting her back. Their usual sitting and rocking only made her cry. With her head on his shoulder, Claire sucked on the pacifier in her mouth.

"More than likely," Margo said, and he stopped for her to rest her hand on Claire's forehead. "Feels like low grade fever. I bet she has molars coming in. I hear they are always the worst."

He and Margo said their good-nights. And, finally the baby went to sleep. He placed her in her crib. Then he took a shower, checked on her, and went to bed, hoping tomorrow would be better for his Claire Bear. But when he got up and checked on Claire later that night, her face was flushed, sweaty and she was burning hot to the touch.

"Hey, Claire Bear, hey, sweet girl."

He lifted her into his arms, and she whimpered and pouted but never opened her eyes and terror unlike he'd ever known filled his chest. Without hesitation he ran toward the stairs and went down one flight, headed down the hall, and banged on the door.

"Margo!" Gideon knocked again urgently. "Margo, please."

She flung open the door, her face full of concern. "Gideon, what's wrong?"

"She's burning up and won't open her eyes…

I—I can't lose my little girl." Gideon's voice cracked.

Margo took the baby and laid her on the bed to assess her while he watched. She ran to her bag and got a thermal thermometer and took Claire's temperature.

"One hundred and three," Margo said just as Micki rushed into the room.

"What's going on?" she asked.

"Micki, call Mia, tell her to come to the house. Find out if Ryan is on call," Margo said urgently. "Gideon, go get dressed, grab her blanket, we're taking her to the children's hospital."

"Margo, is she going to be okay?" he asked, desperate.

"Gideon, go get dressed and hurry," Margo said, while she shoved her feet into her sneakers, then began tapping Claire's tiny foot with her hand. "Come on, sweet baby, open those eyes, there's a good girl."

He breathed out a quick sigh of relief seeing Claire's eyes open before he rushed out the room. "This can't be happening. This can't be happening," he repeated to himself as he pulled on jeans and his boots. He didn't bother to change his shirt—just picked up his wallet, keys and Claire's favorite blanket, before charging downstairs. Margo was already there in the lobby, holding the baby, and Mia had just stepped in the door. Enid and Micki were dressed and waiting.

"Ryan knows we're on our way," Mia said. "Give me the keys. You two sit in the back with Claire."

"I can drive," Gideon said.

Mia plucked the keys from his fingers. "No, you can't. Neither of you can. You're both terrified."

"You all don't have to come." Gideon looked at all the worried faces as they headed out the door.

"If you haven't figured it out by now, we're a family and we stick together," Micki told him. "You guys are our family now too."

That humbled him to hear because for a long time it felt like it was himself and Claire against the world. Now, he was part of a caring family and a community, that was a treasure. He focused on watching Mia drive seamlessly through the dark Charlotte night. He and Margo sat in the back with Claire in her car seat between them. Margo kept a vigilant eye on his baby, looking for any signs of distress. It seemed like they were at the hospital in no time and Ryan was waiting at the door with a nurse and a child's gurney.

Gideon had Claire in his arms as soon as the car stopped, and he rushed her fragile little body over to Ryan.

"She's had a fever and Margo said she's listless." Gideon began to stammer her symptoms.

"Give her to me. I'll take care of her," Ryan said gently.

Gideon heard the words but was frozen with fear.

"Gideon!" Ryan snapped, then gentled his voice. "Let me take her. I promise I will look after her, buddy. I promise."

Gideon let her go. Ryan placed her in the crib and began to assess her while the nurse pushed the gurney. He didn't understand the words Ryan was saying, but just then his Claire Bear began to cry and that broke his heart. With his hand on his head, he watched Ryan head off with his baby. He'd never felt so helpless in his life.

Margo came up behind him and wrapped her arms around his waist and he turned into her arms.

"I don't know what to do," he whispered raggedly. "I could take on any assignment the military threw at me, but this..." He lifted his head and looked at Margo. "How do I fix this?"

Margo took his hand. "You don't. You let Ryan handle it because he's one of the best pediatric doctors in the state. He's going to make sure Claire is okay. I can guarantee you that."

The rest of her family came up to him, and together they went to wait in one of the hospital's family rooms. Each minute seemed like an eternity for Gideon until Ryan finally came in. He shot out of his seat and rushed to where his friend stood. Ryan was the professional right now, wearing his doctor's coat with a sock puppet hanging out of one of the pockets. He would probably find that funny later, when he knew his baby girl was okay.

"Ryan?" The one word was all Gideon could manage.

"Claire's going to be fine. She has a viral infection that we've been seeing in a lot of kids the last few months." Ryan put his hand on Gideon's shoulder. "We have her on a broad-spectrum antibiotic, and I want to keep her for a day or two and make sure her lungs stay clear."

"Why? Is that going to happen?" he asked, looking at Margo for clarification.

She came and stood beside him. "He just means that it *can* happen. It hasn't, so that's good, but they want to be certain the medication does what it's supposed to."

Gideon let out the breath he was holding. "Okay—okay that's good. Can we see her?"

"Yeah, follow me. Don't be alarmed with all the machines. She has an IV and some oxygen to help her breath nice and easy," Ryan warned.

Margo turned to the family. "You guys head on home and get some sleep. I'll stay here."

"Call us if anything changes," Mia said and hugged Gideon and then her sister. "She's going to be good as new."

"Thanks for driving us here," Gideon embraced her.

Mia smiled. "And here are your keys so you can get home. I'll ride home with these two."

"You kiss my best friend for me." Micki hugged him as well. "I'll have the house stocked with mango Popsicles by the time she gets home."

"I'll make sure to do that," he promised.

"And I'll make sure that you have some dessert," Enid added after she gave him a hug. "Her dad needs a little comfort food after this experience for sure."

Gideon kissed Enid's cheek. "You're amazing."

The trio walked out and then he and Margo followed Ryan to Claire's room. The monitors were beeping, and Claire looked so still in the bed as she slept. Gideon covered her with her favorite blanket and sat down in the chair next to the crib, playing with her tiny hand.

"Uncle Ryan says you're going to be okay," Gideon whispered kissing her tiny fingers.

Ryan rocked on his heels with a grin. "I'm an honorary uncle now. I can dig it. Hit the button for the nurse if you need anything and have them page me when she wakes up."

"Thanks again, Ryan," Gideon said gratefully. "For everything."

"You're welcome," Ryan replied and stepped out of the room for an instant. "Margo, here's another chair for you."

"Thanks, Ryan."

Margo took the chair and, before she sat down on the opposite side of the crib, pressed a kiss to Claire's forehead.

"That was the most terrifying thing I ever experienced in my life," Gideon admitted.

Margo looked at him. "I can only imagine how you felt. I was scared as hell myself."

"Thank you for stepping in. I don't know what I would've done without you there." He reached over and took her hand, squeezing it gently.

"The reason I've been so distant since that evening I was with Claire was because she called me Mama," Margo said suddenly. "It felt so good, and also terrifying. What if I fall for her and then you take her from me?"

"I'm not planning on going anywhere," Gideon told her firmly.

Margo met his gaze. "Life changes at the flip of a coin, Gideon, and I can't stand to be hurt, not again."

"I don't know what happened to you in the past that made you so wary, but you and your family have given me and Claire so much in the short time we've been here. She already loves you," he shared in a gentle voice. "I guess it's up to you to decide how you need to protect your heart, but it doesn't have to be from us."

"I already love her and…" Her words fell away.

"And?" he asked huskily.

"I can't help but care for you both," Margo said and laced her fingers with his. "I think this dose of reality has me thinking I don't want to lose out on something that could be amazing. Losing her or you."

"Then we travel this path together." Gideon smiled and ran his fingers over the smooth skin of her knuckles. "With this little Claire Bear here."

As if she heard her daddy's voice, Claire squirmed and puckered her little lips to cry.

"Ssshh, baby, we're here," Gideon crooned and glanced at Margo. "We're both here."

They held hands over Claire and kept a vigilant watch while she was in the hospital. To Gideon, that solidified the way he felt about Margo more than anything else. He wasn't alone anymore, a single father taking on the world for himself and his child. At Ballad Inn, he found kismet with Margo, and a family he never knew he needed until they stood with him.

GIDEON WAS A less worried papa as Claire continued to get better after being released from the hospital and he nursed her back to health. Claire couldn't go to daycare until she was given an all clear by Ryan, so Mia gave him time off. He knew work was backing up. Enid watched Claire each morning and that gave him time to handle some jobs, but Gideon left early so he could spend the afternoons with Claire. He wanted her to know that daddy was there when she coughed too much or if she needed him to help her sleep.

His life had taken an upswing. He was happier, slept better, his baby girl was healing, and it was all because of Ballad Inn. He and Margo were on the same page. But it was much more than that, it was the warmth in the house from the family that embraced them and the close-knit community who had welcomed them with open arms.

Unfortunately, his former in-laws would throw a wrench into a good thing he had going on. Seeing the number of his lawyer come up on the cell while it vibrated on the bedside table made his heart lurch. Gideon moved from the bed where Claire was napping, a light breeze coming through the window across from where she slept.

"Hey, Jean," Gideon said in a low voice, stepping out of the bedroom. "Let me guess, the Wells are making waves again?"

"Big waves." Jean Hargrove was an amazing lawyer based out of Tacoma and she came highly recommended by his previous lawyer who had retired. She'd done everything right to make sure that Claire stayed with him, but this time she sounded worried. "I heard around the courthouse that Judge Wells is looking to get custody of his granddaughter. He's supposedly going to pull in favors from some of his cronies on the bench."

"That doesn't sound good for me," Gideon said slowly.

"Don't worry, yet. I wanted to let you know so if I call saying papers have been filed, you're not surprised," Jean said. "But as for his friends—he made none in family court. He insulted a few female judges with his horrible opinions of women on the bench."

"Knowing Grant, he will try to bully and threaten to get his way," he said grimly.

Jean hesitated before she spoke. "He can't get this case tried by anyone else but in family court, so that may work in our favor. Judge Macy or Fitzgerald are both fair and good. Wells may have friends, but he has just as many enemies."

"What's the worst-case scenario?" Gideon asked in a clipped tone.

"You have to come back for a trial and prove that you're stable as a single father—good job, housing, daycare facilities, things like that," Jean explained. "Ideally a two-parent household would be great, and that's what they will use to say they are good parental alternatives because his wife is a homemaker. But we also have Trudy's unhappiness with them to use as evidence, unless the judge doesn't allow us to use past events as such."

"This is a lot to think about," Gideon said with a sigh. "I guess it would be easier to just move back and let them have their way with my life and Claire's."

"I don't think you're the type to do that," Jean said gently. "As your lawyer, I'm also saying that's a terrible idea. Are you happy where you are?"

"For the first time in a very long time," Gideon said with honesty. "I even met someone. We're taking it slow but it's good, really good, and Claire is happy and thriving."

"Well, we're going to use all of that, plus your exemplary military record. If the family you're with is willing to offer affidavits or even testify…but we don't have to go there yet, not until we have something definitive to argue against."

"Okay, well, you'll keep me updated, right?" Gideon asked.

"Of course. That's my job, and as a friend, I'm happy for you," Jean said softly. "I'm going to fight like hell to make sure you and Claire keep that happiness."

"Thanks, Jean."

Gideon looked down at the phone after the call was disconnected and resisted the urge to throw it in anger. Would they never let him have any peace? He moved across the country, and still they were trying to ruin his life.

After Claire woke up from her nap, he was still antsy. He knew the only way to get rid of the restlessness was to work. To use his hands and build always made Gideon feel better. It reminded him of his deployment in Afghanistan when they built parts of their forward operating base from nothing, and he found a giant hedgehog-looking critter. There were pictures of him holding the animal in gloved hands. He'd have to find the photos to show Margo sometime. Enid was more than happy to have Claire in the high chair in the kitchen as she made dinner.

He left his daughter talking away in toddler speak while eating cut up tangerine pieces. Out in the workshop, he picked up a symmetrical piece of wood and set it in one of the carving machines. He wanted to replace a few of the banisters that were loose and temporarily fixed one too many times. The new pieces would be carved precisely to match the others, and no one would know the difference once they were stained.

"Hey, what are you doing?" Micki entered the workshop.

Gideon looked up, his chisel in hand as the wood spun on the bit.

"Replacing the loose banister rungs with new solid pieces, the temporary fixes won't hold much longer," Gideon said over the whir of the machine.

"I made those fixes," Micki pointed out.

Gideon smiled and tried not to hurt her feelings. "And they were done very well, but the wood is old. Probably why it didn't hold."

"I guess so. I could do this, you know, with that machine," Micki offered up.

Gideon turned it off. "You mean a lathe, have you ever used one?"

"No," Micki put her hands on her hips. "But how hard can it be?"

"Well, with the gouges, you might take off a finger, or launch the tool if it bounces out of your hand, or worse," Gideon said. "This is not a toy, but if you want me to teach you how to use it I can."

"That's what online videos are for," Micki said sullenly. "I was the handyman here for years."

"Yes, I know."

"And I did pretty awesome work like the gazebo extension and some of the barn renovation," she added.

"That was great work."

Micki narrowed her eyes. "Are you trying to

soothe me? That sounds like your sweet baby Claire voice."

Gideon shook his head and tried to look innocent. "Me? Never. We're discussing carpentry, craftsperson to craftsperson."

"Exactly, now we can discuss how *we* can redo the trellis on the barn before the weddings…"

"Hey, Micki, isn't that Mia carrying a puppy?" Gideon lifted the work goggles and pointed.

She rushed to the door. "Oh, wow, maybe she found one. She better not let Margo see it, but I always wanted a puppy."

She hustled outside the workshop but abruptly stopped and turned to Gideon. Realization bloomed on her face.

"Oh, that's sneaky, Holder. Real sneaky," Micki said.

"I know." Gideon grinned. "See you later, Mick."

He shut the door and picked up his tool.

"I'll have revenge, Gideon Holder," she yelled at him. "And I'm telling my sisters that you tricked me with the cute puppy tactic!"

"I'm sure you will," Gideon murmured, still grinning. He pulled his goggles back into place and turned on the machine just as she kicked the door.

The next loud knock he heard was about an hour later and he turned off the lathe and looked at the door.

"Micki, if that's you, I'm still busy with this," Gideon called out.

"No Mickis here, just your friendly neighborhood nurse Margo," she replied. She looked amused when Gideon opened the door. "Let me guess, Micki tried to invade the shop."

"She did." Gideon felt his heart ache sweetly in his chest looking at Margo. "Hey, you can't be everyone's friendly neighborhood nurse, I call dibs."

"Did you now?" Margo smiled at him warmly. "She did rat you out though, to me and Mia."

"To what end?" he asked.

"I told her to concentrate on college assignments and leave you alone," Margo replied. "Unless you invite her, this is your domain now. No interference."

"Thank you." Gideon dusted off the table so he could sweep up as he spoke. He liked a clean workspace, carpentry shed or not. "I have no problem teaching her things, or even taking advice or learning from her when it comes to the house. She's been caretaker for the inn long before I came into the picture. But this has been my profession most of my life and I know what I'm doing."

Margo stopped his movements with her hand over his on the broom handle. "Micki doesn't mean to insult in any way. She's passionate about everything, but it can come across a little bossy."

"I kinda got that." He smiled. "We're still in the get-to-know-you stage."

"That wasn't the reason I came in to see you." She took the broom away from him and put her hands in his so they could begin dancing slowly.

"Well, that's a nice thing to hear, you were coming just to see me." Gideon moved to match her easily to the music that only they could hear.

"And to ask you if you want to go to a concert?" Margo said. "I don't know if you like The Eclipse, but the concert is Saturday, and my client's daughter gave me two tickets."

"I'm in," he said instantly. "I've never seen them in concert, but we blared their music loudly on our base. After a while, even our translators knew the words by heart."

She offered him a small smile.

He smiled sadly. "We lost so much. But the music gave us a taste of home, kept us human."

"Then on Saturday at seven, me and you are going to take a journey to the stars." Margo stepped away, not before he took her hand to kiss it.

Gideon grinned. "I shall dress appropriately to view the cosmos."

"See that you do." Margo rapped on the wooden door a few times. "I'll see you at dinner tonight."

"See you then."

Margo left. Just seeing her made his mood lighter. Gideon tried more than once to recall a time he ever felt that way about anyone. He'd cared for Trudy, without a doubt, but the marriage was more like two people searching for something they never found in each other. And that didn't work out in the end for either of them. He never regretted it though because their union had brought him Claire. And after Trudy passed, his daughter needed him even more. Thinking back to what Jean said, he was determined not to lose Claire but to give her the life she deserved, with Margo hopefully by his side.

CHAPTER SEVEN

"I CANNOT FORGIVE you for this," Micki said firmly as she sat on Margo's bed. "They're my favorite band."

It was a warm Saturday evening and Margo looked from one blouse to another to go with the faded capri ripped jeans she already had on.

"I'm sure you'll survive," Margo murmured before asking. "Pink polka dot with the cute '50s neckline or the spaghetti strap cami with cherries and a bolero jacket?"

"You know I'll pick polka dot all day every day," Micki said with a sigh. "Imagine, you're taking your new boyfriend 'a courtin'' at a concert with music I love."

"A courtin'?" Margo's laughter spurted out. "Have you been hanging with Mr. Webber and Doodle?"

Micki flopped back on the bed. "Might as well, no one loves me in this house."

"We all love you." Margo rolled her eyes in the mirror and Micki threw the cami at her in response. "But see what you did there? Combined with this whole conversation, that's called melo-dramatic. There are more than likely still tickets left, dear sister."

"Is that in invitation?" Micki asked hopefully. "I'm wide-open tonight, no plans."

Margo shook her head. "No. Find your own plans, don't wiggle in on ours."

"I'd be far away. We'd just carpool," Micki suggested.

"Yeah, no. Hang out with your buddy Rabbit or something," Margo suggested.

Micki shrugged. "He's getting married or whatever. I got an e-vite about a week ago."

"Learn to enjoy your own company, then," her sister pointed out. "Micki's self-care evening. Think on it. I wish Mia was here to take my side."

"She wouldn't take your side."

"She so would."

"I'm worried about her...them," Micki sat up with a frown. "Something is going on with them and they're keeping it from us."

Margo pulled the top on. "I know, but we have to wait until she's ready to share. We can't force her."

"True, just like I can't force you to tell me what's going on in your noggin." Micki added. "You, Gideon and Claire are such a perfect fit, but sometimes I can see in your face you're terrified even though you care deeply for them."

"It's nothing," Margo lied. "If it doesn't work out, we'll have to see each other every day. It may get weird."

"Sure." Micki scoffed. "If that was to happen, even though there's no way on earth it could happen, you guys would end up being best friends and you would be best man at his wedding. But that's not going to happen. The wedding will be yours. I could bet two hundred dollars on it."

"I'll take that bet!" Margo held out her hand.

Micki danced toward the bedroom door. "I'm no fool. That's a sucker's bet, you charlatan! Snake oil charmer!"

"Stop hanging out with Mr. Webber!"

Margo was grinning when she rolled her braids into a bun on top of her head. It would be time to get her hair redone soon. She wasn't looking forward to that. It was tedious work to open each of the tiny braids, then wash and comb the thick coil in preparation to go to the salon. She gave herself, and her light makeup, another once-over before heading downstairs. Gideon was sitting on the bottom step playing a word puzzle on his phone. He looked up when he heard her footsteps.

Gideon stood and wrapped her in his arms for a hug. "You look gorgeous."

Margo stepped away. "You look great yourself. Where did you get an Eclipse T-shirt?"

"Amazon, two-day shipping."

He did look great. The black T-shirt was stretched over his broad chest and biceps. He wore faded jeans, and yep, his dusty work boots. Margo wondered if he had another pair, but of course, they were probably the most comfortable pair of shoes he owned. Some men were weird like that, wearing shoes until the soles fell off or wore out. Then hoped the shoes could be fixed instead of letting them go where old shoes went to die.

"Ready to go?" he asked.

"Where's Claire? Does Enid have her already?" she asked.

"Funny story," Gideon said as she made sure her small wristlet had everything she needed, including a bit of cash. "I was on the porch getting ready to bring Claire inside when Ryan stopped me. He and Mia wanted to take her to a place called Discover Zone for the crayons exhibit?"

"Oh man, is it back?" Margo exclaimed. "I hope I can take Claire again. I love it. Plus, I won't look strange being on my own if I take a baby."

"I'm sure she will promptly forget, and it will be new all over again for her," he assured her. "What is it anyway?"

"It's a child friendly interactive museum that

lets kids use their five senses to learn," she explained. "The Crayola exhibit has every color of crayon they ever made. Kids can draw, and there's music and water features."

He shot her a boyish grin. "Well, now at least I know where they took my baby. I handed over the baby bag, and they took the car seat. Micki went with them."

"I'm glad she found something to do," Margo said, relieved. "She was trying to be a third wheel on our date."

"Never," Gideon said. "Oh, Enid said to lock up. She's going to dinner with Mr. Bolton tonight."

"Got it."

Margo locked the front door to the inn using the keypad next to the polished brass knob. It was one of the very few things that wasn't vintage on the house. Together they walked to his truck, and he opened the passenger door for her to climb inside. He was so charming, and much to her delight, he stole a quick kiss. Gideon climbed behind in behind the wheel and started the huge beast. Margo loved trucks, and Gideon's was one of her favorites. She sent a silent apology to her truck, The Rocket.

"Oh! I forgot to tell you!" Margo looked over to him.

Gideon gave her a quick glance. "What?"

"They have scented markers and crayons too," she replied.

His rich laughter filled the cab of the truck. "That seals it for me. We have to go!"

She loved how easily he fell into things no matter how eccentric her family could be, or the neighborhood for that matter. They arrived at the concert pavilion, which was more like an outside stadium with seating on the grass as well as the covered portion. The seats she had were fantastic; they were so close to the stage. The music started. Some of the warm-up bands were really talented. She and Gideon stood with the crowd and moved to the music. Micki was right, her polka dots were perfect.

"I came here to see a reggaeton concert about a month before you got to Ballad Inn," she said, speaking right into his ear. The music was loud. Margo raised her voice a few octaves higher.

Gideon looked surprised. "Really, I wouldn't think you'd like that type of music."

"I love all kinds." Margo smiled. "From classical to heavy metal, I've been known to be in a mosh pit or two."

He laughed. "That would be something to see, you're so warm and sweet. I cannot picture you in a mosh pit with kids dancing like frenzied zombies."

His description made her laugh. "You should see me crowd-surf."

"You are an enigma, wrapped in a mystery, covered in genuine caring, Margo Ballad." He was talking so closely to her that the deep timbre in his voice made her shiver despite the heat.

Margo looked at him. "Is that a good thing?"

Gideon nodded slowly and laced his fingers with hers. "I have no complaints."

The screens went dark before the images for the main band came on and the group appeared onstage to roaring applause. Margo could swear she and Gideon were loudest, especially when their favorite songs were played. At one point she stumbled and fell against Gideon. Margo met his gaze and time stood still. The music and crowd noise that blared around them seemed to fade as Gideon kissed her gently. She certainly didn't know that the crowd cheering was for them, until she saw their image up on the big screens.

"That's what tonight's about friends, fun, rock and roll and love!" the lead singer said.

Margo beamed but she felt a jolt of embarrassment.

"Don't be shy." The lead singer jumped off the stage and came directly to them. "Who are you and what do you do?"

"Margo, I'm a palliative care nurse for seniors," Margo said softly.

"And you, hero boyfriend dude, what do you do in this slice of heaven?"

Gideon answered smoothly. "Gideon, retired marine, single dad and carpenter."

The lead singer held out his hand and Gideon shook it. "Thank you for your service, sir. It's an honor to meet you. I want you guys to come see me backstage when the concert is over. I have something special for you."

"You don't have to do that," Margo protested.

The band leader grinned. "It's already done, darlin'."

"This song is for all military personnel, active or retired in the audience tonight, courtesy of Gideon here, and all the nurses, thanks, Margo!"

The crowd cheered as the next song began and the rest of the night was pure bliss. They left later than the audience because the band loaded them down with so much of their merchandise, one of the roadies had to help them to the truck. As they drove away, she and Gideon glanced at each other with wide smiles.

Ballad Inn came into view once they were on the hill where Rae Road turned into their neighborhood.

"Thanks for going. Tonight was amazing." Margo sighed happily.

Gideon took her hand. "It should be me thanking you. It's been a long time since I even thought about a concert. Let's get this stuff inside. I can smell the rain in the air."

"Me too!" Margo said. "See, now you can tell my sisters it's actually a thing."

"You guys have some strange disagreements." He shook his head. "Or maybe it's normal. I never had siblings."

"You just take my side, and it will all be okay." She laughed.

Inside the inn, with their arms full, Gideon kicked the door closed with his booted heel. The noise brought Mia, Ryan and Micki out of the family room.

Micki's eyes narrowed when she spotted the stuff in their full arms. "Did you buy all that merch?"

"No, Simon, the lead singer singled us out in the crowd..." Gideon began.

"After Gideon kissed me and we ended up on the huge screens," Margo added with a smile. "Simon asked what we did and then he dedicated 'Ritual Love' to the nurses and everyone in the military who was in the audience, as a tribute to us."

"Then he said he wanted us to come backstage." Gideon took up where she left off. "And one of the roadies came to get us. We met the band, took pictures and they signed all these posters and sent T-shirts, hats, tumblers—oh the tumblers are signed too."

"And anytime they're in Charlotte, we have VIP access to the concert," Margo gushed.

"Wow, that's a lot," Ryan said with a wry grin. "And a fantastic time. So, you kissed her, huh?"

"One of many." Gideon's words made her face warm.

Margo shot Micki a hopeful look. "We brought you two different T-shirts and a hat, a tumbler, one band poster and an individual photo of Simon."

"And what about us?" Mia asked. "We spent all day in the Discovery Zone. Claire was fine, but there are some unruly kids out there. Eclipse merch should be a reward."

"I got you." Gideon passed them everything in his hands. "You deserve letters of commendation, some of those kid places are the worst. Like the one with the creepy mechanical alligator."

Margo looked at him in horror. "We don't talk about animatronics here. They are what nightmares are made of."

Mia smiled. "Claire is down for the count. Micks and I even gave her a bath and she drank that milk and was out in seconds."

"We're heading home. Night guys," Ryan said as he and Mia walked to the door.

"Thanks again for taking her," Gideon called after them.

Mia smiled. "It was great, and our pleasure."

"You forgive us, Micks?" Margo asked.

"For now, but next time I go for that VIP access." Micki sighed. "I could've been married to Cameron the drummer by now."

"The concert was only hours ago. How would you have managed that?" Gideon asked.

"Ssssh, let her have her dreams. We can give her that," Margo said with a soft laugh.

Micki ran upstairs with her stuff, humming one of the band's songs.

After she went with him to check on Claire, Margo opted for bed. She stared up at the ceiling with a smile on her face and a special warmth surrounded her. She welcomed it.

While she never thought a family of her own would happen, maybe this ready-made one could fill the longing inside of her, instead of all she had lost. Gideon and Claire were it for her. They'd burrowed their way into her head, and her heart. She closed her eyes and sighed.

Perfect.

THERE WEREN'T MANY times that Gideon was impressed, but he was by the drive up to the mountains with Margo and baby Claire tucked safely in her car seat. He was in awe of the view, and then again at the little Western town they'd built for kids called Toddler Railroad. Today was apparently special because a child favorite was there, Tangerine Tank Engine, a cute train with a sparkling headband would make an appearance and guests could take a ride. Of course, this was all kind Margo's planning.

They parked and got themselves organized. He pushed Claire in her stroller and admired the town built around an old railroad system. Today, it was all things Tangerine, including the large train that came chugging up as they approached the station.

"Tangy Twain!" Claire squealed and bounced.

"Who are you, kid?" Gideon asked in surprise. "I buy her two dolls and she is not interested, but a train with a giant face and she's ready to go."

"We can leave the stroller over in that area while we ride the train," Margo said, smiling. "Little girls don't always want to play with dolls. Mia loved Tangerine. She knew the songs by heart, owned every episode and movie on DVD. She kept all her stuff for when she has a son or daughter. I suspect she's pulled them out for Claire when she was at her house."

"So that's why she been calling stuffed bunny, chug-chug." Gideon laughed. "Your sister has made a train conductor out of my child."

Margo's chuckle was clear and sweet as they boarded the train after procuring a conductor hat. The train route was absolutely stunning with breathtaking mountain views. Claire waved madly to anyone she saw and for the most part they waved in return. His daughter had such a good time that they ended up riding Tangy, as Claire called her, several times that afternoon. They found themselves in a re-created old mining town, eating lunch in the jail cell because they'd *won* the role of the outlaws.

It amused Gideon to no end. No one could look at him, Margo and Claire as outlaws, but they enjoyed lunch with the sheriff. After eating, they promised to reform their awful ways and were let out of the cell where Claire promptly took a badge and hightailed it out of there with them on her heels. At the gift shop, they went a little crazy on the trains and toys they bought Claire. The day seemed to go buy in a flash, and before they realized it, it was five and the park would be closing in an hour.

Claire fell asleep as soon as he steered the truck out of the parking space, and while they headed down the mountain, the sun set over the valleys, causing hues of blues, oranges and pink in the sky and across the canopy of trees. Gideon laced his fingers with hers and she turned to him and smiled. He took a mental picture of that moment. Margo's beautiful face framed by a sunset with eyes filled with love. They hadn't said the words yet, but it was there, between them. Unspoken love, something Gideon couldn't describe, but it felt amazing.

Claire was up about two hours later, and they stopped for dinner at a quaint restaurant. On the way out, Claire made grabby hands at a Raggedy Ann and Andy set of dolls, and said, "Peese." Margo promptly picked them up and paid for them at the cashier.

"You can't give her everything she wants," Gideon pointed out.

"Why not?" Margo asked, casually handing Claire the cloth dolls.

Gideon lifted the baby as they went out the door. "It going to spoil her. She'll think she can get anything she wants."

"I disagree with that child development theory." Margo followed him out the door. "I think a child's wants should be nurtured. Telling a kid no doesn't necessarily teach respect. As children get older and learn how to ask, using please and thank you, and you form proper boundaries, kids will figure out what they can ask for and when. Denying them only builds resentment and they throw tantrums because they don't understand why the parent is saying no."

"That's a different way to think about it," Gideon said, as he strapped Claire into her car seat. "Wish my parents had followed that."

Margo stood on her tiptoes to kiss him before moving over to the passenger side. "Just so you know, anything you want, just ask me and I'll say yes and get it for you."

Gideon laughed. "I'll remember that."

Pulling into Sardis was a welcome sight. The day had taken a toll. They were both tired, and his Claire Bear was a handful on outings. *If only we had an ounce of baby energy, I could accomplish so much*, he thought, amused. As they stopped in front of the inn, he saw a silhouette of a person dash from off the porch and run into the trees.

"Did you see that?" Margo clutched at his arm.

"Yeah." Gideon was instantly on alert. "You call your sisters to let them know what's happening and tell them to stay where they are until I give the all clear."

Margo nodded but he could see concern in her eyes.

He squeezed her hand comfortingly. "It's going to be okay."

She was unclipping Claire when he got out and she had the baby in her arms as he blended into the shadows. He saw the small figure again, and Gideon was instantly a soldier once more, crouching down, watching each step so he didn't draw attention to himself. This person was an amateur, making more noise than a bull in a china shop. When he ran past where Gideon was hiding, he snagged the little would-be burglar.

"Hey, let me go!" the voice cracked.

Gideon pushed back the hood of the black sweatshirt to reveal a young sullen face and glaring eyes.

"You're just a kid," he said. "Come on, let's go."

They walked back through the trees to the inn and found everyone, including Mia and Ryan, outside. Micki carried a baseball bat and Enid a rolling pin.

"I thought I said stay put until I sounded the all clear?" Gideon asked them helplessly.

Micki held up her bat. "In case you needed back up."

Gideon shook his head and chuckled. "You're going to hit a home run and Enid's going to roll them out. Anyway, here's our culprit, no more than fourteen, I'm assuming."

"I'm thirteen," the boy said grimly.

"What were you going to do?" Mia asked.

He didn't answer and Margo frowned. "Are you a runaway?" she asked.

The kid gave a sarcastic laugh. "Runaway from what? I don't have a home, lady. I was just looking to get something to eat. Big place like this, I thought I could raid the kitchen or something. You guys don't look hard up if you lose some food."

"Or, you could walk up and ring the doorbell," Ryan said, gently.

"Yeah, sure. A kid my color coming up to this place." He scoffed.

Margo bounced Claire in her arms. "We're exactly your color. What's your name?"

"Trig."

"Real name," Margo added dryly.

"Omar Barrows," he said. "Rich people stick together no matter what color."

"We're not rich by any means." Micki looked at his sweatshirt. "What's that bulge."

He pulled out four pears. "Told you... I was hungry."

Gideon took them. "Son, they're not even ripe."

Omar shrugged. "If you're hungry, you don't care."

Enid made a sound of distress and Gideon watched her fan her face to hold back the tears. It tore him up too, hearing that from a boy that young. Gideon remembered seeing scenes like this during his tours.

"Should we call the police?" Mia asked.

A look of terror filled Omar's face. "Please, no. I'll go, and I promise not to come back. I don't want to go to any juvie home."

"No." Gideon shook his head. "I saw a news story about these folks who think it's sometimes safer to be on the streets."

"I tend to agree," Ryan said, sadly. "I treat kids from these homes from time to time. Pretty banged up from fighting, and all sorts."

"What he said." Omar looked around. "Sleeping in the slide tubes at the kids' park is safer than juvie. It ain't a great place."

"Isn't," Enid corrected him.

"Yes, ma'am." Omar ducked his head down.

"He's going to come right in, and we're going to feed him and give him a place to sleep," Enid said, firmly. "You girls don't remember but your parents always said we don't turn away those in need, and we definitely don't turn away children."

Margo nodded. "We have more than enough room until we figure out how to help him."

"You guys want to take me in?" Omar seemed shocked. "I just tried to steal from you."

"No, you were desperate to eat," Enid stated. "Is this all the clothes you have?"

"Running away means you pack light," Omar admitted. "I doubt anyone even knows I'm gone, or cares."

"We'll grab you some gear." Gideon addressed Margo, "Can you get her to bed for me, I'll make a run to the Waithe's."

"I'll go with you," Ryan said. "What size shoes do you wear?"

"Eight." The young man looked amazed. "You

guys…are you guys actually talking about taking me in?"

"Till we can find somewhere safe for you to be, yes." Mia glanced at her sisters' faces. "Unanimous decision?"

"I think from the moment Enid wanted to feed him we all were pretty much for the idea," Micki said in a light voice. "But we can't keep the kid without school and stuff, either."

"Let me pull some strings. I know a few people," Ryan said. "This could be what we talked about Mia."

She smiled. "I know."

"Fill us in?"

Mia squeezed Margo's hand and then Micki's. "Soon, I promise."

"Okay it's getting late, we should get this show on the road," Margo said. "Menfolk off to the twenty-four-hour department store. Me, Mia and Micki, we'll be supporting staff and get him a room set up. Enid feed Omar until he's ready to burst, then give him dessert."

"Whoa, there's dessert in this?"

"Kid, I live here for the desserts." Gideon grinned at Margo. "And for her."

Ryan nodded. "Same."

"You also work here, Gideon," Micki teased.

"Obviously." He patted her on the shoulder as he and Ryan passed by. "Stay out of my workshop, unless you'd like to be my assistant. If you're good, I'll even promote you to senior assistant."

"Margo, you gotta make him stop that!" Micki wailed.

"I didn't hear a thing. Taking care of a sleepy baby," she called over her shoulder, walking up the porch stairs. "He's teasing you like a big brother would."

"This is why our parents had all girls." Micki followed her, and Mia was on her heels.

Mia snorted. "I don't think they had a choice in that. Michael became Michelle when you were born."

"Come on, Omar, let's get you warm, fed, a good shower and a comfortable bed." Enid put her arm around his shoulders.

"Okay, thanks," Omar said, staring at the sisters as they entered the inn.

Omar's eyes were as big as saucers. The kid had just gotten the biggest gift of his young life. Ballad Inn would now be his home. Gideon could tell the sisters weren't sending the boy anywhere. Omar had found a family, just like Gideon and Claire.

GIDEON KNEW IT was coming, but the call from Jean still made him sit down in his workshop. His hands trembled as he answered the phone.

"They filed." Gideon stated the fact.

"I got the papers this morning," Jean said. "Do you have a minute to talk."

Gideon laughed but with no happiness. "It's for my child. I'd make the time. So, what have we got?"

Jean sighed. "They're claiming you alienated them from Claire, and then moved across the country so they couldn't see her."

"Really." Gideon's tone was filled with disbelief. "I offered them the chance to come visit her. They could even book a room at the inn."

"Calm down, Gideon," Jean soothed. "You have written documentation of this. Their main claim for sole custody is your lack of a fixed address, and that your work takes you away from Claire. This is where the affidavits from your employer, and the sisters of the inn come into play. Also, the documentation from the daycare. You said it's within walking distance, right?"

"Right around the corner, and I go eat lunch with her daily," Gideon confirmed. "Mia, the oldest sister, basically lets me work around Claire's schedule, and they sometimes take her on outings or babysit her if I need to get something done that day. Claire has what seems like aunts and uncles and even a grandmother in Enid. We have more than enough support. We're not alone."

"This is all good," Jean said, and he could hear her writing. "I'm drafting our counterclaim, including some practices we've found out about Judge Wells. If they're playing hardball, so are we."

"I didn't want to exclude them from Claire's life," Gideon protested. "I just needed them to leave me alone and to let Claire thrive here. They are welcome to be in our lives, but not on their terms. I'm her father. I set the rules."

"It would help so much to seal this if you had a relationship going on," Jean murmured. "I mean you have a seventy percent chance of this going your way. I wish we could lock up the last thirty percent."

"I do have someone," Gideon admitted, thinking about Margo with a smile. "Margo Ballad and I are getting pretty close, but we're taking it slow."

"And Margo is…"

"The second sister, she is a palliative care nurse, with a masters in nursing, including pediatrics," Gideon replied. "Ryan Cassidy is married to Mia, she's the oldest, remember? He is one of the leading pediatric doctors in the country. He works at a hospital nearby."

"I have heard of Doctor Cassidy," Jean said. "All of this is good stuff. Have the Wells tried to reach out again?"

"No, should I call them?" Gideon asked. "I

send pictures to Denise's cell but never get a response."

"No, keep the contact minimal. We don't need this to be more caustic than necessary," Jean said. "Okay, I am going to get our response filed today. I want their lawyer to see how tight the case is. Luckily, we hit the judge jackpot with Judge Fitzgerald. She believes that children need to be with their birth parents as much as possible, and even in cases when children are taken out of custody, she gives them a chance with rehabilitation."

"Sounds good," Gideon said.

"I'll email those affidavits. Have them filled out and notarized before sending them back to me," Jean said. "Don't worry, we're going to win this, Gideon."

"From your lips…"

"To God's ears," Jean said with a soft voice. "Trust me when I say he's looking out for you guys too. Talk soon."

"Bye, Jean."

Gideon stared at the phone in his hand, his frustration growing by the second. Before he realized what he was doing, he scrolled through his contacts and finding Denise Wells's number, he pressed it. Claire's grandmother answered on the second ring.

"Gideon," she said his name simply.

"Why are you and Grant doing this?" Gideon asked. "Can't you see that Claire's happy? We're happy?"

Denise gave a short laugh. "Yes, I can. You're out there having huge fun with my granddaughter and acting like my daughter never existed. Does Claire even now about her?"

"Denise, she's two. Of course, as she gets older, she'll know about her mom, but you can't expect us to live in a gray world of mourning for the rest of our lives," he protested.

"Why not, I do," she shot back.

Gideon hesitated before speaking. "Then you're selfish and this custody case just proves that. You can see in the pictures that Claire is happy. She's playing in the sun, making friends and is so smart. Just come see for yourself and be a part of her life."

"You can move back here, into the house, and we'll drop the case," Denise countered.

Gideon knew he couldn't do that to his daughter or himself. "I won't put her in a prison of your making. We're good here, so I guess we'll see you in court."

"You're going to lose her, Gideon," Denise threatened. "We have a more stable home—a two parent home. You're a single father, a drifter."

"That's where your wrong, Denise. I have more roots here than I've ever had in my life,"

Gideon protested. "And I have someone who loves me and Claire. A family who stands by us. And I'm getting married."

"I don't believe you," Denise said slowly. "So soon after Trudy?"

"Denise, Trudy died when Claire was five months old," Gideon said gently. "I truly, truly wished she was here to watch Claire grow up, but we need to be happy as well."

"Of course, after you drove her away from us and we weren't there to protect her," Denise cried out.

He stopped her right there before she could say anything else.

"Lay blame where you think it needs to be, Denise," Gideon answered bluntly. "I tried to be the best husband I could be. While I was deployed, I begged you and Grant to support us but you both told her and us to work it out. That we'd be fine. But we weren't fine. We were a mess relationship-wise."

"Because you weren't there," Denise threw out the blame.

"I was a marine. When they say jump the only thing I can do is ask how high?" Gideon retorted. "Denise, I didn't call to hurt you or argue. But pretending it was okay until you couldn't look past the truth was yours and Grant's way of handling what was going on with me and Trudy. We both have fault here. I was her husband, and I should've listened to my gut instincts when we got pregnant. I wanted to give us a shot but in my heart I had doubts. We didn't start off on the right foot and it never got any better for us. That is my burden to bear, and I will carry that fault, but I won't carry yours as well."

"Just move back here, Gideon," Denise pleaded.

Gideon ran his hand through his hair. "I won't, Denise. We've found a real, loving home, and you still have the offer to come visit. It's a beautiful place and..."

Denise disconnected the call, and he sat on the floor, emotionally exhausted. The words *I'm getting married* had slipped from his mouth before he could stop them. While he should regret saying them, knowing they held the power to change his life, Gideon didn't. The thought of being married to Margo felt right, not just because of how good she was with Claire, and that it would help his legal case, but because, Gideon acknowledged, he loved her. He wondered how Margo would react—a sense of exhilaration filled him, and Gideon left the workshop. He passed Omar on the way, who was outside the shed, taking care of Margo's bunnies, ducks and chickens.

"Hey, Omar." Gideon slowed down.

"Margo said I could feed them," Omar said defensively.

Gideon smiled gently. "Easy, kid, I know you're good, okay? No one is going to accuse you of anything here. Plus, if you get the basket from Enid, you can collect the eggs from the coup."

"Oh." Omar's eyes brightened. "Cool, I never collected eggs before."

"Have you seen Margo?" Gideon asked.

"She was in the family room, ironing a table-cloth." The young boy shrugged and fell into step beside him. "Who irons tablecloths?"

"People we didn't think existed." Gideon looked at Omar. "I was never in one place for very long, certainly not long enough for my mom or anyone to be pressing tablecloths. We kept things pretty humble in my family, my dad was military."

He nodded. "Lots to like about being here. Although I wasn't sure about Monty. I was kinda scared of him, but he seems like a chill lizard. Maybe we can be friends. Miss Mia and Ryan are applying to be my foster parents. The doc—I mean Ryan, said he has people to help make that happen and at their house I can have a huge room with my own stuff."

"How do you feel about that?" he posed the question.

Omar gave what Gideon considered as his signature shrug. "I don't mind it. I mean, I never had a room of my own ever, and they seem nice.

I just hope they don't get bored of me and send me away."

Gideon stopped and turned the boy gently by the shoulders toward him. "You can trust me when I say, no one here is going to send you away. This is going to be your home. This family, they make quick decisions, and they stick to them. I think Mia and Ryan want to be your forever mom and dad."

Omar gave a hesitant smile. "I'd like that. He said he'd take me to work with him, something about needing a new assistant, and they have a boat on the lake, but first I gotta learn to swim."

"They'll take care of that too," Gideon said, happy for him. "Go find Enid for the basket and I'll go find Margo. Come by the workshop later, and you can help me finish the banisters I'm etching out."

"Yeah tools!" Omar yelled as he ran off.

Gideon couldn't question his reaction to tools. He'd felt the same way when he'd picked up his first hammer. Boys and anything that could possibly drive their parents mad with worry, generally went together. But in his workshop, everything would be done safely.

This was a blessing in the rarest form. Omar would have a home here now and that was the best thing for a thirteen-year-old lacking security and a belief in others. Just like he said, Margo was in the family room with an iron. The steam came up from its flat surface as she moved it over the fabric on the ironing board. A neat stack of tablecloths were already folded and were sitting off to the side.

"Wow, that's a lot of tablecloths," Gideon commented, standing in the doorway.

Margo looked up with a warm smile. "July's coming up fast—first wedding is on the sixth."

"Ah, well then, do you need help?" he asked, stepping into the room.

She shook her head and turned off the iron. "Nope I'm all done. I just have to let this cool—Gosh darn it, Doodle!"

A giant orange puff of fur jumped through the window and knocked over one of the piles of champagne colored tablecloths. He flew out of the room and was heading up the stairs.

"Is that Monty's love interest Ryan was talking about?" Gideon called after Margo, following her up the stairs.

By the time he located them, Margo had a hold of a cat with the strangest orange color he'd ever seen. He still couldn't get over it and with suspicious green eyes, the cat creeped him out a little bit.

Margo frowned at the cat. "Don't believe Ryan's theory. Cats eat lizards. Monty is this one's unicorn. He wants to murder my Monty. This place needs to be a fortress."

"As a contractor I will investigate and bring you my findings on how to cat proof against Monty's feline nemesis," Gideon offered and took the surprisingly heavy animal. "What does he feed this guy?"

"He feeds on his nefarious intentions toward Monty." Margo was on his heels as he took him outside and deposited him back over the fence. "Now I need to go lint roll and deal with the pile he destroyed."

Gideon took her hand. "Can that wait for a minute? I wanted to talk to you, ask you—can we sit?"

"You seem a bit flustered." Margo eyed him curiously as they sat on one of the white porch swings on the patio. "Are you okay?"

Gideon heaved out a breath. "Not really. I got news I was dreading this morning. Claire's grandparents are trying to take custody from me."

"I'm so sorry." Margo took his hand. "Anything we can do? You know we'll help. You're family, all of us, will fight beside you so they know Claire is happy and thriving here."

"Thanks for that. My lawyer will need affidavits from you guys, Ellen at the daycare, and Ryan as her pediatrician. I hope that's enough."

Gideon hesitated for a moment. "I can't believe they're trying to take my daughter from me."

"Do you want me to go with you, back to Washington, when you have to go to court? Is that what you wanted to ask me?" Margo asked.

"Yes." He met her gaze. "As my wife."

"What?" Shock registered on her face.

This time it was Gideon who took her hand and kissed it. "We care about each other, right?"

"We do, but…"

"More than care?" Gideon prodded and gave a soft laugh.

She nodded. "More than care, for you both."

"Well, Margo Ballad, in the span of weeks, I think I've fallen head over heels for you."

"Is this because of Claire?" Margo asked bluntly. "I know you being married looks better for the custody case."

"I'd never lie to you. Yes, that's part of it." But Gideon needed her to understand. To see how much she'd come to mean to him in such a short time. "But that's not the only reason. I've been thinking about this more and more. When I was married before it was rushed, forced, both me and Trudy looking for something neither of us could provide. I was a marine and I wanted someone to come home to, but Trudy and I never really fit. I cared about her, more than her parents realized, and she blessed me with Claire."

Margo looked at his face as if searching for the truth or a lie before asking. "And now?"

"We fit—me, you and Claire." He meant every word and pressed her hand over his heart. "From the moment I met you, this ache started deep inside, and I can see a forever with you, Margo. I want that so much."

"I have to think," Margo protested. "I can't just jump into this. I can't hurt like that again if I lose you both."

"You won't lose us, I promise." Gideon kissed her hand.

"Don't do that, don't make promises you can't keep. Things happen beyond our control. You know that just as well as I do," Margo's voice held tears. "The reason why I have to think is because I love that little girl and to lose that love for her or you. I couldn't come back from that, not this time around."

"Tell me," Gideon prodded gently. "Let me share the load, like you've done for me."

Her voice hitched and she blew out a shaky breath. "I lost my fiancé in a car accident. I was in the car, and I lost something more that night."

"What?"

She pressed a hand against her stomach. "More. And I may never have that again. If I marry you, and Claire becomes my child—if I lose you both... I can't—I need to think."

Gideon pulled her into his arms. "Oh sweetheart, I'm so sorry."

He felt her shake in his arms before Margo pulled away and wiped her eyes. "I'm sorry, I wish I could say yes right now this instant."

"I understand, and even if it's a no, and you need more time, I'm not going anywhere."

"Why?"

"Because I want you to be a part of my life, our lives, however you'll have us, and that's all that matters." He cupped her face gently. "As long as I know I have you by my side, I can face anything."

"It's not a no," Margo said softly.

Gideon held her close again. "I know, sweetheart."

Margo stood. "I'm going to get back to my tablecloths and we'll— Well, you know where I live."

He gave a laugh. "Third floor, right?"

"Exactly," she smiled before opening the front door and heading inside.

He waited for a moment before heading back to the workshop. He'd proposed, sort of, and it was a wait-and-see type of scenario. Gideon tried to put it out of his mind, but Margo, his child, and the looming custody case, made work almost impossible.

"Hey." Omar stood at the doorway, looking

uncertain. "You said I could learn how to make stuff."

Gideon smiled. "Yep, come on in. How about we start with something easy like making a bird-house?"

Omar's face brightened. "Sure, can I paint it and put it next to the other house for the birds?"

"Sure can, and we'll add a patio for bird seed." Gideon handed him a pair of glasses. "Let's start with making the pieces of the house."

Teaching Omar about woodworking was a great way to take his mind off the unknown. He couldn't fathom his life without Claire or Margo, and the thought of losing his child made him hurt worse than any bullet or shrapnel he took when he was deployed. He sent up a silent prayer for intervention, *please don't take them from me*. Gideon had very few memories, moments, or people to treasure in his life, but his child and now the woman he'd fallen for were at the top of the list.

CHAPTER EIGHT

WHEN IN DOUBT, bake it out.

That was Margo's motto and right now all the doubts in the world swirled around her. That night at the dinner table, she and Gideon shared secret looks and soft smiles until Micki rolled her eyes.

"Will the two of you stop with the goo-goo eyes and get married already," she said before biting into a fluffy biscuit.

Her words made Margo flush and her face warmed, if only her sister knew how close they were to that point. But hesitation swirled in her mind.

"Hey, guys." Gideon cleared his throat. "I wanted to let you know, Claire's grandparents have filed a custody case against me for Claire."

"How dare they!" Enid said outraged. "You are a wonderful father."

"They want me to bring her back to Tacoma." He looked at his daughter. "I can't force a life onto her that removes her from the happiness we've found here, so I have to fight it."

Margo looked at them both and said firmly, "I'm going with him when it's time for the trial."

"We'll all go," Mia chimed in. "There's no way we'll let you face this alone, Gideon."

"I've done a few assessments in custody cases as the doctor of record," Ryan added. "I will add Claire's full workup and my medical opinion as her pediatrician. There's also a wonderful child therapist at the hospital I can put you and your lawyer in contact with. She can see Claire and offer her professional diagnosis of her well-being."

"That would be a great help," Gideon said gratefully and looked at each of them. His gaze settled on Margo when he spoke again. "Thank you. You all are amazing."

"This chicken is amazing," Omar said, adding another huge forkful of potatoes and chicken to his mouth.

"You're going to be six feet tall by the time you're sixteen if you keep eating like that," Ryan said amused.

Omar looked at him. "Really, because I was kinda shorter than anyone else I knew."

"You're thirteen. You have more than a few growth spurts coming," Ryan told him.

Omar grinned. "Nice."

"Speaking of which." Mia smiled at the young boy. "Ryan's resourceful contacts have worked quicker than we thought. Guess who are your new foster parents!"

"No way!" Omar cried out. "So, I don't have to go a group home?"

"No. Our background checks were good, and we came through all the other stuff with flying colors," Ryan added. "We are taking the classes at the hospital while you live with us, but it's a formality at this point. If things continue to go well for all of us, with the arrangement, we might consider starting adoption proceedings in about six to nine months, if you'd like that."

"Is that something you may want?" Mia asked Omar with a gentle smile.

Omar dropped the fork and pushed the chair back across the polished floors with a loud scraping noise that made Margo grimace.

"We'll need to get that buffed out." Enid sighed. "A boy in the house means muddy floors, scratches, and the larder empty."

"Just like when we were growing up." Micki grinned.

Enid smiled. "Exactly."

Omar rushed over to Mia and Ryan and put an arm around each of them. "I would like that. I mean really, really love that."

Mia smiled and wiped at her eyes brimming with tears. "Me too."

"Ditto, but you're squeezing me." Ryan's voice was raspy, but his smile was wide.

"Oh, sorry." Omar pulled away. "What should I call you?"

"How about Mia and Ryan to start, and then you just go with what you feel," Margo suggested.

"Sounds good to me." Omar went back to his seat and again the chair scraped against the floor.

"So much buffing." Enid sighed.

The entire dinner had an effect on Margo and that night she couldn't fall asleep. She finally gave up around two a.m. and that was when her baking started. Micki came home about two hours later and walked directly into the kitchen.

"Whoa, are we expecting guests for brunch I didn't know about?" she asked, taking it all in.

"Nope, couldn't sleep." Margo glanced at the doorway where Micki stood before going back to carefully folding whipped egg whites into the Belgian waffle batter. "Eat what you like. We have banana bread and peach muffins. I'll get a fruit compote started when I finish these. Oh, and black current scones, cherry pie, chocolate chunk cookies."

"Margo, you're stress baking. Something is obviously wrong," Micki said slowly. "We're going to have to give so much of this to the neighbors. Will you stop with the batter?"

Margo shook her head. "You know if I don't fold this in just right the waffles won't be light and fluffy."

"Sis, it's like four in the morning. I don't think anyone is expecting breakfast." Micki pulled out her phone. "I'm calling Mia."

"Don't call Mia, and why are you just now getting home?" she asked. The batter looked fantastic. Margo sprayed the waffle irons.

"I went to one of the War World games and it got crazy," Micki answered. "Sally went rogue and started a campaign against Will, and you know he likes to be Dragon King of every new game. A coup followed and we had to choose sides before he unleashed a mutant horde."

Margo stared at her. "I don't know what any of that means."

"Don't worry about it." Micki put the phone up to her ear. "Hey, Mia. No, the house isn't burning. Margo's in a baking loop. Something is up with her. Okay, I'll see you in a few."

"I don't know why you called her," Margo muttered pouring batter onto the waffle irons.

"Uh-huh." Micki picked up a muffin and bit into it before closing her eyes. "I have to say, your baking is always sublime, but when you can't sleep and something is on your mind, it's like a whole new level."

"Thank you, I guess." Thunder rumbled outside before the first patters of rainfall hit the roof. "If Mia is coming and it's raining, best to put on the tea."

"Did you make any of those…" Micki snapped her fingers as if she was trying to remember the exact name. "The chocolate things for storms."

Margo rolled her eyes. "Pain au chocolat, are you going to ever learn the name?"

"Have I ever before?" Micki asked.

"Good point, and yes, I made those first. Look under the cheesecloth." Margo waved her hand at the opposite counter. "At least make some hot chocolate, you always forget the electric teakettle."

Mia came through the back door and left her umbrella in the mudroom off to the side. "It's really coming down out there."

"Ryan going to miss you tonight?" Margo asked.

"He's got night rotation. He won't be home until the morning," Mia said. "Omar is fast asleep. I left a note in case he does wake up. So what's happening here?"

"How goes the room renovation for Omar?" Margo waited for the kettle to finish boiling, and poured them each a cup of their favorite hot chocolate. Micki had been little help, having got distracted with eating the pastries.

"He's going to love it, I hope." Mia smiled and held up two crossed fingers. "We may have gone a bit overboard."

Micki put six of the special pastry treats on a plate. "He's a teen boy, as long as there is a gaming console in there, he'll be good."

"Oh, we have a game set up tomorrow night," Mia said, rubbing her hands. "He thinks he can beat me at *Fate and Fantasy*."

"Ah, you'll be amazing at being a mom." Margo smiled and everything she was trying not to think about came flooding in. Who was she fooling? It never left no matter what she baked or created.

My old faithful has betrayed me, she thought thinking about all the cakes, breads and cookies surrounding her.

"Come on. Upstairs." Mia encouraged Margo. "We'll snack, talk and then you'll sleep. I have to go back to Omar after this."

"The cleanup…" Margo said looking back.

"We'll help in the morning," Micki promised and waved her hand at the kitchen before they left. "You need to talk about whatever this is."

"But first we nibble." Mia smiled while they walked up the stairs. "We haven't done this since that stormy night I decided to go find Ryan in Spain."

"Second anniversary coming up." Margo pushed open the door of what was once her older sister's bedroom. "You guys are amazing together."

Margo could close her eyes and see herself and her sisters sitting on the wide four-poster bed as children. It had been large enough for all of them to sleep in. The lights over Mia's bed were still there, but most everything else was gone. The white bookshelf that now stood empty in the corner once held her fairy ornament collection. Margo smiled at the warm memories. Lightning cut through the dark night, lighting up the room for an instant making them all scream and then laugh.

"Hush, we're going to wake up Enid." Micki fake whispered.

"You know how she sleeps." Margo shook her head. "She's out like a light."

"Amazingly enough, when we used to try to sneak out, she was like a motion sensor." Mia chuckled as she switched on the twinkle lights. "Let's eat."

They talked about a little bit of everything and reminisced about growing up until there were tears in their eyes from laughter. It was all to loosen her up of course, and Margo appreciated that her sisters knew exactly what she needed without her having to tell them.

"Gideon asked me to marry him." Margo just dropped the news and waited for their reaction.

Mia choked on the sip of her hot chocolate. "What? What did you say?"

"Yes!" Micki said around a bite of her pastry.

"No, I said maybe." Margo flopped back on the bed and looked up at the ceiling. "It helps his case. To keep custody of Claire."

"Is that his only reason, because if it is, he gets a good talking-to from me." Mia's lips were in a frown.

Margo turned to her side so she could see her sisters. "No, he loves me—I think. We haven't technically said the words yet. He said even if I say no because it's not the right time, he'll still be here, and will wait until its perfect for both of us. Regardless, I'll go to Tacoma with him when it's time to go to court."

"Why are you hesitant, Margs?" Micki asked gently. "You love them, anyone can see it."

"What if I say yes and I lose them like I did when Scott died…" Margo took a shuddering breath. "The night of the accident, I lost Scott and…a baby as well. I was pregnant and—after that, I just can't even fathom the loss."

"Margo, why didn't you tell us?" Mia put her cup down on the bedside table and instantly embraced her sister. "Why did you face that all alone?"

Micki was on the other side and hugged her, pressing her face against Margo's back. "Oh, honey, I'm so sorry."

"I was reeling, and then it was something I pushed away so it wouldn't hurt as bad." A tear leaked from her eye, but feeling the warmth of her sisters' embrace, Margo continued. "Gideon and Claire are my dream come true. I tried not to care, but it's impossible. If I say yes and then it doesn't work out, I'll lose not only him, but Claire too, who I love with my whole being. I couldn't go through that again."

"I know you're afraid and that you're trying to keep your feet firmly on the ground, but what if you fly, Margo?" Mia asked. "What if this is your forever love, and you let fear keep you from something amazing?"

"You already think of Claire as your daughter," Micki added. "Seems to me, Gideon and Claire Bear are what you were hiding from, and still searching for simultaneously."

"It can't be both," Mia claimed in an amused voice.

Micki shrugged. "Tell our middle sibling that. She's the one doing it."

"Margo, you're not alone." Mia seemed to hesitate before speaking. "Ryan and I have been trying to have a baby, but it's not happening."

"Mia! Is that what's been going on?" Margo questioned.

She gave a sad smile. "Yes, we're both testing fine, but no luck. I'm thirty-five, the doctor said it can be harder at my age. We were going to become foster parents, and then Omar came into our lives. He needs parents and we're them. If the other stuff doesn't work out, adoption is our next step."

"Saying you should've told us doesn't mean anything in this family," Micki pointed out ruefully. "I'll say this ahead of time—don't expect kids from me anytime soon."

"You're almost thirty, don't be so hasty," Margo pointed out. "So far, two very special men have arrived at out inn doors and never left."

"See you just jinxed it!" Mia teased. "She'll be the cool auntie who lets the kids get away with everything."

Micki shrugged. "I'm okay with that."

"Should I say yes?" Margo asked her sisters hopefully.

Mia shook her head. "No, ma'am, we cannot make that decision for you. If it feels right or wrong, the choice has to be yours."

"Ugh, no easy way out." Margo lay back against the pillows again.

"Nope." Micki grabbed the blankets to pull over their legs.

"Life, man, we get zero breaks," Mia added.

There was no place better than unraveling a complicated situation with her sisters. They always had each other's backs, and while she was still uncertain, Margo felt better whether she said yes or no to Gideon. The three of them dozed and talked on and off, as they often would when growing up, tucked into Mia's bed.

As Margo finally drifted off to sleep, she knew her answer could only be the one thing that would make her whole.

Yes.

SATURDAY AFTERNOON, and the house was empty except for him and the animals. Margo and Mia took Claire and Omar to an outdoor festival that was in Union County, just a short drive down the interstate. Gideon was invited but he took the quiet time without Claire to finish installing the banister rungs. Once he was finished, you couldn't tell they were replacements. He chuckled, wondering if Micki would spot the difference and test out his work to give it her seal of approval. Margo still hadn't said yes or no to his proposal, and that worried him. Everything seemed fine. He was heading back outside with his tool bag, when Ryan came bounding up the stairs.

"Hey, I was at the workshop looking for you," Ryan said.

"I thought was the only one here." Gideon stopped at the top step.

Ryan grinned. "One of my few Saturdays off. My friend Matt is taking me to play something called disc golf, wanna join?"

"What exactly is disc golf?" Gideon asked.

"Not sure. He said it's like golf but with discs." Ryan shrugged.

"That makes it all the clearer." Gideon shook his head. "Let me guess, age of the participants is less than thirty?"

"You guessed it." Ryan sat on the top step. "He's come back from a Doctors of the World humanitarian project and is trying to slide into his old hobbies. He's been talking about it for days. Apparently, there is a group of guys here who play. And I don't want to face it alone."

"So, you decided to pull me into the fracas," Gideon said. "Thanks for that."

"Be a pal," Ryan implored. "I'll owe you one."

Gideon thought for a minute. "Okay, I can go with that. If you'll go to the mall or somewhere close by to find a jewelry store."

"Why? Are you buying me best friend bling?" Ryan's smile was wide.

Gideon tightened his grip on his tool bag. "Maybe next time. I want to get Margo an engagement ring. Wedding bands too, possibly. I don't know."

"Well, look at you! Are you planning on proposing to my sister-in-law?" Ryan hopped up and shook his hand. "Good man!"

"I asked her already. We're just in a stalemate or holding pattern." Gideon sighed. "I'll be honest. It helps the custody case if I'm married, but that's not the main reason. I love her, and I told her yes or no, doesn't matter, I'd be here for her. I have a good shot to win the case with all of my support."

"But she's still hesitant," Ryan surmised.

He nodded. "Parts of the past are a burden on our shoulders. I think together we can work past it and become a family."

"There you go." Ryan slapped his hand against his thigh and stopped. "I've been hanging out with the neighbors too long. I've began knee slapping."

"Soon you'll be playing chess and going fishing with them." Gideon smiled. "Let me get changed and we'll go to this disc thing."

"They need to stop mixing things together. Disc and golf..." Ryan scoffed.

Gideon thought for a moment. "Yeah, if they

create three-way checkers, you and Mr. Bolton and Mr. Marley can have a real game."

"Go change." Ryan pointed at the door.

Ten minutes later, they were in Ryan's Land Rover heading toward Freedom Park. It was an easy Saturday ride, traffic was pretty good. Charlotte was becoming like many cities though, wrought with congestion and busy streets. To Gideon, no matter how the city progressed, places like Sardis Woods would always offer a quaint small-town feel. Good people and Southern hospitality.

At the park, he and Ryan walked past the soccer fields and volleyball courts where groups played with zeal under Carolina blue skies and hot sun.

"I hope they're wearing sunscreen," Ryan commented as they strolled past the players.

"I'm sure they are. More people are skin conscious these days," Gideon commented.

Matt was waiting for them on open grass where there were metal baskets with chains, and flags set up at various points.

"Let me guess. The hoops are like the golf holes." Ryan pushed his sunglasses back on his head. "Who's throwing Frisbees at it."

Matt held up a smaller disc. "We are."

"Gideon this is Matt, doctor, cowboy, and line dancer extraordinaire." Ryan introduced them.

"How did you find out about the dancing…?" Then Matt laughed softly. "That fast-talkin' friend of ours is also a narc."

"I warned you. He's a wild one." Ryan chuckled. "Now, teach us how to play this game. We gotta go to the mall after to help him pick out an engagement ring." He pointed at Gideon.

"Engagement rings at the mall works, but when we're done, I'll take you some place that will blow your mind," Matt said excitedly.

"My colleague here knows everyone and everything." Ryan slapped Gideon on the back. "It's the only price to pay now that he's your best friend."

Matt walked backward and spread his arms wide. "Like I'm not the most awesome person you've ever met in your life."

"He has an ego to boot." Gideon followed the two men and paid attention to the finer points of disc golf, which was basically frisbee with metal basket hoops low to the ground for scoring.

There were, surprisingly, a lot of men and women playing the game. They had backpacks that held discs of various sizes and shapes. Think golf clubs, but sailing through the air, and not because an angry golfer threw one in frustration.

"It's all in the wrist," Matt explained as he let a disc loose from his fingertips and it hit the chain basket perfectly. "The more consistent you are. This will be easier than running a stent into a heart valve."

"I've never done that," Gideon pointed out, but when the disc he threw landed on top of Matt's, he pumped his fist in the air. "Yeah!"

Ryan hadn't landed one shot yet and grumbled. "I thought we agreed this was ridiculous."

"Sorry, I got caught up in the moment." Gideon held up his hands and grinned.

"Uh-huh, it's a mutiny," Ryan accused.

Matt laughed. "Bro, we're not even on a boat."

"Plus, we're all friends now, so technically any type of betrayal can apply," Gideon added.

"I dislike you both right now." Ryan threw his disc and landed the shot. "Yeah, that's the ticket!"

"See, I told you!" Matt cheered. "Now we've got a game!"

An hour later, they were packing up Matt's discs and getting ready to go to Matt's destination for the perfect ring. They ended up following him for thirty minutes to South Boulevard, past all the new breweries and outdoor eating areas where there happened to be food trucks parked for the afternoon.

"We just had a rousing game, I could eat," Gideon said, slowly looking around. His stomach rumbled, reminding him he hadn't had lunch.

"The pulled pork nacho looks pretty good." Ryan eyed a guy who passed by with a large plate. "Though we can never speak of this in the presence of the Ballad sisters, or Enid."

"This could be our Saturday thing," Matt pointed out. "Saved by our secret bro code. Shake on it?"

Handshakes were given all around. It was very hard to hide anything in Ballad Inn, and Gideon knew they would fold at one-to-many questions, but for now the secrecy held. The ladies, Omar, and Claire would be enjoying the festival's edible treats. Why couldn't the guys indulge? Their trio decided on nachos and frosty cold beers that they enjoyed at one of the picnic tables under a huge red umbrella.

"I've been here for about two years now, and it always amazes me how Carolina weather works," Ryan commented. "Spring is kind of late March to the middle of May, and right after Memorial Day the heat comes in until around late September. Then we go to the depths of winter."

"Hey, now," Matt piped in. "Fall is the best and can give us weather in the low seventies until December. Then the bottom falls out and we get our version of winter."

Gideon chewed before speaking. "What you guys are saying tells me I won't be in a thermal coat by September. In Washington, we have cold and rain, and then maybe just maybe we get blessed by a few weeks of sunshine, but not all together."

"I get you man. St. Paul was the same," Ryan commiserated. "I've soaked up the sun, with the right sunscreen, of course. I'm never going back to deep dark winters."

They raised glasses in solidarity and Matt joined in, making Gideon grin. He'd just met Matt, but he could already tell they would have a good friendship. In the Marines you had friends—no brothers, and sisters, because while you served every man and woman became like a sibling. They shared their joys and sorrows within their ranks. When your tour was up, the comradery shared usually stayed on the base. A mere memory even though many often promised to keep in touch.

Gideon had no doubt that if he saw any of his military buddies right now, it would be like they'd never left the base. Old deployment stories would make them laugh at some points, and somber the next, and again they'd promise to keep in touch. But they were living all over the country. After his parents passed, he never really had anyone close enough to him in Tacoma to call more than an acquaintance, until Trudy. Now Ryan and Matt had extended their friendship to encompass him.

"So, how are you going to propose?" Matt asked.

"Again," Ryan added.

Gideon looked from one to the other. "What do you mean?"

Matt sighed. "Are you sure you two aren't brothers? You can't be both this clueless about women."

"Hey, I married mine," Ryan defended.

Matt rolled his eyes at him. "After you almost mucked it up. Luckily, she gave you a second chance."

"Good point." Ryan went back to his nachos. "Carry on."

"You have to do something great if this is an again," Matt said. "Horse drawn carriage where you step out, dressed as the prince, bend down on one knee and ask her to marry you."

"Where am I supposed to get all that on short notice on a Saturday?" Gideon asked.

"I know a guy…"

Ryan cut Matt off. "To clarify, that's not Margo's style. Micki, maybe, Margo no."

Gideon nodded. "Margo is very down-to-earth."

"What's her favorite movie?" Matt asked.

"I don't know," Gideon replied.

"Can we find out?" Matt asked. "Then we can dress you up like the hero, play the theme song from the soundtrack, and you propose."

"Why do all of your scenarios end with me

dressed up like something I'm not?" Gideon asked.

Matt shrugged. "Women like men who put in an effort. I guess the next question is, who are you, Gideon Holder?"

"A father, a soldier, a carpenter," Gideon replied instantly. "Just a simple guy."

"Do you have your dress uniform with you?" Matt asked, a slow smile began to spread across his face.

"Yeah, I do." Realization bloomed over Gideon's face. "Oh, I get it."

Ryan grinned. "Gentlemen, we have a plan."

"This evening—sunset—we propose the right way," Matt announced.

"We?" Gideon questioned.

"I'm not missing this, and I'm sure there'll be food after," Matt said without hesitation.

"And there you have it, folks, it leads back to his stomach." Ryan shook his head.

Matt showed no shame. "Listen, the last piece of peach cobbler I had was so divine I dream about it still. The flaky crust, the peaches that were cooked to perfection with just a slight crunch and not too soggy…"

"Your food spiraling again, buddy, rein it in." Ryan looked at Gideon. "He tends to do that."

"I can't blame him. The peach cobbler is heaven in a bowl," Gideon agreed.

They finished their nachos and threw the disposable bowls in the trash and headed back to the cars. At Matt's jewelers, Gideon found a beautiful set with an engagement ring and wedding band for Margo, and it came with a wedding band to match for himself, if she said yes, this time around. Gideon felt apprehension fill his chest when they were back in the car. The little white bag sat in the center console between Ryan and himself.

"What if she's thinking about it because it's going to be a no?" Gideon asked suddenly.

Ryan was quiet for a moment. "Which part came out first, the custody of Claire, or the fact that you're in love her?"

"I didn't actually say I love you," Gideon admitted.

Ryan sighed. "Matt's right. We're buffoons. She has to know how you feel. The words need to be said to solidify the foundation you want to start on."

"I get it, but…"

"No buts," Ryan interjected. "Do you love her? If you had just met her and it was only you and her, no custody mess, no baby, would you still love her and want to marry her?"

"Yes."

"Then you lead with that," Ryan spoke firmly. "No woman wants to kinda hear I love you while skating around the words. Say it, man, and then ask her to marry you."

"Okay." Gideon blew out a breath. "Are you this tough on your residents at the hospital?"

"Worse." He laughed.

The plan was set. He would need to hide out at Ryan and Mia's house until it was time to ask Margo to be his wife the right way. Claire would be involved because together they were a package deal. Tonight, they were going to propose to the woman they loved. He hoped they would become a family.

CHAPTER NINE

EXHAUSTION WASN'T THE WORD. Try taking a two-year-old and a thirteen-year-old to a country fair, along with a younger sister who wants to ride every ride. She and Mia barely made it through the hot day with cold peach tea slushies, and a prayer. *Why do we do that to ourselves each and every year?* Margo wondered with a smile as she soaked in the tub. They each promised it was the last time, every year for different reasons. Margo because of the heat, Micki because she always ate too much junk and ended up with a tummy ache, and Mia because they got rid of the twenty-five-cent thrift bookstore tent.

"It's the fact that they took it out when I was almost done my collection of old noir mystery books," Mia had complained.

"Don't you have enough books?" Micki had asked.

"You bite your tongue," Mia gasped. "There's no such thing as too many books. That's why my office has walls and walls of shelves."

"One of these days we're going to have to dig you out from under books like rescue crews digging out a skier in an avalanche," Margo warned. "Just stick a hand up through the mound of books and we'll find you."

"You are a riot," Mia said dryly.

Smiling at the memory, Margo laid her head back and let the warm water soothe her aching muscles. She recalled another event when Omar moved into his revamped room in Mia and Ryan's house. Even as young girls the Ballad sisters promised to live close to each other so their children could be best friends and the family could continue to be close-knit. The Crawford property gave them the opportunity to do so while spreading out the homes for privacy. Gideon and Ryan were both gone when they came home, so Mia showed Omar the room herself. Margo, holding Claire, and with Micki in tow, were with them and watched as the young boy looked around the room in awe.

Posters of superheroes graced the olive green walls and his bed sat in the center of the wide space. There was a TV on the wall across from it and on the shelves below, a video game console and tons of games. There were two gaming chairs situated in front of the space. Margo looked at the black-and-green curved leather seats and knew that Mia picked them. The secret gamer in her sister possibly wanted one, and this was the way to share her love of video games with Omar. There were other action figures placed on shelves set into the wall like steps, Mia and Ryan left many of them bare.

"You've got space to put things and make the room yours," Mia pointed out gently. "What do you think, Omar?"

"I love it!" He breathed out slowly. "You promise this is all mine and you won't make me leave?"

Margo turned and blinked away tears at his questions. The Ballad women grew up with each other in a loving home, and never felt alone. It put their blessing into perspective, given the point of view of a boy who slept in the tube at the playground to feel safe and stole young pears to eat because he was hungry. He'd never known love like this or had anything in his life that compared.

Mia put her hands on his shoulders. "You are never leaving. You're ours now. You'll always have us. I promise."

He moved forward and hugged Mia and a soft sob escaped him. They all looked at each other and wiped away tears. Omar was home.

"And you better call me Aunt Micki." Micki said with a watery laugh. "Makes me feel older, and I can get cool cat eyeglasses."

"You got it." Omar hugged her, then Margo while she held Claire.

Back at Ballad Inn, she gave Claire a cool bath and dressed her in a light cotton pull over before she went down for a nap. When she woke up, Margo planned on giving her dinner, but Micki plucked the toddler from her arms.

"I'll feed her. We're going to go see Mia and Omar and eat there," Micki announced.

"Hold on. I can get changed and go with you," Margo told her sister. "Gideon is still out with the menfolk. Enid was here and now she's gone, so we can all walk over."

"No, you relax. Take a bit of time for yourself." Micki gave her a broad smile. "We'll see you in a little bit."

Margo frowned. "You look funny. What's going on?"

Micki feigned innocence. "What? Can't I want my big sister to have a breather and relax in a tub?"

"No, no, you can't, Michelle." Margo put her hands on her hips. "What do you have up your sleeve? It's not my birthday so you can't be pulling your usual prank. I'm still getting confetti out of my hair from last year."

"Yeesh, forgive me for being a wonderful, exciting sister." Micki turned to take Claire downstairs. "You'd want confetti, wouldn't you, Claire Bear?"

Margo called down to her. "Not with confetti. Confetti should never be in the mix."

"It was a glitter bomb!"

"Confetti, glitter, it's all the same!"

Margo sighed, so here she sat in the tub. The water had cooled noticeably, and it was time to get out. The house was all too quiet, but it was a good type of peace as she took care of her skin regimen and put her hair up in a high bun with a few of her braids loose to frame her face. She wondered if she should still go over to Mia's anyway for dinner. There was more than enough she could find to eat in the fridge. *Maybe cold pasta salad and chicken with one of my puzzles until my missing family comes back?* Margo pondered. But a commotion of feet on the porch and low murmured voices pulled her from the direction of the kitchen to the front door.

"I'll check to see where she is." She heard a low voice say.

The doorknob turned and Margo asked, "Where who is?"

Mia screeched in surprise and held her chest. "Aren't you supposed to be in a bath relaxing?"

"Well, I was, but one can only soak for so long," Margo supplied. "I was going to get something to eat since I wasn't invited to your house."

"There was a reason." Mia looked behind her

and gave a nod. "Okay, you can come out. Dinner can wait."

"But can it? You already ate, I suppose, and I don't want to be part of Micki's pranks. I'm surprised she got you in on it." Margo put her hands on her hips. "I'm going to eat, and subsequently thwart whatever you and our little sister have cooked up."

"Just get out here." Mia grabbed her hand and dragged her out the door.

Margo stumbled forward onto the porch and stopped in her tracks. Gideon stood on the second step, wearing his marine dress blues, including the crisp white gloves. He stood at attention, the marine emblem on his hat gleamed as much as the polished black boots he wore. Margo's breath caught at the handsome picture he made. Beside him, Claire stood in a pretty blue dress that matched the color of her dad's uniform. She held a small bouquet of flowers in her hands. Margo was quite impressed that Claire hadn't taken off with her flowers in tow. Toddlers weren't known for being patient or still.

"What's all this, then?" Margo asked, her heart racing.

Gideon looked at his daughter. "Go give Margo the flowers, sweet girl."

Holding her tiny hand in his, he helped his

daughter up the stairs and she handed Margo the flowers wrapped in silver ribbon.

"Thank you, baby." Margo bent and took the bouquet.

"Mamamama," Claire wrapped her small arms around Margo's leg and wouldn't let go.

All of a sudden, from a speaker somewhere, soft romantic music filled the air. Of course, as if sensing something big was going to happen, Mr. Bolton, Mr. Marley and a few other neighbors wandered over. Mr. Webber arrived also, and Margo breathed a sigh of relief that Doodle wasn't with him.

She noticed Ryan was here too, and his co-worker Matt.

"Now hit it," Matt whispered loudly.

"Okay, I get it." Gideon looked back at him before clearing his throat and focusing on her. "I didn't expect an audience..."

"Son, its Sardis Woods, and the Ballad sisters. You're lucky it's just us," Mr. Marley said dryly.

"Right." Gideon took a deep breath. "Margo Ballad, you have been a whirlwind in my life. One of the sweet, gentle kinds, that tied your heart to mine and Claire Bear's."

"Oh, Gideon, you both are amazing," Margo whispered.

"As are you. I know the last time I proposed it seemed like caring for you came second, but it's far from the truth." Gideon moved farther up the stairs and took her hand. "I love you, Margo. Every happy breath I've taken from the time I got to Ballad Inn, it's been because of you."

Margo wiped away the tears that filled her eyes as he got down on one knee on the porch of the home where she'd grown up.

"As I told Ryan and Matt, I am a father, a soldier and a carpenter. That all boils down to me being a simple man." He continued, "A simple man who is asking the woman of his dreams to marry him. To make a home, a family, and to spend the rest of our years growing old together. Marry me and make me and Claire the happiest people in the world?"

Margo looked at him and then down to Claire who still had her arms wrapped around Margo's leg. Even she seemed to be waiting for an answer, and it could only be one word.

"Yes." Margo nodded and swiped at her happy tears. "I'll marry you both."

"Well, just me, but Claire is in the package." Gideon teased as he opened the ring box.

Margo's jaw dropped as he put the vintage ring on her finger and both her sisters oohed and aahed.

"There is a wedding ring to match," Gideon said, briefly kissing her finger before standing. "And a matching band for me."

"When I left here this morning, I thought you were going to play disc ball or whatever." Margo couldn't help the wide smile on her face.

"It's not random, it's amazing!" Matt called out.

"If you want dessert here, hush," Ryan told his friend.

"Good idea." Matt made the motion of locking his lips shut.

"So, we're getting married?" Gideon asked.

Margo nodded happily. "We're getting married."

He wrapped her in his arms and kissed her while lifting her off her feet. There were cheers all around, but Margo focused on the love that filled her heart. She would have a family of her own with a loyal, loving man. Margo turned to her sisters who held her hand and looked at her ring before they all hugged and jumped in elation.

"What's our timeline? I have a wedding to plan," Mia said. "I wonder if mom and Dad could get back from their latest trip in time?"

"We can sort that out in a few days." Gideon took Margo's hand. "Right?"

"We could," Margo said slowly, and looked at Mia as she pulled out her phone. "But she has a wedding folder for all of us. Welcome to the family."

"Oh, boy," Gideon breathed out.

"We married off two of the Ballad sisters. One more to go," Mr. Bolton nodded at Micki, chuckling.

"You did no such thing, and stay away from me, just in case you have some courting juju," Micki warned.

Margo let the world fall away as Gideon lifted Claire and then pulled her into an embrace. Her dreams were coming to fruition under the canopy of love and family. What she had lost, she was blessed with once more. Margo's happiness overflowed making a burst of joyful laughter escape her.

"THIS ISN'T PRE-WEDDING JITTERS. No, this is me stressing out." Margo paced the guest suite they used for wedding parties.

"Here, drink this." Micki gave her a flute of champagne. "It will settle your nerves."

"I don't have nerves. I want to marry Gideon with all my heart." Margo took a quick sip. "It's Mia and her idea to make my wedding the photo spread front and center on the inn's website, not to mention all the minor details she keeps springing on me. I don't want to be the template. It was supposed to be simple and sweet under the gazebo. Now we have a string quartet and a harpist. My simple dress is now these layers of taffeta and…"

"This isn't what you wanted," Micki concluded.

"Exactly."

Margo lifted a trembling hand and took another sip from the glass, while Micki and Enid exchanged a worried glance.

"Where is the dress you wanted to wear?" Enid asked.

"It's hung up in my standing armoire," Margo said with a sigh. "Don't get it, Mia wants this. It's only one day."

"But it's *your* day," her mother said. "Enid, please get the dress, and I'll get the oldest. We're going to have a quick meeting."

"I don't want to make any trouble," Margo said earnestly. "I can deal with it."

"You should look back on your wedding with happiness, not be focused on the stress," Micki said. "Mom's right."

Margo sat down in defeat. "You may have been right about your plan to get married in Vegas by a cool impersonator."

Micki nodded. "Don't put me down for any of this."

Margo quietly sipped the champagne and the bubbles helped settle her stomach even though she would prefer ginger ale. Gideon proposed seventeen days ago, and from the moment it happened, Mia was planning. She'd come into Margo's room with all sort of suggestions, plus two catalogs of wedding dresses and while Margo picked one gown, Mia still brought another. The simple family ceremony with a few friends that had started at eleven people, was now several dozen folks from the whole Sardis Woods neighborhood.

A special photographer was hired so that they could have candid and formal pictures and some that would show Ballad Inn in a vintage light. Enid needed help in the kitchen. And Margo wanted to be the one to do so, but Mia refused, saying the bride had other, more important duties. While Enid didn't say it, Mia's words hurt her feelings and Margo's. The inn was built around a sense of home, and this wedding was slowly losing that.

The part that still made her happy was not only that she would be Gideon's wife but that her parents had rushed back as soon as they heard the news of her upcoming wedding. Her father already adored Gideon, and his carpentry, and everyone loved Claire and Omar. Having grandchildren definitely thrilled her parents, and the kids had already seen two mall trips for things they surely didn't need.

Maybe her mother would be able to talk sense

into Mia, but the thought of any confrontation made Margo's stomach topsy-turvy with anxiousness. Rosie Ballad came in the room once more, dressed in a dark burgundy dress with gold lace overlays. Mia followed and closed the door behind her.

"Mom said you were unhappy," Mia said, sitting beside her and taking Margo's hand. "I know it's not what you expected for a wedding but it will end up being a benefit to the inn. The pictures alone…"

"Could be reenacted, Mia," Rosie said. "You were happy at your wedding. Margo needs the same opportunity. Instead, she's distracted and not thinking about walking down the aisle to the man she loves."

"I'm going to wear the dress I want today, and not the one you chose specifically for the photos," Margo said firmly. "You get tunnel vision sometimes, Mia, and both Enid and I were hurt by what you said about the food."

"We certainly do not need a catering chef in my kitchen." Enid emphasized the word *my*.

"I second that. We're paying out the nose for things that Enid and Margo can create with their eyes closed," Micki added.

"I wanted everyone to enjoy the day and not be stuck in a kitchen or doing the hard work," Mia interjected.

"And you also saw this as a great opportunity to build up Ballad Inn's reputation as Charlotte's wedding destination," their mother said with a small smile. "My lovely firstborn daughter, you are so business orientated, and we love that about you. But this is a family occasion, we have two new members of the family joining us through marriage and one who is now going to be your son. We have more to celebrate with these new blessings. The inn and its growth can wait."

Mia looked at them all and her shoulders relaxed. "You're right. Let's have the bride and groom have their day exactly as they want it. We should be thankful because we're all together. Margo, I'm sorry if I ruined your special day."

"It's not ruined, everyone I love is here. Plus, catered food *can* be good food."

"Bite your tongue," Enid chastised and then smiled. "It will do fine."

Margo stood and held out her hands. The women shared an embrace. She instantly felt her anxiousness abate and with her family at her wedding, nothing could go wrong.

"Let's get you dressed. Your groom and daughter are waiting," her mother said, and then fanned her face. "I never thought I would see our family grow in this way."

"Mom don't start crying because then we'll start crying," Margo begged with a laugh.

Her wedding was back on schedule, and she was helped into the dress she truly wanted. A classic sheath dress of satin, and a veil that ran down her back into a short train.

"You look beautiful," her mother said.

"Beyond that, gorgeous," Micki added.

"Exquisite," Mia concluded.

A knock on the door sounded and Mia went to peek out. "It's Gideon."

"He can't see her before the wedding," Enid cried out.

"I just need to hand her something," Gideon said loudly enough that they all could hear.

"Okay, stay where you are and, Mia, you come stand here on the opposite side of the door, now each of you reach around…" Her mother directed the action. "You can't see each other, but still, make this quick, Gideon."

"This is for you." Gideon pressed a metal object in her hand. "Tradition of my Marine unit when anyone got married, so pin it anywhere you like. It means that no matter where I am in this world, my heart is always with you."

Margo opened her hand to reveal one of his medals. "It's your bronze star. Gideon, I can't take this."

"You're going to be my wife. That star is like the North Star or a compass, I can always find home," Gideon said in a low voice. "I love you with all of my heart, Margo."

"I love you too," Margo answered.

"Okay, so, bye-bye, Gideon," Micki said quickly. "The wedding is in thirty minutes."

"Ok, baby sis," Gideon teased.

"Ugh, you are going to be one of those nosy big brothers, aren't you?" Micki moved around the door. "I know where you sleep, Gideon, and I am the prank queen."

"Bring it on, baby sis," he called over his shoulder with a laugh.

Rosie clasped her hands. "And now we have a second son as well, and I can see he already loves your sisters."

Micki went back to fixing Margo's train. "I love him too, but I'll get him for sure. Maybe for Halloween."

There was more of a surprise for Margo when she began her walk to the gazebo. The music started, and she followed the cream-colored carpet that had been laid across the grass and down through the middle of the chairs where the guests sat. Claire was the cutest little flower girl, except that went a little askew, when she dumped out the burgundy-dyed rose petals, dropped the basket, and took off between the chairs with a loud scream of triumph. Luckily, she was captured by

Ryan, and now she sat between him and Omar, happily sucking on a cold applesauce pouch.

Flowers of gold, cream, and burgundy decorated the gazebo, and a gasp escaped her when she saw the man she loved. Marines, dressed in their military blues, stood on each step leading up to where Gideon stood waiting for her in the very same uniform. With her sisters as maids of honor, each was helped up the stairs by one of those Marines, while her father made sure she was secure on their walk down the aisle and up the steps.

"Take care of my baby girl, soldier," her father said before kissing her cheek. "Be happy, baby girl, love your new family as hard as you can."

Margo nodded; her eyes misted. "Thank you, Daddy."

Mia took her flowers and then Gideon held her hands.

"You look…" Gideon shook his head slowly. "How lucky am I to be marrying the most beautiful woman in Charlotte?"

Margo smiled. "I could say I'm marrying the most handsome man who has ever come to this state."

"Well, since we can obviously tell you love each other, how about we get you married?" Pastor Bashir was the local preacher of Sardis Woods church.

"Please do." Gideon grinned.

The nuptials began and the service was short and sweet. As they exchanged vows, Margo never felt so sure about where her life path was leading her.

"Do you, Margo, take First Lieutenant Gideon Holder as your husband, to have and to hold, now and forever?" Pastor Bashir asked.

"I do," Margo answered easily.

Pastor Bashir turned to her soon-to-be husband. "And do you, Gideon, take Margo Ballad as your wife, to have and to hold, now and forever?"

"I do with all my heart and soul," Gideon promised.

"Then by the power vested in me, I pronounce you man and wife." Pastor Bashir smiled wide. "You may now…"

Margo rushed into his arms, took his lips in a fierce kiss and the guests laughed in response.

Pastor Bashir cleared his throat. "Oh, okay… kiss the husband."

Clapping ensued as they turned to the guests.

"Raise arms!" the marine commander ordered.

The marines pulled their swords from their sheathes and raised them to crisscross above their heads, so she and Gideon could walk under the saber arch. It was all so gloriously wonderful, that Margo knew no matter what shots the photographer took, each moment formed a memory that would last a lifetime.

CHAPTER TEN

GIDEON LOOKED AT the revised plans for the extended kitchen in the new house that would one day be his, Margo's and Claire's. He was excited to use his hands and talents to make this a special home for his wife. *Wife*, the thought made him smile. This wasn't what he'd expected when he moved to North Carolina, but it seemed the universe had other plans for him and Claire. Yes, he'd been married before, but it felt nothing like this. Thinking about Trudy in this sense made him sad.

He wished she was still around to see Claire grow. By now, they'd have figured out a custody agreement, and maybe she would've found her own happiness. He sure would have hoped for it. No one should go through this life alone. Margo had shown him that.

Everything had happened so fast. It was the reason they hadn't and wouldn't consummate the marriage unless they thought they were ready. They were even keeping their own, separate bedrooms at the inn.

He put down the plans and picked up a sander to smooth off the rough edges of the wood on the worktable. Focusing hard, he kept his attention on his task until he looked up and saw Margo was there in the workshop doorway. She was still dressed in the scrubs she'd left in that morning, but now she held up two cups from what looked like a local coffee shop.

"Iced coffee?" Margo offered with a smile.

"Do you know you're the best wife ever?" Gideon moved to kiss her and take the plastic cup she offered. "Thanks for this. Why didn't anyone warn me that the humidity was so thick here you could swim through it?"

"It's the South, honey." Margo took a sip of her drink. "It's always been in the travel brochure. North and South Carolina summers are the place to be if you like pea soup."

Gideon grinned. "Hmm, I don't remember seeing that?"

"How are the picnic benches coming along?" Margo asked.

"This is the last one," he answered. "After it dries in the sun, I'm going to put it in the gazebo tonight so the smell of the polish can go away completely."

"Good idea, we're going to have one of those fast, fierce storms tonight," Margo said, and looked to the far end of the worktable. "Hey, what're those plans for?"

Gideon moved to roll them up quickly. "Nothing, well just something I was thinking about doing."

"Yeah? Let me see. I might have some insight for whether it will work on the inn grounds," she offered.

He tucked them away in a slot over the table. "It's okay, when it's all done, you can see it. I promise."

Margo smiled. "Keeping secrets from your wife already? It's only been a little over a week."

"It's a good secret," he answered. "When we built our first FOB, it was just an open area of desert. By the time me and my guys were done, we even had a dedicated water source for bathing and each living space had air-conditioning."

"FOB?" Margo repeated the word.

"Forward operating base." Gideon nodded. "I should've mentioned that the first time around."

"We leave for Tacoma on Tuesday, next week." Margo looked at him as if trying to assess his feelings as she broached the tender subject. "Anything else we need to go over?"

"I think we have it covered. Jean said she has all the affidavits from everyone, even the daycare, and our marriage certificate, and she's filed all the paperwork. Hopefully, when we go to court it's over sooner rather than later so we three can get back to our lives."

"Are you scared?"

Gideon looked at her and expelled a slow breath before admitting, "Terrified. What if I have to leave without my baby in my arms? They don't know her favorite blanket, or the songs to sing her at night. They don't know how she likes her milk, or that she's already a finicky eater and she likes her food separated. It's killing me to think she'll be crying for me, and I won't be able to be there."

"Oh, Gideon, that won't happen." Margo stepped into his arms and held him tight. "The judge will see that Claire is best with you. You are an amazing father. You put her first in everything."

Gideon kissed her temple. "Denise and Grant painted me as a bad father long before Trudy passed because of my deployments. They refused to understand that you can't chose where to go and what to do in the military. You do what they say, when they say it."

"Isn't it due to fear, mostly? Of change, and then a loss of control of their daughter, after holding the reins for such a long time," Margo analyzed. "Then, when Trudy passed, they wanted to hold on to a piece of her by any means necessary. I feel so sorry for them because they aren't thinking rationally, but from a place of grief."

"How are you so amazing, to see the good in

people when we're facing so much bitterness and anger?" Gideon asked.

"I've always been taught to be kind and look past the surface hurt to the root cause." Margo looked up at him. "It's sort of like being a nurse. You know the patient is in pain, but the symptoms lead to the source of the injury. For them, it's their broken hearts."

"It should be guilt for not listening to Trudy, or us, when we tried to tell them we were falling apart. But they just wanted to play happy families." Gideon's voice was full of frustration, even he could hear it.

"I'm sure guilt plays a part as well," she replied, and laid her head on Gideon's chest. "We have to worry about you and Claire first before we can deal with how we'll interact with Denise and Grant in the future. I know you don't want them out of Claire's life for good, we'll just have to push a little harder for them to come visit and see her. I feel, when this is all over, everyone will be able to meet in the middle for Claire Bear's benefit."

"I'm the luckiest man in the world." Gideon smiled at her.

Margo laughed. "Glad you know that. Now I'm going to let you get back to work, I'll see you when you pick up Claire and maybe we can take a walk this evening."

"In the pea soup?" he teased.

She stood on tiptoe to kiss him gently. "The soup cools when the sun starts to go down. See you in a bit. I love you."

The words made his heart sing as she headed for the open door.

"I love you too," Gideon called after her and she turned with such a radiant smile on her face, it took his breath away.

It was all for him, her love, and so much more. Margo was willing to stand with him in a battle that was being thrust upon him and which placed his daughter's happiness in the balance. Gideon had to believe that it would work out for the best, and then their lives could truly begin as a family. He wasn't trying to erase his past, Trudy, or her family, but for all of them to heal, a solution had to be found.

THEY WERE IN a two-car caravan heading toward Sydney Park. One vehicle carried Margo, Micki and himself, and in the other was Ryan, Mia and Omar. They were going to take part in the annual zombie run, whatever that meant. Margo was practically vibrating with excitement. Gideon didn't know if he was supposed to be worried or not. Especially when she stretched her neck and cracked her knuckles.

"What exactly are we doing?" Gideon asked

casually. "Because you're kinda stretching like you're getting ready to run for your life."

"That's because she's going to win this year," Micki said and leaned forward to lightly punch Margo's shoulder. "I've got your back this year, mate."

"Uh-huh," Margo said and chuckled. "To answer your question, Gideon, it's a charity run, where some people are dressed up as zombies to do the chasing, and the rest of us move as fast as we can to escape them."

"You should have been here when we explained it to Ryan." Micki sat back.

"Well, that was when Ryan first got to Charlotte," Margo pointed out matter-of-factly. "And we don't get to choose if we are zombie or prey. It's random. Participants select a band from the bucket when signing in. Bands are all mixed together so it's luck of the draw whether you're running or doing the scaring. Makeup artists are there to get the zombies looking authentic."

"Margo is always lucky. Never been a zombie yet. She came in second last year because she stopped to save Mia," Micki said. "Margo's a beast. She's never been tagged by a zombie, either."

Gideon took her hand and squeezed. "That's my wife for you."

"Thanks, honey, I'll protect you." She squeezed his hand.

Gideon shook his head. "You're super excited."

"We train for this all year." Margo smiled.

"When?" Gideon glanced at her in surprise. "I have been at the inn for more than a few weeks, and I have never seen you train."

"Us," Margo pointed to herself and then her sister. "And no one is usually up at five in the morning when I have us out in Crawford field."

"With leg weights," Micki said from the back seat. "You forgot to mention the leg weights."

"I hope I can keep up." Gideon maneuvered the car into a parking spot in front of Sydney Park.

It was a big race, for sure. He could already see huge banners set up. The trail was marked with tall red flags.

Ryan pulled into the spot next to him, and he and his family got out. Omar looked just as excited as Margo, and the two of them high-fived when they got close to each other.

"I hear you've done this before?" Gideon asked Ryan casually.

"Last year, and let's just say they take it seriously." Ryan eyed Mia. "She sacrificed me to finish faster."

"You were already doomed, babe." Mia leaned her head on his shoulder. "You were two steps away from being tagged."

"Where's the love?" Ryan teased and then directed his next comment to Gideon. "Your wife will sacrifice you too, friend."

"I'm here to make sure she wins, or at least, survives." Gideon grinned.

Mia gasped. "How come you don't say that about me?"

"He's a marine, honey. I'm sure he can save us all," Ryan said simply. "The bro code has been broken. I'm telling Matt."

"Tell me what?" Matt jogged up to their group.

"Gideon broke the bro code," Ryan answered. "He chooses to be cannon fodder to help save Margo, so she can win."

Matt shrugged. "I already worked that out with Micki. Margo is winning today."

"This is great!" Omar snickered.

The group moved to the starting line to pick their bands, and Margo's luck continued to hold out. Matt, Ryan and Micki got chosen to be zombies, and the rest of them would run the race much to Omar's delight.

"There's a mud pit," he said, pointing. "Zombies follow you in!"

"That's the spirit!" Margo took Omar's hand. "Stick with me and your mom, we got this."

Omar looked up at Mia shyly. "Can I call you mom?"

She kissed the top of his head. "I would love

that, but when we get home, you get hosed down before you step inside."

"Awesome!" he said excitedly.

"Only kid I ever saw who was excited by being sprayed off by a hose." Mia chuckled. "Except for us growing up."

"Kids and mud." Gideon wrapped his arm around her shoulders. "I would've loved to have had siblings like yours when I was growing up."

Mia smiled at him. "You've got a huge family now with two very annoying sisters."

"You guys are great. Even when the youngest one is trying to tell me how to run the workshop." He raised an eyebrow at Micki.

Micki pointed at him. "I'm going to get you first."

The zombies went off to their positions so they could catch the flags of the runners. Gideon could see Margo's determination written all over her face as she shook out her limbs. She was ready to race. He was more than a little impressed at how she threw herself into everything with gusto.

The announcer went through the rules and thanked the sponsors before the starting pistol signaled the beginning of the race. Gideon ran, focused on his task of escaping the zombie horde that was intent on pulling his flag away and knocking him out of the race.

"Only the strong survive!" Micki screamed

and tackled a runner to snatch the red flag from the Velcro band around her waist.

"Wow, she does take this seriously," Gideon muttered as they sprinted.

"She's going to be your demise." Margo laughed. "She's eyeing you already."

Gideon picked up his speed. "She's got to catch me first."

There was a rope that swung you at least half-way across the mud pit and Gideon had flash-backs about being at bootcamp. Omar reached it first and with a cry, he swung a short distance and landed in the mud, landing with glee. As soon as he reached the edge he was tagged, but he'd made it to the midpoint of the race.

"Sorry, kid," Gideon said.

"I don't care. I'm going to stay in the mud!" Omar stretched out his arms and fell into the gooey mass.

"Thankfully, those aren't the good pants," Mia said, laughing, as she ran by.

"Go, Mom, go!" Omar yelled in support.

Margo sprinted past him with a zombie player on her heels. When the zombie grabbed for her flag, she ducked, and combat rolled to the side. She was back on her feet in an instant and took the mud rope easily.

"Who are you, and where is my wife?" Gideon called after her, pumping his legs to catch up.

Her wild laughter echoed over the screams and cheering of the others on the course. *Well, I can see what Claire will be doing when she's older,* he thought. There was no better role model to teach a young girl how to be independent, brave, and live in her happiness than Margo.

Near the finish line was when things got dicey. He noticed that Mia ran interference for Margo with the fake zombie horde. He did the same and didn't even notice he was about to be tagged until Margo dragged him out of the way almost getting caught herself. She deftly maneuvered ahead and turned to flash him a big grin before moving on. *Was she even out of breath?*

"Gotta think on your toes, brother-in-law." Mia ran up beside him. "Okay, Gideon, the zombies are ganging up to stop anyone from making it to the finish line. It's between Margo and Viking dude again."

"Why is he dressed like a Viking for this thing?" Gideon asked between panting breaths.

"Who knows? He does it every year," Mia answered. "Less talk, more distractions!"

The race was winding up in earnest, and he could see Margo was tiring but she pushed on, using the last of her reserves. The colorful finish line tape was now in sight.

"You can do it, babe!" Gideon yelled, excited for her win.

And she did. Mia propelled herself in front of the zombie that was going to get Margo and he did the same with another one, letting their flags be taken. At the last minute, Viking dude got tagged, and Margo threw herself across the finish line and took the ribbons down to the ground with her while the crowd whooped and cheered. She stared up at the sky, breathing hard and raised her fist in victory. Gideon took that arm and pulled her up against him, kissing her and then hugging her as he swung her around. She laughed more, clearly elated.

"You are outstanding!" Gideon exclaimed. "You could outmaneuver anyone in my platoon."

"That's a pretty hefty compliment." She smiled at him.

Gideon hugged her once more. "Because you deserve it."

The rest of the family was just as tired and dirty as they were as the gang crowded around Margo to hug and congratulate her before she received the 2024 trophy and an assortment of gift cards.

"Hey, this one is for Murphy's. We can use it now." Margo waved the gift card in the air. "Outdoor seating and barbecue with sweet tea—and it's within walking distance."

"I'm in, and we can clean up and change in the sports center. They open it for the event," Mia suggested and gestured at Omar. "Which is good, because I think he's even got mud in his ears."

Margo nudged Gideon. "Think about it, in a few years Claire will be old enough to do this."

"Like how old?" he asked slowly. He'd imagined his daughter doing the zombie run but as an adult.

"The youngest here was five and there is a kiddie run," Micki pointed out.

"Let's get her to that age first, and we'll revisit the issue." He put his hand on Omar's shoulder but lifted it quickly, looking at the thick mud and how damp he was. "Did you soak up the whole mud pool?"

"You guys, there are showers in the sports center for the teams who practice here, can you please make sure he uses it?"

"Sure thing." Ryan kissed her.

The group parted ways with males and females going in opposite directions to clean up. Thirty minutes later, after saying their goodbyes to their race friends, and promising to see them next year, the Ballad Inn crowd was finally back at their cars to drop off their grimy stuff. They began walking for what was said to be the best barbecue joint in Charlotte. After ordering sweet tea and their meals, Margo pulled out her winnings in the form of gift cards.

"Okay, so for helping me win, we share the loot." Margo spread the cards on the table.

"This sounds like we're in an old gangster movie and we're dividing up our ill-gotten gains," Gideon commented, and everyone looked at him. "What? I read and watch a lot of old noir books and movies."

"Is that what's in those boxes in storage, your book and DVD collection?" Margo asked.

"Yes, I'm collecting all the goodies. Though I am missing a few," he admitted.

"You know, I collect the same books. I was mad when they got rid of the thrift store book tent," Mia said. "Maybe we could see if we can finish off each other's collections."

"I do have double of some editions, like *Lotus the Spy*," Gideon said.

Mia reacted, almost falling of her bench. "I'm looking for that one!"

"Okay, you two, you can go gaga over books later. Trust me, Mia won't let you forget, and I need to remember to buy more bookshelves," Ryan said.

"I'll build them." Gideon took a long drink from his glass. "This is the best sweet tea I've ever had."

"I'm taking the Fashion Floor card," Micki interrupted. "Margo, you said the dresses in there were not your style."

"Please do. I won't even step in there," Margo said. "Omar, which ones do you want?"

"Can I get the video game store one, and the sneakers one?" he asked hesitantly.

"They're yours," Margo handed them over. "Enjoy, nephew!"

"You guys say the best stuff." Omar smiled widely.

Margo's heart warmed just looking at the thirteen-year-old, before she focused on her sister. "Look, Mia, there is a chocolate shop one. Gideon, which one do you prefer?"

"The hardware store," Gideon answered automatically. "And the rest are yours. You can't not have something for yourself."

"Me and Enid will share the gourmet store cards," Margo said.

"I have to get her something marvelous. She's been so good with watching Claire," Gideon said.

"She loves it. I'm sure they're in the kitchen making mini cupcakes like she did with me and my sisters when we were young." Margo linked her hand with his. "Family means everything to us. Enid will never let you forget it if you try to give her a gift for babysitting."

"Then it will be a 'just because she's amazing' gift," he suggested.

"Add some flowers to those gift cards. It may work." Micki rubbed her hands together as their meals came. "If you weren't already married, Gideon, Mr. Bolton might think you were trying to steal his main squeeze."

"You have got to stop hanging out with Mr.

Webber," Mia said, shaking her head. "You're two steps away from a fedora."

"A black fedora would be pretty cool." Micki picked up a rib. "I'm starving after all the running and dodging."

Together they laughed and enjoyed a meal of what he had to admit was the best barbecue he'd ever had. This was family. Something he never truly experienced even when he had one. The group shared bites from their plates and teased each other without mercy. He watched Omar bloom even more under this umbrella of love and attention. How could Trudy's parents want to take his Claire away from all this?

He pushed those thoughts aside, refusing to let the dark cloud mar a great day. Things would work out in his favor, he had to believe that, because to think otherwise would break his heart. He and his daughter deserved to be happy and loved the way Margo loved them both. She looked at him with sparkling eyes filled with merriment, and his world tipped on its axis. The universe wouldn't give him a life—one that had changed him for the better—just to take it away.

CHAPTER ELEVEN

MARGO STUDIED THE skies over Tacoma, which were blue, but somehow not the Carolina blue she was accustomed to. The weather was mild, not the boggy humidity that always plagued Charlotte in the summer, and there was a slight chill in the air after a rainy spell the day before.

This was their second day in the city. Gideon's demeanor had seemed reserved from the moment they stepped off the flight with Claire. Margo could truly tell he didn't want to be there at all. Claire seemed to have tapped into her father's mood because she was fussy on the plane. Even in the hotel room, she was not happy with the crib, or, well, anything.

"She's miserable," Gideon said as he walked and bounced the baby in his arms.

"She's kind of feeling your energy of not wanting to be here." Margo stood and moved over to him. "Here, let me take her. Kids are adaptable, but she can feel how tense you are and how your mood has changed."

Gideon ran his hand over his short military cut. "Can you blame me? I'm stuck in a place with two people who are trying to take my daughter away from me. Not for her best interests, either, but to be spiteful because they don't want to accept the truth."

Margo managed to settle Claire and gave her the sippy cup filled with milk. "I know, but you can't stress every minute until Friday. It's going to be okay. How about you put the TV on and find her favorite show. Hopefully, we get her to take a nap before Jean gets here."

"Yeah, that sounds good."

He looked at her and Margo could see the fear in his eyes. She didn't want to make it worse by pushing the subject. She loved Claire. She looked down at the child in her arms who stared up at her with so much trust, and her heart hurt just thinking about not being able to hold her like this. Knowing this, Margo couldn't even fathom how Gideon was feeling.

"Maybe we should run. I mean move to Bali if we have to so we can keep her," Gideon said suddenly.

"I would follow you anywhere. I love you that much. But I also know that you're scared and not thinking clearly. Do you want Claire to live a life like that? All of us away from the people who love us?" Margo asked gently.

Gideon leaned back against the headboard. "No, I'm just frantic at this point."

"Here, she's falling asleep." Margo handed him Claire so the little girl could lie on her daddy's chest. "Hold on to her tight. She's your anchor."

Gideon took Margo's hand quickly. "So are you."

His words warmed her, and she left the bedroom of the hotel suite for the small living area and put the television on. Margo sat on the sofa, twisting her hands with worry, when she noticed how they were shaking. She was so in love with him and Claire both, but if she showed any of her own insecurities about the situation it would affect Gideon even worse. He was a strong man, but not with this. Facing the past and all he went through with Trudy and then her parents was too much for anyone.

He was not okay, and for now she had to be his rock. There was a soft knock on the door, and she opened it to reveal an older woman, carrying a business satchel, dressed in an immaculate power suit. This had to be Jean. Her reddish-brown hair, smattered with gray streaks, was pulled back into a neat bun. She looked like a force to be reckoned with. Margo instantly felt better that she was on their side.

"Margo, I presume," Jean said warmly and

held out her hand. "Jeanette Hargrove, Gideon's lawyer."

Margo shook the woman's hand. "Nice to meet you. Come on in. Gideon is getting Claire down for her nap. Can I get you a cup of coffee, water?"

Jean stepped inside. "Water would be great, thank you. It's getting steamy out there."

"You've never been to the South, I see." Margo grinned. "This feels like early fall for us."

Jean took the bottle that Margo offered. "I've actually had to second chair a case there, to help a fellow lawyer, and it was in the height of summer. It was then I knew I could never live there for any extended period of time."

Margo nodded. "It's not for everyone."

Gideon came out of the bedroom and closed the door before greeting Jean with a hug. "Hey, Jean, how is everything?"

"Wonderful." Jean grinned. "Very happy we're not having this case in the South."

Gideon gave a fleeting smile. "It's hot, but we love it."

Jean patted his shoulder. "Sit down, let's talk. I can see you're ready to crawl out of your skin with worry."

"Yeah." Gideon took Margo's hand, and they sat down together on the sofa while Jean sat in the armchair.

"Friday, we meet outside the courthouse at eight thirty. Claire will not be allowed in court because tensions may be high," Jean said in a soft but brisk tone. "Do you have childcare?"

Gideon nodded. "I reached out to her old daycare, and they can watch her for a few hours. I already paid for that."

Jean nodded and pulled a file from her satchel. "I have all the affidavits from everyone, including you, Margo, but I'd like for you to testify. I added you to the witness list so the lawyer for the Wellses has notification."

"You want me to testify?" Margo felt her stomach clench.

Jean smiled reassuringly. "You and your family have been with Gideon and Claire the most. I want you to testify from the heart. Why you married him, and how Claire's life, your lives, are in Sardis Woods. Lovely, quaint name, by the way."

Margo smiled. "It's a wonderful place where my sisters and I grew up. All the neighbors know us. Some from when we were children—we grew up with their kids. Anyone new that comes into our little slice of heaven is welcomed with open arms. My sister and her husband just brought a foster child into our family in hopes of adopting him soon."

"Do you have pictures on your phone? Of you,

and of your life since Gideon moved there?" Jean asked.

Margo nodded. "Yes, we both do. Of the fair, when we got our faces painted, or I have one of all of us at the little train theme park we took Claire to. Oh, and I've got one when he was feeding her on the porch swing."

Margo picked up her phone and skimmed through the pictures quickly. "The sunset was to the back of them, and it was perfect. I planned on getting it framed when our house is finished."

"Can you send me pictures of the house being built and any other family-type photos?" Jean asked. "I want to have them so the judge can see. I'm going to blow a few of them up and put them on easels. Everyone should see you all as a family unit."

"The one with the entire family should be one of them," Gideon suggested. "The one Mr. Bolton took that Sunday after dinner, and we were all outside."

"Stop! Your life sounds too perfect to be true and I want it," Jean teased. "Email me your favorites so I can send my assistant to have them blown up."

"Can you tell us how the trial will work?" Margo asked, curious.

"Each side has an opening statement, then the Wellses' counsel will present their case. They will put their witnesses on the stand, and we get to cross-examine them and vice versa." Jean sat back. "Their witness list is spotty. Your old boss saying how many hours you used to work, the daycare saying that Claire was there late. But now we can counter with all these affidavits, the pictures, and having your wife on the stand. Plus, we have Ryan as Claire's pediatrician, and the child psychologist he recommended flew out to speak in person. She does this quite often, evidently, and we paid for her fare and accommodation."

"So, our chances are good?" Gideon asked, sounding hopeful.

Jean's expression was full of reassurance. "You're walking out of that courtroom, with your wife's hand in yours, and going directly to your daughter. Then on back to North Carolina to begin your new life."

"After I finally get my VA records moved over to the clinic in Charlotte," Gideon added. He drew Margo close. "Transfer accounts, put everything in Charlotte, then we go home to our lives."

Margo smiled at him. "Sounds perfect to me."

"You guys are so stinking cute." Jean stood. "I'm going to go before I get a sugar rush from the two of you. See you Friday."

"Thanks, Jean." Gideon followed her to the door and closed it behind her.

"She's amazing," Margo said as she stood.

Gideon came over to her and slipped his arms around her, burying his face in her neck. "It's almost over. It's almost over."

Margo felt his shoulders relax as she rubbed his back. "We'll be going home soon."

"I want to take Claire to see her mom. I don't know if you'd be comfortable…"

Margo stepped back and gave him a reassuring smile. "I'll go with you. She needs to know who her mom was and how much she loved her. Regardless of how it ended between the two of you, there's one thing for certain, she loved her baby."

"You are one of a kind, Margo Ballad," he murmured. "I don't know how I got so lucky in my life."

"I do, it was fate, for both of us." She patted his chest. "How about we have lunch first and then we'll pick up a lovely bunch of flowers to put on her grave?"

"Perfect." Gideon smiled. "I feel like I can take a breath for the first time since we got off the plane."

"I'm sorry that you have to go through this," Margo said sadly. "I'd hoped that they would reconsider visiting the inn to see how Claire was thriving."

"Maybe one day they will," Gideon said with a sigh. "No matter the outcome, I don't want her to lose her grandparents and the last connection to Trudy."

"And that proves what a good man you are," she told him.

CLAIRE WOKE UP in a much better mood and the three of them left the hotel to eat before choosing a beautiful bouquet of sunflowers and pink dahlias to place on Trudy's grave. Gideon parked outside of the rolling hills that made up the cemetery and they walked to the grave site of his former wife. Claire held a single flower in her hand as they stood in front of the marble gravestone. Trudy's face was etched in the stone, and Margo could see the beauty of her smile. Right then and there she silently promised to care for Claire as if she was her own—and her father as well. While there were problems at the end, Margo chose to believe that they saw something in each other to create such a beautiful child.

Gideon laid the bouquet against the stone, and following her father, Claire did the same with her single sunflower before plopping down in the grass.

"This was your mom, Claire Bear. She loved you more than anything," Gideon said, crouching next to his daughter.

"Mama," Claire put her hand on the etched face like she could still remember, and maybe she did. Margo had no doubt that even if the little girl didn't recall her mother, her little heart did. She looked up at Margo and held out her hand. "Mama."

"Two mamas. Aren't you a lucky girl?" Gideon gave a soft laugh.

"Only one," a voice said from behind them.

She and Gideon turned, and Margo saw the hurt face of a woman who was still grieving. She knew immediately it was Denise Wells, Trudy's mother.

"Denise, no one is trying to make Claire forget Trudy." Gideon stood and lifted Claire in an almost protective move. "You and Grant are doing that by trying to separate us and choosing not to be in her life except on your terms."

"We'd still be in her life if you hadn't moved across the country," Denise pointed out.

"It was best for both of us. Look at her, she's grown since you last saw her and she's happy," Gideon stated.

"And you brought your new wife to where Trudy is laid to rest, adding insult to injury," Denise snapped.

Margo had to interject. "Mrs. Wells, I am truly sorry for your loss, but my being here is in no way to disrespect your daughter. I came to honor her memory, with Claire and her father. No one wants Trudy's memory to be lost, especially not me."

"You need to leave," Denise said stiffly.

Gideon frowned. "Let's go, so Denise can have her peace. Claire, can you give Grandma a hug?"

Denise held out her hands eagerly for Claire, who ran into them, giggling. She held the baby tight and closed her eyes, as if savoring the moment.

"Denise, speak to Grant. He will listen to you. End this before it begins," Gideon begged. "Come back to North Carolina with us and spend a few days at the inn. We can come to an arrangement as she gets older, for you guys to take her in the summer for a few weeks. You could even spend holidays with us. Just please, let's not do this and drive a deeper wedge between us."

"I—" Denise hesitated, then firmed her lips, with another quick squeeze she handed Claire back to her father. "I'll see you in court, Gideon."

He shook his head sadly. "If that's what you want, Denise."

As she and Gideon, with Claire, walked away, Margo looked back to the woman whose hand was on her daughter's gravestone, her shoulders slumped. Denise Wells was steeped in grief, so much so, that she couldn't see past it. Margo felt tears threaten to fall.

"I just want to hug her and tell her we'll always be here," Margo said and wiped her cheeks quickly.

"Friday is going to be a hard day." Gideon looked at Claire. "But I have to fight for her, and I hate that it's come to this."

"I'll be here every step of the way," Margo said, glancing back once more. "Even for her, though she doesn't see it right now."

They got Claire strapped into her seat in the rental car and slowly drove away from the cemetery. Margo could see why Gideon needed to start over somewhere new for him and Claire. They'd only been in Washington a few days, and while the sky was clear and the air light with a soft breeze, Margo could feel the weight of difficult memories permeating around them. It would be good to get back home, put all this behind them and move forward into the future.

She only hoped that the Wellses would change their minds in time to be in that future. It would not only heal old wounds but make Claire's life richer, having everyone around her who loved her.

FRIDAY MORNING, they stood nervously as the judge's gavel echoed through the room. On one side were Grant and Denise Wells, his former in-laws, and on his side was Margo and the witnesses who were there to support him being able to retain custody of his daughter. Judge Eleanor Fitzgerald was an older woman with a stern face, but she would manage the proceedings fairly, they were told.

After opening statements, Mr. Cameron, who was the lawyer for Judge Wells and his wife, began bringing witnesses to the stand, and Jean was ready to counter each one. The first being his old boss, Jack Sealy, from the construction company who brought in records to show his long work hours. Gideon chose not to be mad at the family man and grandfather. He believed in family. He was also a friend of Grant Wells. Still, with each question, Gideon felt his anxiety rise.

"Mr. Sealy, how long has my client not worked for you?" Jean asked.

"For four months now. He left for North Carolina." Mr. Sealy leaned forward so his answer made it into the mic.

"Was he a good employee?" Jean rose with a document in her hand.

Mr. Sealy answered, "Very much so, one of my hardest working employees—dependable, trustworthy and easy to get along with."

"Why was he working such long hours?" Jean took slow steps back and forth in front of the witness stand.

Mr. Sealy smiled. "He was doing everything for his baby girl. I never saw a man work so hard."

"Hmm?" Jean made a disapproving sound. "Then why was he paid only fifteen dollars an hour? Standard rates for anyone with the skill Gideon brought to the table would be thirty dollars at the minimum."

"Well, um…" Mr. Sealy flushed red.

"Why did Gideon tell you he was leaving Tacoma?" Jean asked.

Mr. Sealy cleared his throat and regained his composure. "To make a better life for his daughter. He was working too many hours here to make ends meet and he wanted to be able to see her. I couldn't fault the man."

"Why are you testifying for the plaintiffs?" Jean asked.

Mr. Sealy shrugged. "I didn't want to. I want no part of separating a father from his child. I have too many employees having child support being taken from their checks. They fuss about it, but they never see their kids. Gideon isn't like that. I was subpoenaed to testify, and I did."

"Ah, understood." Jean stood before the judge. "I'd like to offer into evidence, Mr. Holder's new employment record. It shows a pay increase to thirty-five dollars an hour, and less work hours. I also offer signed and notarized affidavits from his employers in Charlotte, which state that he has proper housing for himself and his daughter."

Judge Fitzgerald nodded. "So entered."

Judge Wells sprang to his feet. "You cannot

take those into evidence. You have no proof that they are even real! They'll all lie for him."

"Mr. Wells, you will sit down immediately." Judge Fitzgerald rapped her gavel on the wood block and pinned him with a stare. "While you may be a judge in this district, this is not your courtroom. I'm the judge of record and I would suggest your attorney rein in your behavior."

Mr. Wells sat down, face red and glowering defiantly, while his attorney spoke low in his ear.

"Judge Fitzgerald, to validate these statements are true, we have been in contact with the staff of the Social Services Department in Charlotte, whom we asked to evaluate Mr. Holder's new home, Claire's daycare, and to interview the extended family who live on the grounds of the inn." Jean handed the judge a folder. "We had no say in who was sent to the home to do the assessment, and the results were sent via registered mail from their offices to ours. The file was also sent to the Wellses' attorney who could have made a motion for it not to be entered if he had concerns about it not being certified through proper channels."

Judge Fitzgerald opened the file and scanned it briefly. "This, and the previous evidence, are so entered."

"I have no other questions for this witness."

Jean turned away and the judge dismissed Mr. Sealy.

The next witness that was called was Claire's previous daycare provider, who said that she had agreed with Gideon's request for Claire to stay with her a little longer each day when he worked overtime. Jean countered that he worked longer hours to provide for his daughter, and asked if he ever didn't pay her fee for the extra time. Then the affidavits for Claire's new daycare with Ellen at Tiny Tots were entered into evidence. The new daycare had stated that Gideon usually finished work early and picked her up to spend quality time with her.

With each of the Wellses' witnesses shut down, Jean introduced her own, starting with himself and Margo. He was called first, and as he took the stand, he made eye contact with his former in-laws. Their attorney tried to trip him up—to make him angry, and maybe aggravate his post-traumatic stress disorder. But he was ready for that, and besides, the veteran affairs clinic in Charlotte offered him more services. He held his composure easily under the questioning, although it seemed more like harassment. After the same question was repeated for the third time, even the judge got irritated.

"Mr. Cameron, it's obvious he will not change his answer no matter how much you try to poke the bear," Judge Fitzgerald snapped. "I don't like these tactics in my courtroom, and it ends now."

"I'm not done questioning the witness," Mr. Cameron said defiantly.

"Oh, so you do have other questions beyond this one?" Judge Fitzgerald asked. "What is your next question?"

Mr. Cameron flipped through his notes. "I, uh—well he needs to answer the question."

"No, he doesn't. The question of his PTSD has been asked and answered, so noted in the court transcript," the judge said firmly, and cast a look of disdain toward Grant Wells. "And if your client Mr. Wells has told you these are the tactics that work best, they don't in my courtroom. It casts aspersions on you as a lawyer, and him as a judge. The court will now hear questions from the defendant's own lawyer."

"Thank you, Judge," Jean said in a respectful manner. Jean asked Gideon, "Why did you move?"

"This was never my home. It's where I was stationed at Joint Base Lewis-McChord," Gideon answered. "I met Trudy and we got married rather quickly. It was our intent to move, but Trudy's parents didn't want us to."

Jean frowned. "Didn't want you to? Even so, you both were grown adults."

"Mr. and Mrs. Wells had a very strict hold on their daughter. I was married to her, but she still put their views and decisions ahead of our marriage." Gideon shrugged. "To be with my wife, and my child, I had to stay."

Jean gave him a sad smile. "The plaintiffs blame you for her death, why?"

"Her death was no one's fault. She was driving upset, in bad weather. No one could have known what would happen," Gideon explained. "We'd had an argument. I'd asked her again to go to marriage counseling. I even set up the appointment. But after she mentioned it to her parents, they told her nothing was wrong with her marriage."

"I offer into evidence the paperwork proving my client's claim." Jean handed the judge the documentation showing the appointment, and the police report from the accident. "What else, Gideon? It's time to have your say."

"They ignored the signs of our troubled relationship. They didn't want us to be honest about it, instead, they only cared about wanting it to look and sound happy. To be successful, that was what was important to them. When I was deployed, it made it worse. I even asked for two weeks personal leave to go home and try to figure things out with Trudy," Gideon replied. "I'm sure my commanding officer has sent you a copy of my request. By then, they had persuaded

Trudy I was the problem, not the two of us, and not their continuing interference."

"Have you tried to keep Claire's grandparents from her?" Jean asked bluntly.

"No, ma'am, I have not," Gideon insisted. "I have made many attempts to offer her grandmother and grandfather a chance to visit us in Charlotte. I offered for her to spend part of the summer with them when she's older. The offer still stands. I've made every attempt for this case not to happen. I don't want them to be out of Claire's life, but they won't understand that we can't stay here. I want her to grow up smiling and happy, not mired in their grief at the loss of Trudy. We all lost her that day."

Jean nodded to her assistant who put the blown-up images of the collected photos on easels. "These images are also entered into evidence, Judge. As well as more affidavits, from family, friends, even the pediatrician and child psychologist's assessment who will also testify..."

"Oh, this is utter nonsense," Mr. Wells declared loudly and pointed to the pictures. "These have all been doctored to make him look good."

The judge slammed the gavel down hard. "One more word out of you, Mr. Wells, and you will be placed in custody for contempt of this court. Mr. Cameron, this is your last warning—control your client."

"Grant, please," Mrs. Wells spoke the plea and put her hand on his arm.

Grant Wells chose to sit down and folded his arms.

"You may continue." Judge Fitzgerald inclined her head to Jean.

"Thank you, Judge." Jean moved to the enlarged photos. "Tell us about these images, Gideon."

Looking at the pictures, his heart warmed at the sight. "That's Claire. The first one is her and Margo after the spring festival. We had just arrived in town, and it was kind of like a get to know the neighborhood event for us. It's a very close-knit community that welcomed us in."

"It looks like a great place to live." Jean nodded and then asked. "Who took this picture of everyone on the porch?"

"That was Mr. Bolton from across the street," Gideon explained. "He and Mr. Marley play chess on his porch every day, and he's courting Enid, part of the Ballad family. He saw us all, had her grab her camera, and took the picture of the group of us lounging around after dinner."

"Is that a lizard wearing a coat with tails and a top hat?" Judge Fitzgerald asked, clearly curious.

Gideon chuckled. "That's Monty, Margo's bearded dragon. The picture doesn't show his monocle. My wife loves animals, currently, she has a turtle and two bunnies. She's also a nurse and is a certified chef. Dinners are the best every evening, and we all eat together."

"Even the sister that moved away?" Jean asked.

"The inn property is large, and houses are being built so the main house can fully be an inn one day. The older sister is still on the property—within walking distance." Gideon smiled at Margo. "Distance enough so we're not on top of each other, but to keep a close-knit family close by to enjoy each other's company."

"So, you're happy and Claire is happy?" Jean asked.

"Happy and thriving," Gideon replied. "We don't forget Trudy. Her picture is in Claire's nursery on the dresser her mom painted and decorated herself. We hold no ill will toward Grant and Denise. I understand they are grieving, but we all have to move on and do what's best for Claire. Instead of just hearing about her mom from me, we want her to learn about her from her grandparents as well."

"Thank you, no further questions," Jean said.

Judge Fitzgerald excused Gideon from the stand and then it was Margo's turn to give testimony. Jean was quick and to the point.

"How long have you been married to Gideon?" Jean posed the first question.

Margo answered smoothly. "Three weeks exactly."

"The plaintiffs are going to say you married him to act the stable family for court," Jean informed her. "What do you say to that?"

"It couldn't be further from the truth." Margo smiled at Gideon, her love for him clear on her face. "The day I met him, in his eyes, I saw the love he had for his daughter, but there was also such sadness and a burden that he carried. I watched that slowly fade away as he and Claire began to truly live. I watched him feed her, rock her to sleep, be patient with her when she fussed. He even bought her a little set so she could pretend to work alongside him when he was busy. He showed her the flowers on the property, the fish in the koi pond, and in the evenings, they'd walk to the ice cream shop. I fell in love with a father who put his child first in all things, even us."

"You said 'even us,' how so?" Jean asked.

"We did decide relatively quickly to get married but we didn't rush into anything. We spoke about it. Discussed how it would affect Claire and her future," Margo answered. "She was the best part of our wedding."

"I can see that from the wedding photo of you and her together," Jean said in a quiet voice. "Do you love Claire?"

"As much or more than Gideon." Margo laughed softly. "They're tied for first place in my heart, but I would do anything for her and for the family that surrounds her. That includes Mr. and Mrs. Wells if they so choose. Our family home is a large Victorian bed-and-breakfast inn. Just like when my parents visit, they'd have a room there anytime they want to come to town."

"A very generous offer," Jean said. "I have no further questions."

"Mr. Cameron." The judge waved him forward. "None of your shenanigans while questioning this witness."

"Yes, ma'am." Mr. Cameron got up and approached the stand. "Three weeks, hmm, seems a bit fast. I think that maybe you were trying to help Mr. Holder make the perfect family in a desperate attempt to try to keep custody."

"Your beliefs are just that Mr. Cameron, yours. I don't lie," Margo said firmly.

"These pictures were staged, weren't they?" His question was overly loud in a courtroom with only them, the judge and a few others present.

"No, they were not, and I have an entire community that would swear under oath to that," Margo replied crisply. "Unless you're saying that a few hundred people in a small community would lie."

"You never know." Mr. Cameron tried to goad her.

Margo never wavered. "It's obvious you've never lived in a place where neighbors can go to each other's homes for a chat, and a glass of sweet tea and a sticky bun."

That's my love, Gideon thought with pride. If this lawyer thought he could shake Margo, Mr. Cameron had another think coming.

"What about how you were raised? Mostly by a hired housekeeper while your parents traipsed around the world, isn't that right?" Mr. Cameron asked, and Gideon made a fist on his lap not to jump to Margo's defense.

"My mother has lupus. In the South in the sixties, seventies and even eighties, her care was not the priority it should have been—being a woman of color." Margo met the lawyer's stare with a direct one of her own. "My parents traveled for my mother's health care, but they came home every time they could. There were—"

Mr. Cameron cut her off. "That's all well and good."

"You didn't let me finish—"

He cut her off again. "Ms. Ballad."

"Mrs. Holder," she corrected. "You trying to avoid the fact that I am married to the man I love doesn't change the fact that we are married."

"Judge, please direct the witness to only answer the questions I ask," Mr. Cameron demanded.

"I would, but you didn't let her finish answering the first one," Judge Fitzgerald said. "You can finish now, Mrs. Holder."

Margo nodded her thanks. "My parents were there for our wedding. Mr. Cameron, we were raised with love, by my parents, in our home, neighborhood and by Enid who's like a second mother. Even from a distance, there is love in every part of my life, and there is enough of it to share with Gideon and Claire. And the Wellses, if they choose to accept it."

Mr. Cameron paused but then said, "I have nothing further, Judge."

Judge Fitzgerald waited until everyone was seated before she spoke. "I have all the evidence from both parties in front of me. Mr. Wells, Mrs. Wells, is it correct you both choose not to testify?"

"We're not the problem here. It's him! He's an unsuitable father," Grant shot back. "Just because he has some sunny pictures, and a new wife doesn't make a difference."

"So noted, you chose not to testify." Judge Fitzgerald wrote quickly on her sheet. "I will see you all tomorrow back in this courtroom at one in the afternoon so I can render my verdict. No contact between parties until then."

The bailiff ordered them to rise, and after the judge left, Jean ushered them out quickly.

"How much did he pay you for this so-called marriage, huh?" Mr. Wells said loudly behind them.

"Don't answer, don't react." Jean stopped Gideon from turning around and responding.

Margo took his hand. "We're fine, they don't know me or us."

Gideon kept going and they walked out of the courthouse together, Jean going to her car and they to their rental. After picking up Claire, instead of eating out, they ordered room service and stayed inside, watching Claire play before she went to bed.

"I can barely think past this might be the last night I get to be with her like this," Gideon murmured. His voice cracked saying the words.

"It won't be," Margo said. "Today went well for us. His lawyer was a joke, and they didn't have any actual evidence."

"I hope the judge sees it that way." Gideon was pessimistic.

Margo rubbed his shoulder. "Tomorrow will be here soon enough. Let's try to get some sleep until then."

But Gideon didn't sleep. He stared at the ceiling the entire night, and then in the morning tried to put on a brave face. This time, Claire was at the courthouse. They'd left her in an assigned room with a social worker while they sat in the courtroom waiting silently for the judgment. He bounced his foot nervously until Margo put her hand on his knee to stop the movement. Finally, Judge Fitzgerald entered.

"I see two sets of people who definitely love Claire Holder," Judge Fitzgerald said. She looked at each person at each table. "I also see two sets of people who could work together for the betterment of the child in question. The olive branch has been held out and offered by the defendants, only to be slapped away by the plaintiffs. That speaks, more than anything else, to the heart of the case. A father and his new wife who are willing to embrace his former in-laws for the sake of the child."

"Oh, that's utter nonsense," Mr. Wells burst out.

"You will be quiet, Mr. Wells. Your continued ruckus makes me question your ability to have a gentle temperament around your grandchild," Judge Fitzgerald snapped. "I saw pictures of a loving family, read affidavits and records from professional child advocates and her doctor all communicating that Claire Holder is a happy, healthy child, suffering no neglect. With that said, I rule in favor of the defendants. Mr. Gideon Holder will retain custody of his daughter. Any visitation is at the discretion of the custodial father. I would suggest, Mr. Wells, that you and your wife work with them and take the offer generously given by Mr. Holder and his wife. Case adjourned."

"I'm going to appeal this!" Mr. Wells shouted.

"Mr. Wells, you know that's not possible, but if it was any new judge would have the transcript of this trial documenting your behavior." Judge Fitzgerald gentled her voice. "I am truly sorry about Trudy and her death. I remember seeing her with you on the days you worked, you were so proud. Grant, Denise, work with your granddaughter's father to see her and be in her life. Don't let bitterness cause you to lose her forever."

Jean led the way out of the courtroom. Gideon expelled a shaky breath. "Oh, I'm so thankful this is over. Thank you, Jean, thank you so much."

"Just doing the right thing." Jean embraced him. "You guys go be happy and raise your little girl in peace."

Margo hugged her. "Jean, you're going to get the biggest basket of baked goods at your office."

Jean laughed. "Now that I won't refuse—a person who feeds my bread and pastry addiction."

Gideon stepped aside as Grant and Denise went by. "Please, the offer still stands. Call us and come visit anytime."

"We don't want charity from you," Grant snapped.

"It's not charity. It's about being in your granddaughter's life," Gideon grated out. "Please, let's bury this."

Gideon watched as they walked away. Denise looked back forlornly. This would be another sort of grief for her, not seeing Trudy's child because of Grant's stubbornness. He couldn't focus on that now. He couldn't make them see he truly cared and wanted to share Claire's growing up with them. He could only pray that someday they'd come around.

He and Margo picked up Claire from the social worker and stepped out into the drizzling rain. They'd be going home soon. Back to the sunshine. He was even looking forward to the humidity as long as there was sweet tea on the porch in the evening with his family. He smiled at Claire, and then pressed a kiss to Margo's lips. Their lives, together in happiness, started today.

CHAPTER TWELVE

"ARE YOU SURE you don't need us to stay?" Margo asked Gideon while they stood in line at the Tacoma Veterans Center.

"No, she'll get fussy standing around for too long." Gideon stroked Claire's cheek. He was back to his old self but still ready to leave Tacoma as soon as possible. "There's a park across the street. Tons of play stuff, and a coffee shop just along from here. You guys hang out and have fun, and I'll run across and get you when I'm done."

"Our flight leaves tomorrow at four. Will they have everything transferred by then?" Margo asked.

"It should be. Dealing with the government and the military sometimes is a hurry up and wait process, but I won't have to come back to Washington. My doctor at the Gold Clinic has the portal open so it should go through," Gideon answered. "My DD-214s will be updated with you as my wife and all that good stuff through the Department of Defense."

Margo shook her head. "All this stuff… You'll explain to me in small bites. We'll go over to the park and I'll let this little Claire Bear run off some energy, then we'll have a bite to eat at the coffee shop."

"If I get done in time, I'll join you." Gideon leaned down to kiss her and then made a smacking sound on Claire's cheek when he gave his baby girl a kiss, making her squeal.

Margo got Claire into her stroller and over to the park. They followed a paved walking path to the first vacant bench. A plaque at the entrance had said the park was dedicated to all veterans, and was set up especially so those who were disabled could easily access and enjoy the beautiful open space. Claire was eager to get out and play. Soon Margo was helping the toddler down the red slide and playing peekaboo through holes in huge colorful square blocks.

Claire stopped long enough for a few sips from her cold applesauce pouch, only to go again with seemingly boundless energy. *At least she'll be asleep quickly tonight*, Margo thought to herself happily.

"Hello, M-Margo," a voice said from behind her.

She turned to see Mrs. Wells in jeans and a navy wool cardigan over a soft pink blouse. Denise's arms were folded as if she was warding off a chill or maybe holding herself together the best way she could. She looked longingly at Claire and Margo's heart instantly went out to the older woman.

"Mrs. Wells." Margo straightened. "How are you?"

"The best I can be. Call me Denise," she said.

"How did you find us?" Margo asked.

"It's the closest place to the hotel for a toddler to run around," Denise replied. "May I h-hold her."

Margo knew that Gideon wouldn't mind. He'd offered them the option to visit Claire in Charlotte multiple times.

"Of course. Would you like to sit and maybe talk?" Margo spoke gently and gestured to the bench.

Denise nodded. "That would be nice. I assume you will be heading back home soon."

"Tomorrow," Margo answered as Claire ran over to them. She picked her up and sat down before handing the toddler to her grandmother. "I'm sorry how this all worked out—for all of you. Gideon means it, you know, and I do as well. Come see us anytime. You're more than welcome."

Claire's grandmother kissed the top of the toddler's red curls. "Maybe one day. Grant is still so angry."

"Aren't you?" Margo prodded.

"More grief than anger now," Denise admitted. "My bitterness once matched Grant's, but my heart has been torn to pieces, and now I'm losing this sweet baby too."

"You're not losing her. Please just think about visiting, and I'll talk to Gideon about traveling here as well," Margo said. "Don't let hard feelings keep you away from your granddaughter."

Denise admitted, "I let myself be blinded for so long. I could see things weren't working out for Trudy and Gideon, and she was so unhappy. But Grant wanted the perfect daughter, so her marriage had to be perfect too. But I could see in her eyes—the longing to be free, who she wanted to be. She was creative, more a free spirit. Did you know she made such beautiful art?"

"No, I didn't," Margo answered.

"She hid most of the pieces from her father." Denise frowned. "He said being an artist was a fine hobby, but only a fool would do it as a job. A surefire way to stay poor and always struggling. Trudy simply saw beauty in everything. It was marvelous to talk to her about it. I have two pieces of hers hung in the dayroom. Her father still doesn't know they are hers."

"Claire likes paints and flowers. She loves anything with color," Margo said with a smile. "She must've gotten that from her mother."

"How I wish I could go back in time and nurture that instead of forcing activities like rowing so she could get into an Ivy League school," Denise said suddenly.

"I'm sure she knew your heart." Margo covered her hand with her own. "But taking Claire from Gideon was not the answer. We can work together."

"I hope we can." Denise smiled. "Gideon sends us pictures—well, me. I don't want to miss her growing up."

"You won't have to. Even if you have to come by yourself, Claire will always be available to you," Margo promised.

"Going back…wishing for it…" Denise gave a soft laugh as she bounced Claire on her knee. "If fishes are wishes, then we all would be fed."

"Enid says that, and it took me a while to figure out what it meant," Margo said. "May I have your phone? I'm going to put my number into it, that way if you need to talk to me about anything, or just to hear Claire babble, you have a way to get ahold of me."

Denise nodded and passed it over. "I would like that. I don't talk to many people anymore."

Margo looked at her. "Don't you have friends in your life?"

Denise gave a short laugh. "The wives of my husband's friends aren't the sort of people I want to share my feelings with. We have a certain reputation to protect."

Again, Margo's empathy caused her to reach out and take Denise's hand. "I'm sorry to hear that, but to heal you have to move on and not focus on the bad parts, but instead, on the parts you shared with Trudy that were truly happy, before and after Claire."

"I see why Gideon loves you. Your heart is pure gold." Denise smiled.

"You look cold. How about if I go across the street and grab us two coffees, and maybe a chocolate croissant? Those always seem to help me and my sisters when we're upset," Margo suggested.

"It must have been nice to grow up with people you can confide in and know will always support you," Denise said. "I wonder how much better Trudy's life might have been with a sibling, but alas Grant and I only had the one—we'd always held out hope for a boy to add to our family."

Margo stood. "I don't think you could put an order in for the exact gender."

Denise laughed. "Very true."

"I'll be right back." Margo dropped a kiss on Claire's hand. "I'll be back soon, Claire Bear, and maybe if your daddy gets done soon, we can all have lunch."

Margo set off across the street, lucky the café

was at the end of what looked like its busy rush, she got her order in quickly. After picking up the tray with the coffees and the bag with the pastries, she hurried back to the park. Claire's stroller was exactly where she'd left it by the bench, but Denise and Claire were not.

"Denise, Claire!" she called out. Margo's heart began to race. "Denise, Claire Bear!"

She turned and looked at the stroller, noting the mint-green baby bag was no longer there.

She took her. Margo went numb as she looked around in shock. "She took Claire."

With trembling hands, she pulled her phone from her pocket pressed the symbol next to Gideon's face.

He answered on the second ring. "Hey, almost done. Just signed the last paper."

"S-she took her," Margo stammered.

"Who took who?" Gideon asked slowly.

"Denise!" Margo's voice rose. "She came to the park, and we were talking. She wanted to hold Claire and I let her. It was okay. She seemed good. I went to get coffee and when I came back, she'd left the stroller but took Claire!"

"Oh no, Margo, what did you do!" he shouted and hung up the phone.

She began to cry. *What had she done? Why did she always see the best in others, and...*

Gideon showed up and she stared helplessly

in one direction and then another. "Did you see which way she went?"

Margo shook her head, speaking between her tears. "I was in the coffee shop…"

"Why did you leave her with Denise?" he yelled. "We won custody!"

"She just wanted to talk!" she cried out. "She was so alone and unhappy. We talked about her coming to visit us."

"How could you be this gullible? She was playing you," Gideon said, his exasperation showing.

"She was acting normal. She just wanted to talk. I thought it would be okay for Claire to stay with her while I got coffee," Margo protested.

"Why didn't you call me?" Gideon demanded.

"Because Claire was with me, and I thought it would be okay," she said. "I'm her mother now too."

"I'm her real father. I'm the one who has to make these decisions," he ground out. "It wasn't your choice to make."

"So I'm just her…what, exactly? Babysitter when you need one, but not a partner to share important decisions with?" The hurt that Margo felt shook her to her core, but she tried to speak calmly. "I called you. I called the police. What else could I do?"

"I think you've done enough," Gideon said and jogged away to the corner to look, obviously hoping to see Denise holding the baby and walking away.

Margo made another call, trying to catch her breath between the tears.

"Hey, Margs, how's it going?" Mia asked in a singsongy voice. "On your way home yet?"

"Not yet," she managed to gasp out.

"Margo, what's wrong?" Mia asked instantly. Margo knew her sister could tell she was upset.

"Denise took Claire. We were talking in the park, and I went for coffee. When I came back, she had and Claire were gone. Gideon blames me and it's my fault. I shouldn't have believed her."

"You stop that right now, Margo. You couldn't have predicted or known that was going to happen. You felt for a grieving woman," Mia said firmly. "She's acting out of that grief and fear."

"He said Claire's not mine to make decisions for, but I love her like she's mine," Margo whispered, her heart broken in a million pieces. "We got married to be a family, but he seems to think I'm—I don't know what he thinks."

"Margo, I'm filling Micki in and we're taking the next flight out," Mia said. "I'm putting you on speaker, everyone else is here."

"What's going on?" Micki asked. "Sis, are you okay?"

"Claire's grandmother took her and ran after

we were talking in the park. Gideon blames me."
Margo gave the condensed version of her story.

"He can't blame you. You didn't start this, he
brought you into this," Micki said in outrage.

"I went for coffee, and she took off." Margo
felt tears clog her throat. She swallowed before
speaking. "I explained why I trusted her, and he
said I couldn't make decisions when it came to
Claire. That she was his child."

"Oh that…" Micki didn't finish her sentence,
but Margo could tell her sister was furious.

"If it wasn't for you—this family, all of us…"
Ryan's tone was serious. "I understand he's
upset, but that was a low blow."

"But he's right. She's his daughter and he has
custody. I just don't know where I stand right
now," she admitted.

"You're her mother in every sense of the word.
You love her, you've been there in her sickness
and to pick her up from daycare. She even calls
you Mama," Enid pointed out. "Me and Gideon
are going to have a talk when you all return home
with Claire safe and sound."

"Don't do that," Margo sighed. "I'm an adult,
I'll figure it out."

"Text me your hotel information and we'll be
there." Mia huffed. "Your sisters are coming."

"You don't have to—"

Mia cut her off. "We're coming. You need us

there. Ryan will be here with Omar, and Enid can take care of anything else."

"That I can do. Come home soon, sweetheart. You are not at fault here," Enid consoled.

"Okay."

She hung up and sat on the bench as police cars stopped and uniformed men and women swarmed the park. They took her statement and then talked to Gideon who explained about the Wellses' custody hearing being lost. He made eye contact with her for an instant, but she saw anger, hurt, and fear in his gaze. Could she blame him?

No, she couldn't, because maybe he was right. She wasn't Claire's mother, after all. Was her marriage a sham for Gideon to just get what he wanted—custody of his daughter? Because when the chips were down, he pulled being a mother away like a rug from under her feet. *He can't even look at me*, Margo thought. She was hurt and afraid as well. As people rushed around them, and Gideon coordinated with the police, Margo put her hands on her knees and cried.

HIS MIND COULDN'T comprehend why Denise would take Claire like that or why Margo would leave his daughter alone with her. He got it, Margo was kind and saw the best in every-one and wasn't jaded enough to see Denise as a threat. But right now, as she sat beside him in the car totally devastated, he couldn't comfort her when his mind was racing a mile a minute. Denise and Grant had the financial resources to take Claire anywhere, including out of the country. Would authorities, would anyone help him get her back?

They were following the police, who were heading toward the Wells house, with the hope that Denise went back to a place she considered secure. He could only pray that was the case, while his mind went back to what he'd said in anger and fear to Margo. Essentially, he had implied that Claire was his child only, and she had no say. He saw her rear back in shock and knew, without a doubt, he'd hurt her.

"I didn't want for this to happen, you know," Margo spoke up suddenly. "She admitted that they were wrong about how they treated Trudy, their crazy expectations for her and how she should've nurtured Trudy's creativity instead of stifling it to smooth things over with her husband."

Gideon gave a caustic laugh. "Now she figures this out. After two and a half years of awful behavior from both her and Grant?"

"You can't be like that or expect me to feel like that with you. I don't know about Grant, but Denise is hurting. She's wishing for a way to go back and fix what happened," Margo implored. "She lost her daughter and now her granddaughter. She is acting out from a place where she only sees despair."

"Are you on their side?" Gideon demanded.

"Of course not!" Margo exclaimed. "I'm trying to make you see she didn't plan this. She is acting on a gut-wrenching impulse a person, a mother in this case, faces where there's loss. I can understand where she's coming from. If I recall, you asked me to run away with you and Claire because you were afraid of losing your daughter. Imagine how Denise feels? She's losing more than even you can imagine."

Gideon was silent.

"I may not be Claire's mother, but I love her, and I can have empathy," Margo said between stiff lips. "One doesn't exclude the other."

The police cars parked in the driveway of the Wells home, and they could see a black escalade ahead. She and Gideon got out of their rental and stood behind the detective who knocked on the door. Grant Wells opened the door and his eyes widened in surprise. When he saw Margo and Gideon farther down the steps his face became a mask of anger.

"What do you want? Get them off my property right now," he said, lifting his chin high into the air. "Do you know who I am?"

"Yes, Judge Wells, we do," the detective said and showed Grant his badge. "I'm Detective Tyrell Bradshaw, I work in Missing Persons. Where is your wife, sir?"

"Why? She's not here." He looked from them to the police, worriedly. "Did something happen to my wife?"

"No, sir, your wife has taken your granddaughter and has not been seen since," Detective Bradshaw said politely. "Mrs. Holder told us that your wife was upset. I need to know if she is on medication or would do anything harmful to herself or the baby."

"That's not right." Grant looked at Margo. "You must've done something to her."

Margo shook her head. "No. We were talking and going to have coffee. She misses your daughter."

"And *he* is taking our grandchild." Grant lay blame at Gideon's feet.

"You had options, Grant," Gideon replied. "You are so stubborn you refused them and now Denise feels like she doesn't have any control in her life. Just tell us where she is."

"I don't know." Grant passed his hand over his hair and Gideon could see the concern on his face.

"We're going to have to search the house and interview you," Detective Bradshaw said.

"Fine, you come in. They don't." Grant's voice was weary but still filled with stubbornness.

Together, she and Gideon waited outside, and Gideon looked up at the sky. "It's getting late. Is she even going to feed Claire, give her milk? She doesn't have her favorite blanket, it's not in the bag."

"She is Claire's grandmother. She's going to make sure Claire is safe above herself." Margo took his hand and squeezed it.

"Yeah, you're right—you're right," he murmured. He knew Margo was hurting just as badly as he was, but—she'd let Denise take Claire and he couldn't come to terms with that yet. His Claire Bear needed to be safe, or his life would crumble into nothingness.

Detective Bradshaw and the police officers who were helping with the search came out of the house. The detective was frowning.

"She's not in there," Detective Bradshaw said. "We're putting out an Amber Alert with their pictures, make and model of the car, and financial forensics has Mr. Wells's approval to run a trace on her credit cards and any activity with their bank accounts. We're also leaving an officer here in case she contacts him. We'll know immediately."

"Can you do that?" Margo asked.

The detective nodded. "In the case of an Amber

Alert with a noncustodial parent we can. This is essentially a kidnapping."

Margo looked at Gideon in alarm. "Are you going to press charges against her?"

"Why shouldn't I? If our positions were reversed, they would do it to me," Gideon replied.

She placed her hand on his. "We don't have to stoop to that level, match people's bad behavior with our own, you're better than that."

Gideon felt foolish. "So, what happens now?" he asked.

"We wait." The detective sounded apologetic. "Until we get a hit, or a tip called in, that's all we can do."

"I can't sit in a hotel room and wait for my child to maybe show up," Gideon ground out.

"Mr. Holder, I know you're frantic and feeling helpless right now…" Detective Bradshaw tried to console him. "But go back to your hotel. Stay put with your wife, and we'll contact you."

"I'm not leaving this town until I have my daughter." Gideon felt it in his bones, he had to do something. "Find her, Detective, but I will also continue my search."

"How?" Detective Bradshaw asked.

"Some old marine buddies might be able to help," he answered.

"I'm helping too," Margo said. Looking determined.

"I should take you back to the hotel so you can—"

"Can what? Sit there and worry when I can be with you," she countered.

"You've done enough."

"That's the second time you've said that to me. I don't know if that means it's my fault or you really think I can't contribute anything else." Margo gave him a direct stare and folded her arms. "Either way, I'm your wife. She was my responsibility, and I'm going with you."

He didn't know how he'd meant it. All he was thinking about was Claire and how Grant Wells looked him at him with accusations on his face.

He and Margo turned and walked back to the rental car.

"How about we go by Trudy's gravesite? Maybe she went there to feel closer to her daughter with Claire with her," Margo suggested. "We saw her there before the custody hearing, remember?"

"Good idea," Gideon said. "Why don't you drive, I'm going to call a few guys I know from my platoon. After they left the military, they formed a security business. I can at least ask for their advice. Maybe they'd even add their resources to the search."

"Okay."

Margo started the car, and he placed his first

call. He gave her directions to the cemetery while waiting for someone to answer.

"Fordham and Hart Security," the voice said.

"Tom? This is Gideon Holder."

"Gunny, is that you?" Tom laughed. "How are you doing, man?"

"Was doing pretty okay. I moved to North Carolina, got married," Gideon explained. "I came back for a hearing with Trudy's parents. They were trying to take custody of Claire."

"I'm sorry, that's rough. I thought after Trudy passed, they would stop their interference and making you miserable." Tom's voice held concern. "They didn't win, did they?"

"No, but Denise ran off with Claire after my wife left them to get coffee," Gideon explained. "I need help finding my daughter because it's been hours. The cops want me to sit and wait, but she could be on her way to who knows where with my kid right now."

"We got your back, Gunny. So, you know the make and model of the car?" Tom asked. "Also, can you send a picture of Claire Bear? I can find one online of Denise. I know for a fact I saw them on TV at some charity thing a few months ago."

"I can do that." Gideon breathed out. "Thanks, Tom, I owe you one, or several."

"Take me out to dinner when I get to Charlotte," Tom teased. "But seriously, Gunny, you don't owe us a thing. If it wasn't for you, we wouldn't have made it home from that last deployment."

"We got each other home," Gideon replied, flashes of their last mission were still clear in his mind. "Let me know if you find anything, please."

"We're on it," Tom assured him.

Silence reigned in the car until Margo spoke.

"Why did you never mention Tom or his business partners before?"

"He's more of an acquaintance than friend," Gideon answered stiffly.

"Please don't downplay your friendship. He called her Claire Bear." Margo sighed. "He obviously knew about Trudy and the issues with your marriage. I thought I'd heard about all the important people in your life."

"It's not like that at all," Gideon denied. "I'm worried about my kid."

"I am too, but you haven't said you don't blame me," Margo pointed out.

Gideon was silent. She was right. Even going through this, he should have acknowledged her, told her he understood. Still, he couldn't say for sure he didn't blame his wife for Denise taking Claire.

"You know everything about me, and my family and you never once spoke of these friends. I honestly thought you were alone here, but you had close buddies you never mentioned to me. You've never talked much about your deployments, the good times or bad, and I'm starting to see that I don't really know you at all. Only what you wanted me to know."

"Margo, that's not how it is. I'm slowly learning to navigate a new life, and I wasn't going to dump a lot of details on you." Gideon stared out the window.

"But yet, you asked me to marry you, to help with the custody." Margo sounded as if she was reevaluating the moment. "The actual proposal was amazing, but now I don't know if it was another way to get what you want. I don't like doubting my choices, or people that are supposed to love me."

"I do love you, Margo, but this is a lot to handle right now."

"It is for me as well," she replied softly and turned the corner where he'd indicated.

The sky was settling into twilight, he noticed.

Gideon couldn't give her any more of an answer. He loved her, but Claire was gone and there was no simple way to find her. At the cemetery, more of their hope was dashed when Denise wasn't there. He ran his hand over his head as panic filled him. *Where did she take my daughter?*

Margo drove them around Tacoma, even going back to the park and every ice cream place and toy store he could think of.

They even went to the mall, hoping to see Denise holding Claire or having her ride in one of those little toy cars she liked so much. But there was nothing. No sign of her, and he felt his hope start to dwindle. He wanted to search all night if he had to—from one side of the city to the other—until he had his girl, but Margo was weary. Even if she didn't say it, he could see it on her face combined with the look of sadness and worry. She loved Claire just as much as he did, and he knew he needed to give their relationship the time and trust it deserved.

He'd handled their first real argument badly. He knew he had to fix it, but how could he when Claire was out there? He asked her to drive them back to the hotel. When they entered the lobby, he saw Mia and Micki. Both had concerned expressions on their faces, but Micki's disapproving frown was directed at him.

"Any word?" Mia asked, pulling Margo into her arms.

"No." There were tears in her voice when Margo answered. "I trusted her and believed her. Now Claire is gone."

Mia cupped her cheek and wiped her sister's tears away. "You see the best in people…"

Micki looked at him. "*All* people…"

Okay, direct hit, he thought glumly.

"Denise's reaction is the sum total of years of bad things that just overflowed with the tragic thought of losing Claire," Mia said. "This is not your fault."

"Do you guys have a room?" Margo asked.

"Right next door to yours," Mia replied. "Let's go up and get you both something to eat and you can regroup."

"Let's hold up. I have a few things to say," Micki spoke in a serious tone.

"I'm sure you do, kiddo," Gideon tried to tease.

"No, you don't get to call me that," Micki said. "That's reserved for someone that I consider a brother, not someone who would hurt my sister. I don't know what you are going to be after this."

Now he saw it—what Ryan said would happen if the Ballad sisters went into protection mode when one of the three was facing something difficult. They were connected in a way he had to admire because they never let each other face anything alone. Gideon felt like he was on the outside looking in.

He knew that his words and reaction had placed him at arm's length from a love that would've embraced him in his time of fear and sorrow. There would be a lot to make up for when they found Claire, if he hadn't ruined it already.

CHAPTER THIRTEEN

THE TENSION WAS thick in the hotel suite. Gideon stayed downstairs to speak to Reservations to book another day or two, all the while knowing that it may be a long haul to get Claire back. Margo sat down on the love seat they'd shared just a few days before as Jean assured them about the hearing. Now she didn't even know where Claire was. That, and the uncertainty of her marriage and the love she thought was hers, broke Margo's heart.

"Margs, you look exhausted." Mia sat beside her. "Are you hungry?"

Margo shook her head. "No, but thanks for asking."

"You're going to eat anyway," Micki insisted. "I'm ordering you and Gideon some soup and a sandwich, and for you a big hot cup of tea. I know it's your comfort drink."

"Okay." Margo's smile was fleeting. Her eyes felt gritty from all the tears she'd shed. "This is my fault."

"No, it's not." Mia rubbed her back reassuringly. Gideon came into the room and she looked at him. "Tell her it's not her fault."

"It's not," he stated. "I just thought you'd use better judgment when it came to Denise."

"How exactly?" Micki demanded to know. "The case is closed, and you'd said your in-laws could still have a role in Claire's life. Nothing about that says keep my kid away from Denise. Margo's judgment wasn't flawed."

"We talked about Trudy, about losing a child," Margo offered up her explanation to him again. "She said she didn't blame you. That she let Grant stifle Trudy, trying to make her into something she wasn't and how it was wrong as well."

"At least she admitted something," he muttered.

"And what about you, Gideon? What do you admit?" Mia's lips were a tight line. "You don't make someone you love feel like this when times get tough. Can't you see she's hurting too? She loves Claire, we all do. But you chose to push her away when this is the time you should hold on to her all the more. Weather this storm together."

"Maybe Trudy and her family were right. I'm not good at relationships," Gideon said.

"No, you can't use that as an excuse." Micki jumped back into the conversation. "No one else makes the decision about the man you are or can be. You prove them wrong. You are a loving dad to Claire, and you can be a loving partner too, if you choose it."

"I am a good father. I know how to be that, and right now, my baby girl is out there without her nighttime milk and her blanket...without me..." His voice cracked. "She's my world, and I lost her."

Margo stood quickly and went to him. "You didn't lose her. Denise will come to her senses soon."

"Not if Grant gets to her. They're going to run off somewhere," Gideon said in frustration. "I just need to hear something...anything."

There was a knock on the door, and Micki went to answer it. The waiter pushed the room service table forward and the smell of food filled Margo's nose, making her stomach rumble.

"You guys are going to sit and eat," Mia directed them. "You, Gideon, are really going to think about how you react to things. You're not alone. You're married now, and to my sister who is the most amazing woman in the universe. Ryan and I had to find our middle ground, and you both can too."

"I know."

Gideon said the words, but he didn't look at her, Margo noted. She understood his mind was on Claire. She tried to remind herself of that as they sat down to eat. Margo ate her soup and just nibbled at her sandwich while Gideon ate while he paced. He spent the time on the phone asking his friends for updates, any little crumb that could lead them to Claire. At one point he walked into the bedroom talking and left the sisters in the living area of the suite.

"He's not thinking straight." Mia tried to console her. "Claire was all he had for such a long time. It was the two of them without anyone. We can be supportive, as a family, but I don't think he understands what that means yet. He'll figure it out. Family is there through the good and the bad."

"I love him," Margo said softly. "But I also feel so very alone right now. Like he's pushed me out of the house and locked the door. When Claire's back, how will I fit in? Where?"

"As her mother." Micki and her usual brass way of speaking gentled when she sat on the opposite side of Margo. "You're her mom, just like Mia is Omar's mom, or Enid is our mom too. You don't need blood to form the bonds of family, Margs. If Gideon can't see that, he's the poorer for it, and he's taking Claire Bear away from someone and something beautiful."

"Look at you, Michelle Ballad, being all sage and full of wisdom." Margo gave a watery laugh.

The two sisters wrapped their arms around

Margo and she felt the comfort of their love. If they were back at the inn, they'd have piled into Mia's old room to have tea and to talk this out. She missed their home right now. She wanted to hide away from all that hurt her, find sanctuary within the walls that nurtured them all their lives. She wanted that for Claire, even if it was a bed-and-breakfast. To be able to run inside and go to the kitchen for a snack from Enid, or to play on the patio while it rained. Margo didn't even know if she would be able to have that wistful dream anymore.

In a mere matter of hours, she was feeling a chasm being formed between herself and Gideon, and each minute that went by without Claire it grew larger. Margo didn't know if a bridge could fix it.

Gideon came out of the room holding up the phone. "Tom's people spotted her car at the airport. I called Detective Bradshaw."

"I'll get Claire's coat. It gets chilly here at night," Margo moved quickly.

Gideon hesitated. "Stay with your sisters and…"

He didn't get to finish the sentence because her phone rang and when Margo pulled it from her pocket, it was a Tacoma area code.

With her pulse racing, she hoped it was Denise when she answered. "Hello?"

"M-Margo, it's Denise. I'm so sorry, I—I just looked at her and saw my Trudy."

Margo's heart leaped in excitement, but she kept her voice calm. "It's okay, Denise, I know you were upset. It's a lot to deal with all at once. Where are you?"

Gideon moved closer as she put the phone on speaker, while holding her finger to her lips.

"I'm at the airport, South Terminal. I'm parked right outside the cell service lot where people wait to drop off departures," Denise answered.

Mia was helping Margo put on her coat as she spoke. "Okay, that seems like an easy place to find."

"Can you come?" Denise asked hesitantly. "I know Gideon is mad, and this is all a whole mess. I just want to talk to you."

"I'll come to you. Is Claire okay? Is she hungry? Should I bring her something?" Margo asked gently, trying to keep Denise calm. She could just hear it in her voice, any stress and Claire's grandmother might just bolt.

"She's okay. I got her dinner, and she had a chocolate milk box and apple slices," Denise gave a soft laugh. "Apple slices and chocolate milk are her favorites, just like her mom."

"Yes, they are." Margo smiled. "We're on our way."

"Can you tell Gideon I'm sorry for making him worry," Denise asked.

"I will, see you soon," Margo said and disconnected the call.

"I texted Detective Bradshaw, he'll meet me there," Gideon said.

"Meet *us*, Gideon. If you show up alone, she is not going to hand over Claire easily. Let me talk to her, she trusts me," Margo insisted. "Please, let me help."

"Fine, you're right. I'm not in a good mind to talk to Denise." Gideon frowned. He looked exhausted.

"I'll be back," Margo told her sisters and placed the key card in Mia's hand. "In case you need to leave and get back in."

"We'll be here," Mia promised in a firm voice.

Margo followed Gideon out of the door, elated that there was finally contact, and they were closer to bringing Claire home. One step at a time, she told herself, it was the only way she could cope.

GIDEON DROVE WITH INTENT, barely staying beneath the speed limit trying to get to the airport. The matter of what's next hung in the air. She and Gideon would need to talk, that's for sure, but when and where it might lead worried her. Even the silence that used to feel comfortable between them was filled with tension. During the twenty minutes it took to get them from their hotel to the airport and Denise, still nothing was said. How could she console him when he blamed her for Denise taking Claire?

"That's her car," Gideon said and pulled in behind it.

Detective Bradshaw and two other police cars showed up right as they were exiting the car.

"Okay, we'd prefer to get her to give the child over before we arrest her," Detective Bradshaw said.

"Do you have to arrest her?" Margo asked. "She's been through so much, she's not okay and she needs help."

"We have responsibility here and a job to do, she will be arrested," Detective Bradshaw explained. "But we will get her help, I promise."

"She asked to talk to me, and I think I can get her to give Claire over safely," Margo said. "I don't think she's a danger to any of us, or Claire."

Detective Bradshaw hesitated before he spoke. "Gideon, its your call."

He nodded. "Go talk to her, Margo. Like you said, she asked to speak to you."

The rain began to drizzle. Margo pulled the hood of her windbreaker up for cover. Luckily enough, Denise was parked beneath the stone walkway that went from the terminal to the upper carpark level. Denise rolled the window down as Margo approached. Margo could hear the grandmother singing to Claire.

"It's a beautiful song, what is it?" Margo asked.

"'All the Pretty Horses.' I used to sing it to Trudy every night." A wistful smile passed over Denise's lips. "She's almost asleep. She's such a good baby. She asked for Mama. I know she meant you."

"I take care of her like she was my own."

"I almost tried to run away. Booked tickets and everything to Key West so she could grow up on a beach like Trudy wished she could." Denise spoke like she was talking to herself. "But then, I couldn't hurt more people. We've been selfish, and I can't do that anymore."

Margo nodded. "Why did you take her, Denise? You know I would've made sure you could see her."

"I know, I panicked." Denise turned to look at her. "I looked at her and saw Trudy smiling up at me. I just thought, I can't lose my baby again. So, I took her. My mind was telling me I was wrong to do it, but I couldn't help it. I want my Trudy back so badly, to fix the mistakes I made. I miss her every day. It's like my arms ache to hold her."

Tears slipped down Margo's cheeks. "I know what it's like to feel that kind of hard loss. It takes so long for you to take a good breath again. But it gets better. I know you can't see it now. I couldn't see it for a long time."

"I don't know what happens after this, but maybe in a few years, I hope I can make this up to Gideon and to you," Denise said. "I know things are going to be challenging. I can see the stress and hurt on your face. I'm sorry I did that to you, Margo, and Gideon."

"We'll get it all sorted out." Margo smiled and put her hand on Denise's shoulder. "I'm going to take Claire so they can come to you. The detective promised they're going to get you help."

Denise nodded and kissed the sleeping baby's cheek. "Bye, my sweet girl. One day I will see you again."

Margo opened the car door and took Claire.

"Here's her bag, and I got her a blanket so she wouldn't be cold."

Denise handed over the items. The soft pink blanket with green elephants Margo used to cover the baby's head. Gideon moved eagerly to take his daughter and hugged her against him. The look of relief was evident as he kissed her cheeks.

"It's okay, Claire Bear, Daddy's got you." His voice cracked with emotion. Claire lifted her head and gave him her wide grin, showing more gum than teeth.

"Dadeee."

He laughed and kissed her again. "Yep, that's me, Daddy, and I'm never going to be anywhere else but with you."

Margo watched as Claire, smiling, laid her head on Gideon's shoulder. An ache in her chest continued to grow. It was obvious to Margo that it was him and Claire against the world. Margo didn't feel like she had a place in that, not anymore. But this needed to end before she could completely shatter. Firming her shoulders, Margo went back to Denise and helped her from the car so the detective could handcuff her. Grant Wells showed up right at that time, screeching to a halt in his black Mercedes and jumping out from behind the wheel.

"You will uncuff her this instant," he demanded, waving his arms at Detective Bradshaw.

"Judge Wells, that's not how this works. Your wife kidnapped the child," Detective Bradshaw said calmly and professionally.

"Because of them!" He pointed an accusing finger at Margo and Gideon. "They pushed her to the edge! The handcuffs should be on them!"

"Mr. Wells, they've done nothing but be kind to your wife." Detective Bradshaw's voice held irritation. "Mr. Holder has just told me he's choosing not to file charges and asks for your wife to get help. But she still has to be processed and booked. Hopefully a judge like yourself will give leniency where you do not."

"How dare you speak to me like that," Grant raged. "Do you know who I...?"

"Oh, for mercy's sake, Grant, shut up!" Denise snapped and sighed. "I hope they put me somewhere nice, where I can get a little peace from you. And in the time I am gone, Grant, you will go work on yourself. Then we will do couples counseling. Forty-two years of your bullying egotistical ways are quite enough. That's how we lost our relationship with Trudy, and unless you want to lose me too, we—you've got to change."

Grant stared at his wife, clearly in shock.

"Wow," Detective Bradshaw muttered.

"Take me away, Detective," Denise said with her head tilted in defiance. As she was walked past Gideon, she halted her steps. "Thanks for understanding. Thank you for being an amazing father to Claire. I'm so sorry I never said that sooner. Most of all, thank you for being there for Trudy when we were too ignorant to be. I hope in time, we can form a relationship and you'll allow me...us, to see Claire. As long as Grant works on himself as well."

"I'm sure we can work our way to that," Gideon said. "Be well, Denise, and we'll be waiting when you call."

"Go, Denise." Margo gave her a quick hug and

whispered in her ear. "Way to take your life into your own hands. You got this."

Denise beamed. "I do, don't I?"

An ambulance was called to transport Claire to the hospital and Gideon rode with her. Margo followed in the car. As she drove, she blinked tears away. First in relief, then because she was hurt by how Gideon had made her feel in the middle of a crisis. She married him for love, and maybe he did love her in a way, but she felt like a means to an end, to keep custody of Claire. When the chips were down, they didn't come together like a husband and wife should. He'd pushed her away.

Margo felt as if she was at the window looking in. Not a mother to a girl she loved, and maybe not a wife. Her sobs wracked her body, and Margo had to pull over so she could cry because she was unable to see through the tears. Finally composed, she continued on her way to the hospital. Approaching the ER door, she calmed herself enough to be numb and called her sisters.

"Hey, any news?" Mia asked in lieu of hello.

"We have her safe and sound. She's at the hospital now for a checkup," Margo replied.

"Oh, thank the heavens," Mia said. "Micki, they have her and she's okay."

"Huzzah," Micki said in the background.

"I'm going to check in on them and then...we

can head to the airport," Margo said. "Can you get our tickets changed to an earlier flight?"

"You and Gideon?" Mia asked.

"Just mine. I think he may have to stay a little longer for police stuff or… I don't know." Margo took a deep breath and willed herself not to cry. "I just need to not be here right now."

"Okay, yeah. We have half of Mom and Dad's miles they gave us for emergencies. It will be an easy change," Mia said. "Margs, you should stay. Talk to Gideon and let him know how you feel."

"I don't think that matters." Margo felt the weight of her words. Her happily-ever-after was shattering before her eyes. "All that needs to be packed up is my makeup. Can you leave me out some jeans, undies and a T-shirt so I can shower and change before we go?"

"Margo are you sure you want to do this?"

"I have to." Margo's breath left her lips with a shuddering sigh. "I need to, Mia. I'm barely holding myself together as is."

Mia hesitated for a moment. "Then we'll take care of you first, until you are more solid in your steps. Then you can face everything else. One step, then another, until you get where you need to be."

"Thanks. I'll take a rideshare back to the hotel."

Margo disconnected the call and then asked the charge nurse which room Gideon and Claire were in. Once outside the room, Margo slowly cracked the door open and peaked inside. Claire was lying in a small bed, railings up on both sides, her eyes closed. There was an IV in her tiny hand. The situation brought back memories of when Claire was sick with the viral infection. At that moment, she and Gideon were getting closer, now, it was all just falling apart for them.

"Hi, she's asleep again?" Margo asked.

"Yep. They said she's good, but they want to keep her a little bit longer so she can have the yellow stuff in the bag," Gideon said.

"It's called a banana bag. It's just water with some vitamins in it. Just in case she was dehydrated," Margo said and went to the opposite side of the bed. "May I?"

"You never have to ask, Margo," Gideon said.

Her smile was fleeting. "After all that's happened, I feel like I should."

"Margo…" he began.

"Not right now." Margo held up her hand. "I can't do this right now, not after today."

She bent over to kiss Claire's cheek and, as if she sensed Margo being there in her sleep, she lifted her hand and grabbed Margo's braids like she often did when falling asleep.

"You're the sweetest baby in the world." Margo untangled the tiny hand from her hair and pressed a kiss on it. "I love you so much."

She could feel Gideon watching her as she straightened, those gorgeous eyes seeing everything, but not understanding her at all.

"Thank you for helping get her back," Gideon said huskily.

Margo hesitated. "I love and would do anything for her. The flight home…"

Gideon sighed. "I don't know, we might need to change them. There's what the police will need, plus, I thought I was finished at the VA, but I kind of ran out of there when you called."

When you told me I wasn't Claire's mother and shouldn't make any choices.

"Yeah, I get that," Margo said instead.

"We need to talk, to sort this out."

"I—um." Margo turned and swiped the tears that escaped down her cheek. "I parked in the emergency lot. It's to the left of the ER door." She placed the keys on the small tray table. "I'm going to take a rideshare back to the hotel."

"Margo, look at me," Gideon begged. "Please."

She shook her head. "I can't right now. I just need to sleep and think. You take care of Claire and yourself. You've been through the ringer."

She went to the door but his voice stopped her.

"Margo, stay." Gideon held out his hand as she turned.

She almost said yes, almost ran into his arms, but in the time that Claire was gone, it showed her the truth. Their foundation was shaky—built on sand. They hadn't known each other long enough to stand firm through a crisis. Maybe they needed time to get to know each other, to build their love so it was solid and could weather any storm. But right now, she felt battered. Like a wave hitting the rocks at high tide, over and over again.

So, she left and let the door close behind her. She walked away quickly, begging her tears to stay put until she could find a place to lick her wounds. When would she ever learn to put a wall around her heart though it made her who she was?

The rideshare was fast, and she was soon back in the hotel lobby, so tired she could barely think. A clerk at reception gave her a new key card to get into the room, but her sisters were there to meet her with their warm embrace as soon as she opened the door.

"We packed up our things, you need a few hours of sleep before we leave. We got the earliest flight possible," Micki said. "I know you want to go home and sleep for days."

"Many," Margo answered. "I'll try to sleep."

As her sisters went to their room nearby, Margo showered and lay in the bed wrapped in the bathrobe that came with the room. She didn't sleep. Closing her eyes just brought back old hurts to pile onto the new. The way he distanced from her so easily… *Okay, don't think about it*, she chastised herself. Knowing she wouldn't be able to sleep, Margo got up and got dressed before making a cup of tea from the little Keurig on the desk. By the time her sisters came knocking she was already at the door.

"The reservations desk knows Gideon's coming back and he still has his key," Margo said. "I tried to pack up their things so it would be easier for him when he leaves with Claire."

"Does he know you're leaving?" Mia asked.

"I texted him and he didn't answer, so I'm assuming they got him a recliner or something so he could sleep in her room. Ready to go?"

"You didn't even sleep, did you?" Micki asked.

"I'll sleep in my own bed," Margo tried to smile. "Let's go home."

"Margo, you're kinda scaring us, acting like you did when Scott first died," Mia said calmly as they walked to the elevator. "Don't pull away from us, Gideon, or, well…life. Sometimes it's okay to face things head-on."

Margo turned to her sister as they got on the elevator and headed to the lobby. "Not all of us are as practical and strong as you. I have to deal with things in my own way."

Micki glanced at Mia, but neither sister said anything, and they kept it light at the airport and while they grabbed some food at a small diner close to their gate. Margo pretended to sleep the whole flight, but she was well aware of her sisters beside her. When the flight landed, Ryan was there in his Land Rover by the purple cement pylon marked number one outside the airport at arrivals.

"Hey, it's my favorite baby sister," Ryan said with a warm smile.

Micki cleared her throat. "Hello, you said that to me two days ago."

"I meant it, I can have two favorite sisters." Ryan laughed.

"We're your only sisters," Margo said, more to be a part of the levity even though she didn't feel it. She didn't want them to worry about her more.

That got a chuckle from her family, and she stepped out into the sunshine, appreciating the Carolina blue skies the whole drive home. At the inn, Enid greeted her with a warm hug, and Omar tackled her around the waist. Finally, she was in her room, replaced her dirty clothes in the small bag with clean ones and grabbed her keys off the dresser. Margo wondered if Gideon had seen her last text or did he even care that she was gone. No matter. She would come back with a clear head. Right now, she needed seclusion— her own little world. Downstairs, when the family saw her with her suitcase, they were instantly alarmed.

"Margo, no. Don't go off, please," Enid begged. "You don't have to do this."

"Are you going to be close by?" Mia asked.

"Wait, what's going on?" Ryan asked, obviously confused.

Micki sighed and used the band she was holding to push her hair back into a loose bun. "Margo handles things by running away to hide. She has a secret spot, and she goes off to lick her wounds there."

"I'm not hiding. I just need to not be here right now," Margo explained.

"Especially when Gideon comes home?" Ryan asked.

"I need—I need to think, okay? A lot went on." Margo felt the panic rising in her chest. "I need to just do what's right for me at this very moment in time."

"Then you go and heal how you need to," Ryan said with a nod. "I can't say how I'm going to act when Gideon comes home, but I don't like how he treated my sister."

Margo shook her head, picking up her bag. "It's not his fault. He went back to basic instincts, and I wasn't part of... I'll see you guys in a week or so. I'll check in, I promise. I love you guys."

"We love you, Margo. Remember that." Enid called out. Her voice was filled with sadness.

Outside, she went to her truck, it'd been waiting for her under the tree where she usually parked. Gideon's truck was close by, and she stared at it longingly for a moment before pulling away. If she returned, and decided they were no longer together—she'd be able to handle it. But now, she needed to grieve. Three hours later, she was in her secret place where she felt safe, where the pretty blue-and-white art deco wallpaper made her feel at home. The rocking chair in the corner held bright yellow cushions and a matching afghan for her to wrap herself up in when she sat and stared out at the water of Myrtle Beach through the sliding glass door.

Margo pushed open the glass door now and stepped outside. People were enjoying the beach, playing volleyball, getting a good tan, or swimming, taking advantage of the warm water. She smiled at the family close by who were under the shade of a cabana. Mom was rubbing suntan lotion on her little girl before putting a floaty duckie tube around her daughter's waist and leading her down to the water's edge.

The baby's squeals filled the air. This was clearly her first experience with the slow, lapping waves, Margo could tell. She wanted to do the same for Claire one day. Meanwhile, Dad ran down to the shore with their older son. She was looking at the family she wanted to have. Claire might have been the older sister running down to the water's edge with her dad, while Margo took care of a new sibling born into their loving family. She turned away from the scene and went inside, closing the sliding door firmly.

With the dull noise, a soft bed, snacks and all the food delivery services at her disposal, she could settle in to heal herself. Starting with a good cry.

Margo kicked off her shoes and curled under the thick comforter. The first hard sob she was holding in escaped, and she covered her mouth with her hand. Here she was free to feel and not have to show anyone her weakness. Margo cried, giving into the pain of a tattered heart.

CHAPTER FOURTEEN

GIDEON OPENED HIS eyes and Claire was sitting up in her hospital bed, smiling at him. Seeing her wide grin and her chubby hand waving at him made his heart sing. He pushed the plush recliner back up to its sitting position and moved to the toddler.

"Hey, sweetheart. You're up and ready to go, aren't you?" he asked with a small laugh.

Claire pressed her small forehead against his. "Daadee, go."

"You're ready to go?"

Claire nodded and put her hands on his cheeks before giving him a drool wet kiss on his face. "Daadee, Mama, Clbear, go."

"Clbear, that's a new one for your vocabulary." He laughed.

Mama, the word made him instantly think of Margo and he pulled out his phone to tell her they were okay and would be at the hotel soon. That's when he saw the message and his heart dropped.

Reservations knows that you will be back to the hotel.

I packed you guys up as best as I could.

I left with my sisters for home.

Gideon stared at the message for the longest time. Knowing that Margo had left put a fear in him that he couldn't describe. He'd faced some terrible things during his deployments, this kind of fear he'd only felt once before when he'd been afraid of losing Claire, and now here was the prospect of losing Margo. He'd reacted like a jerk, and in the process, hurt the woman he loved. How much? *Well, she's gone, you fool. She's very hurt*, he chastised himself.

The nurse came in with a tray and a smile. "Hey, you two. I have breakfast for the little one and coffee for you. The doctor came by last night to discharge her, but you both were well and truly asleep. So, he signed the paperwork and said to give it to you this morning. After breakfast you can go."

"Thanks so much," Gideon said gratefully as she exited the room.

While he helped Claire begin to eat, his heart raced. Their flight home was later this evening. What was he returning to? Angry family, that's for sure. He could deal with that. But what would he face with Margo? A goodbye? Gideon felt broken at the thought, so while Claire ate, he fixed his coffee and made a call to the only person he could think of that would listen and help him in this situation. He took a deep gulp of the coffee and grimaced at the bitter taste.

"Hello?" Ryan answered.

"Hey, it's Gideon," he replied.

There was a moment of silence before Ryan spoke. "I know, I'm just trying to figure out if I want to talk to you or hang up."

He expelled a breath. "That bad, huh?"

"You hurt a woman who doesn't have a malevolent bone in her body," Ryan explained. "You didn't see her when she got home yesterday. She's really upset, Gideon."

"I didn't even think. I just fell back into protection mode when dealing with Grant and Denise. Put up the walls and spoke out of turn, said some things I shouldn't have. Things I didn't mean," Gideon confessed. "It was a gut reaction, and now I might have lost a special woman that I love with every part of me."

Ryan sighed. "I guess I still like you after all, but you know those sisters and Enid protect each other better than any Spartan army. It's them you're going to need help from. Margo, she's the one that loves hard and hurts the most. Micki, Mia and Enid, they'll stand up for her against anyone. Even you, if they think you don't love her enough, or in the right way."

"I can accept that. I just need to come home and face her, and them." Gideon wiped Claire's face.

"You'll be dealing with them first, bro. Margo is gone," Ryan told him.

His breath stilled in his chest. Ryan's words were like ice-cold water being doused over his head.

"Gone where?"

Gideon added the rest of the fruit to the oatmeal that Claire was devouring. Claire clapped in happiness and continued her breakfast. All the while he couldn't quite comprehend the words, *Margo is gone*.

"That's the big question, my friend. She came home, but looking at her, you could see she was barely holding it together. The next thing we knew she was holding her suitcase again and said she needed to be alone. Enid begged her not to go. Micki said she's done this before, gone away. Mia seemed to understand and reminded Margo to check in. She has a place she likes to go to escape the world, until she can shore up her feelings."

"So, they let her go, not knowing where she will be?" Gideon asked incredulously. "Why?"

"Because that's what she needs," Ryan snapped. "Gideon, your words hurt her beyond measure.

Take responsibility for that. You made her feel like she didn't matter. She has nothing to make up for, you do."

Gideon listened to Ryan's blunt words and knew his friend was right. He didn't want to lose Margo. She loved him and Claire completely, and he had to show her that he would do the same.

"Thanks, Ryan, for being so honest," Gideon said. "I'll see you later tonight."

"Sounds like a plan, brother," Ryan encouraged. "I'll have your back. Travel safe with the Claire Bear."

"Will do," Gideon said. "And thanks again, Ryan."

Deservedly, he would face a lot more hurt and anger from Mia and Micki when he got home. He was ready for it because he knew he was in the wrong. The only thing he wanted was to see Margo and ask her to forgive him. He'd promise never to hurt her like that again. After Claire finished breakfast, he got her dressed so they could leave. Just like Margo said, the rental car was parked close to the ER door.

Without too much fuss, he got them back to the hotel so they could get cleaned up and changed before leaving for the airport. Between check-in and the flight, it would take hours for them to reach the inn. Gideon had a sandwich delivered by room service, and Claire ate again, while he made sure her cold cups were clean and ready for her milk once they got through TSA. Checking out of the hotel was a simple process. Gideon turned to walk out with Claire and their bags, but stopped abruptly when Grant Wells came through the revolving door. He and his former in-law stared at each other. Gideon noted the older man's haggard look as he approached them.

"Gideon," Grant said.

"What?" Gideon knew his tone was clipped, but from all he'd faced from Trudy's father, he didn't trust him.

"I came to say…" Grant hesitated and shoved his hands in his pockets, took them out and stared at Gideon once more. "I came to say sorry for everything. For the way we treated you—I treated you. For interfering at every turn with you and Trudy. Blaming you for her death was wrong. We—I couldn't face the truth, because it hurt too much to think that my rigid ways caused more harm than good."

Gideon couldn't believe what he was hearing and frowned. "Why now, Grant? Just yesterday you were blaming me for what Denise did and wanted me arrested. You made my life awful, before and after Trudy, and you are not the apologizing type. So what game are you playing here?"

"No game." Grant's expression softened. "I got

to see Denise this morning, and she was quite adamant that if I didn't change my ways, like she'd said, she was gone. I've loved that woman for over forty years and to hear her say that made me really think about how I hurt my family, and that includes you."

"You have never called me family," Gideon pointed out. "It's kind of unbelievable that you changed your way of thinking overnight."

"I dreamt of Trudy last night." Grant looked at Gideon, who watched tears settle in the older man's eyes. "She was in a field of sunflowers and the light cast a halo around her red hair. She looked at me—stared—a wide smile spread across her face, and she said 'Daddy' as if she was genuinely happy to see me."

"Grant, you don't have to…" Gideon began.

Grant raised his hand. "No, let me finish, Gideon. This has been a long time coming, even if I didn't want to admit it. Trudy—um." He cleared the emotion from this throat. "She said, 'it's okay, Daddy, I forgive you, but you need to stop being so angry. It's okay to let me go and let Gideon be happy so my Claire is happy.' Then the image of her faded as she went off to join people in the distance. Then I woke up."

Gideon nodded, seeing that Grant was truly affected by his dream.

The older man shrugged. "Maybe it was just

a dream. Or my subconscious trying to give me what I need to face my own guilt. Whether it was either or both, I felt different when I woke up. I cried like the day we put her in the grave, and then I went to see Denise."

"What did she think?" Gideon asked.

Grant smiled. "That the dream was a gift because Trudy wants us to live and be happy. I choose to believe what Denise believes so we can move on and try something different in our lives. It meant, first, I had to apologize to you, and if you let us when we're through the process, we'd like to visit you, Claire and Margo. To let our extended family know we love them, and we want them in our lives."

His words floored Gideon. "I, we would like that Grant, truly. It's all I ever wanted."

"That wife you have, Margo, she is a keeper." Grant grinned. "Reminded me of what I loved about Denise. A kindness wrapped in strength, a real partner who will always keep you grounded but uplift you, too, for the rest of your life."

"I know, she's amazing." Gideon smiled, knowing he was close to losing all that if he couldn't make amends with Margo.

"Do you mind if I give Claire a hug?" Grant asked. "I've missed that."

Gideon handed her over to him. "Hey, Claire Bear, look who's here? It's Grandpa."

Claire smiled and patted Grant's nose as if playing a game. Grant held her tight and rocked her a little before pressing a kiss on her head.

"You remind me so much of your mom. I know your daddy will do right by you," he whispered and kissed her hair again. "Go to Daddy, now. Time to go home, but we will see you soon."

"Yes, you will," Gideon promised and held out his hand to shake Grant's. "Thanks, I appreciate you coming to me like this. We'll make it work."

Grant nodded. "We sure will, I have a lot of work to do, but this was an important step."

"For both of us," Gideon replied. "We have to get going. But you and Denise video call us anytime."

"I don't know how to do that. I can barely use my cell." Grant chuckled.

"We'll talk you guys through it." Gideon smiled. "Say bye-bye to Grandpa, Claire."

"Bye, Pa." She waved.

Gideon laughed. "She's learning, but it's usually the first word and the last syllable."

"She'll figure it out," Grant said. "Travel safe."

Claire waved until they got outside and into the car. An hour later, they were through the TSA PreCheck, another thing that Margo had taken care of and made him appreciate her all over again. He had so much to thank her for and apologize for. When the plane finally took off, heading toward Charlotte, he started to count the minutes until he was back at Ballad Inn and finding the woman he loved.

GIDEON STARED AT the heavy mahogany door of the Ballad Inn before he put the code into the keypad lock and stepped inside with Claire and their luggage. The wide entryway to the family room allowed the people inside to see that they had come in. Micki was the first to rush over to him and Claire.

"There's the sweetest Claire Bear in the world!" Micki gushed and took the baby from him. Claire was excited to see them all, and she kicked her little legs to get down so she could run to everyone, especially her favorite friend Omar.

"Hi, Micki," Gideon said politely.

She inclined her head. "Gideon."

Ice cold.

He followed Claire and Micki into the family room. Enid looked at him while her hands crocheted with the soft wool she worked on in the evenings before bed.

"Gideon, there is dinner being kept warm for you and Claire. Dessert is in the fridge," Enid said, even the usual warmth in her voice was absent.

"Ryan said you know Margo isn't here, so we're going to need to talk," Mia said briskly.

"We need to know where things are with you, so when she comes home, we have a plan."

"A plan for what?" Gideon asked.

"In case you plan to break my sister's heart even more than you have already," Micki answered bluntly.

"Shouldn't I be discussing this with her?" Gideon asked with a frown.

"Abort!" Ryan tried to cough the word out a second time. "Abort."

Too late.

Mia stood. "Yes, but it was the two of us, who brought her home. Who watched her hold herself together so she wouldn't shatter in front of anyone. We were the ones who saw the distance you placed between you and her while Claire was missing. While I understand you were under an enormous amount of stress then, you hurt my sister so much that she left home so she could put herself back together again."

"It's only happened one other time," Micki said. "When her fiancé passed, and now we know the extent of that hurt. For her to leave this house, and us… Gideon, she's in a bad way."

"So, yes. *We're* going to talk," Mia finished.

"I'm going to take Claire to the kitchen so she can eat. And Omar will help keep her company." Enid put her crochet things back in the basket by her favorite chair.

"And I get a second dessert?" Omar asked hopefully.

"One more small piece of peach cobbler," Enid said firmly. "I swear, all the men in this family have such a sweet tooth."

"Save me a piece?" Gideon asked, shooting Enid a quick smile.

Enid returned the smile. "I will, you big lovable man. Even though you don't think sometimes and acted without considering the consequences. But you better fix it with my Margo, or you will be banned from desserts for life."

"That's a hard punishment," Ryan murmured. "You still love me, right, Enid?"

"You're not getting a third piece, Ryan," she called over her shoulder.

"Foiled again," he said under his breath.

"Everything settled in Tacoma?" Mia asked.

"Yes. I don't have to go back. Things are even settled with Grant and Denise, which is a shock, but it's all good on that front," Gideon answered. "I know I made Margo feel like she wasn't part of the new family we're creating. But I love her, guys. She's my world and I was wrong, I behaved out of panic and fear."

Mia sighed. "Family is super important to Margo, the family dinners at night are to make sure we never grow apart."

He nodded. "She told me a lot about when

you all were younger, and that it's changed here in the last year and you're closer with your parents now."

"We are," Mia confirmed. "Margo remembers more of our parents jumping in and out of our lives than Micki. Sometimes when it hurt, Margo just needed to go and be on her own. Your attitude back in Washington caused hers in a way. She gives so much of herself to everyone, to help them heal and recover, sometimes there's not enough kindness and thought left for herself. That and she doesn't like for people to see her break."

"I did that to her." Gideon sat down and put his head in his hands. "I never wanted her to feel like this."

"When she comes home, you tell her that," Ryan encouraged. "I've read about some cases where past trauma events have been especially tough on those in the military and their partners. Also, other family members and even co-workers."

He sat back. "That gives me an idea. I should ask her if she'd be willing to try couples' counseling at the Veterans Center, so we can communicate better. Learn to cope with each other's triggers and understand one another more. Especially in the tense times. It's one of the main things that the military advises when troops come home to reintegrate into family life. I should've thought of that sooner. But we were caught up with everything else and focused on the hearing."

Micki nodded. "Sounds like a solid plan. Just as long as you love my sister."

"I do. I see my forever with her." Gideon meant every word. "Does that mean you forgive your new brother, and I can start teasing you again?"

"I forgive you, but no." Micki mock glared at him, and her mouth twitched with a smile. "Even though you're going to do it anyway."

"I definitely will. I won't deny it." He grinned at her but sobered quickly. "No one knows where she is? Waiting for her to come home will kill me. I don't know how to feel without her here with me."

"No, none of us know where she is," Mia said. "You might just have to wait and give her the time she needs. But it's getting late, and Claire needs her bath and bed."

"True." Gideon sighed. "I'll tackle the problem of her whereabouts tomorrow."

Mia yawned. "I've been exhausted. Flying back and forth from one coast to the other in a matter of twenty-four hours has taken it out of me. We can talk more at breakfast."

"Let's get you home." Ryan stood with Mia. "We're tired, and our boy will be hopped up on cobbler."

"Nothing stops Omar from sleeping," Mia said dryly. "When he starts school in a month, it's going to be a trial to get him up in the morning."

"At least with middle school, he can get up at seven," Ryan pointed out. "High school will be the kicker. G'night, Gideon, glad to have you home."

"Glad to be back," he answered.

He followed the others from the family room. Mia and Ryan collected Omar, who finished his glass of cold milk and went with his parents happily. After they left and everyone else adjourned to their rooms, he ate his dinner with a very messy Claire before taking her upstairs and getting her cleaned up and into her pajamas. With the traveling and all the activity, gratefully, Claire was snoozing as soon as she was in her crib.

It was when he went to bed and stared at the ceiling, not knowing where Margo was in the world at that moment, that Gideon realized he missed her so much he ached. It was obvious his life had changed in the best possible way after meeting Margo. He had to prove his love wasn't fleeting when the chips were down. He drifted off, into a troubled sleep.

GIDEON'S EYES POPPED open the next morning. He had a plan—well, a notion. Claire was standing in her crib, bouncing around, when he got up and went over to her. As he lifted her high, she began to squeal.

"Hey, my sweet girl." He made kissing noises at her neck, and her baby giggles grew even louder. "Today, I'm going to get your mommy home."

"Mamamamama," Claire repeated and then pursed her lips to make the pfffts sound she seemed to enjoy.

"Yep, we should get our day started and see if I can make this work."

He washed and changed Claire and after breakfast, took her to Ellen's Tiny Tots Academy. He wanted her schedule to get back to normal as quickly as possible, and today he had an important mission in mind.

"Everything went well in Tacoma?" Ellen asked as he signed his daughter in.

"Perfect, I got full custody. The case is all over," he said, smiling while Claire toddled off to join the other kids without saying goodbye. "She didn't even give me a kiss bye-bye."

Ellen laughed. "Oh, Hun, toddlers have tunnel vision, and it only gets worse as they grow up."

"I guess I'll have to savor the affection now as much as I can."

"Please do, because teen girls have the ability to break even the strongest man or woman," Ellen teased. "Tell Margo I said hi."

"Will do. Bye, Claire Bear!" he called and got no reaction from his baby girl.

Now it was time to put Operation Margo into play. He walked back to the house quickly and found Mia in the office. Luckily Micki was there as well perched on the corner of her sister's desk.

"Hey, shouldn't you be on campus?" Gideon asked.

"Apparently, it's summer, so only the one class and now she's done with physical therapy for her hand, so she is here to generally annoy me," Mia answered.

"I am not," Micki declared. "I'm asking her to go to a conference in Atlanta with me."

"No, she's asking me to go to some sci-fi, fantasy convention, and she needs me to dress up with her to match some anime thing she watches or reads," Mia explained. "I stopped listening when she wanted us to be painted pink under the very skimpy costumes, she showed me."

"Are *these* inappropriate?" Micki demanded showing Gideon a picture on her cell.

His eyes widened. "Pretty sure that's the definition of inappropriate, kiddo."

"It's like the dress all over again," Mia pointed out.

Micki threw up her hands. "I can't win in this house."

"Has Margo checked in today?" Gideon asked, changing the subject.

"She texted around six a.m. asking if you guys had made it home safely," Mia said. "Sorry, but no disclosure on her whereabouts though."

"Do you guys share locations on your phone?" Gideon asked.

Mia nodded. "Yes, we do, primarily to make sure Micki hasn't run off to join a band of travelling renaissance faire performers that sell their arts and crafts across the country."

"One Ren-Faire idea at eighteen and they never let you forget it," Micki muttered.

"I can find her from your shared locations. I just need to see your phone and access the map feature," Gideon said in excitement.

"Are you sure we should do this and not wait for her to come home?" Mia asked hesitantly.

"Ryan told me how he almost lost you. Would you want him to wait?" Gideon asked. "Or would you want him to come sweep you off your feet, declare his love, and promise to fix whatever he broke."

"Kinda what he did," Micki pointed out to Mia. "And why didn't we ever think of this?"

"Good point, Gideon." Mia handed her phone over to him. "Find her and bring her home. Our wonderful sister has got to stop hiding from the world when she's hurt. And we didn't think of it, Micki, because we haven't had to find your location in years."

Micki looked proud. "I call that growth."

Mia shook her head at her sister before turning her attention to Gideon. "Any luck?"

Gideon pressed the location feature and saw the pin icon with Margo's face. His heartbeat picked up as he pressed the icon, and it took him to the map feature and stopped on her location.

"Sand Piper Resort?" Gideon said and looked at her sisters.

Mia's face bloomed in recognition. "That was the first place she worked after she became a chef. It's about three hours away. She figured out she hated how they ran the kitchen and treated people, so she came home. Six months after that we turned our house into the bed-and-breakfast, then she cooked while in nursing school."

"She's been crafty all this time." Micki chuckled. "She said she loved the views, remember? Let's go get our girl."

"Not us, just me." Gideon looked from one sister to the next. "I love you both, I really do, but I need to do this alone. I have to fix it by myself."

Mia nodded. "Yes, you do. We can pick up Claire from daycare if you're not back in time."

"Thanks, that would be perfect. I sent Margo's location to my phone." He went around the desk to kiss Mia's head and then lifted Micki off her feet in a hug that made her squeak. "I'm going to bring Margo back to the place and people she loves. If she'll let me."

"I don't think you'll have any problem with that," Mia said, smiling. "Drive safely and below the speed limit."

"Roger that."

Gideon rushed to his truck. Once he was behind the wheel, he got his phone positioned in its holder so he could see directions without messing with it while driving. Turning out of Ballad Inn, he was focused on the road and a small smile crossed his lips. In about three hours, he would see his Margo and pull her into his arms and ask for her forgiveness. Their love was worth saving and he hoped she felt the same way too.

MARGO WATCHED THE scenes from the flat-screen change from one to the next. She usually loved her old murder mystery shows, but today, it was just a way to pass the time. The vertical blinds to the balcony were open and so was the door to let the sea breeze in. She didn't hide away in the darkness, in fact she needed the sun more than ever. Yesterday she sat on the balcony and watched the sunset, it filled her with peace. Enough to let her know she would survive this too, regardless how it turned out with her and Gideon.

It would take time because thinking about losing him, and Claire, was something unbearable. The exact thing she didn't want to have happen did. She fell in love with a strong, loyal, kind man and his sweet daughter only to lose them.

Her taking a break before facing the world again had steps. She did all the crying the day before, ate through most of her snacks the day after that, and today was the quiet stage where she didn't even want to think. She'd texted Mia to let her know all was well and found out that Gideon and Claire were back. Margo knew she would have to go home sooner rather than later. To deal with the consequences wherever they led. *Later. I should go walk on the beach*, Margo thought looking to the open door. Maybe strolling along the surf with the waves washing up on her feet was what she needed to make her smile. A knock on the front door made her sigh, and she looked at her phone screen. Twelve thirty. It was around the time for the cleaning service to come to her floor. More often than not, most guests were already out enjoying the sun, surf or activities in Myrtle Beach.

Margo opened the door, speaking as she did so. "Thanks, but I don't need your cleaning services today, just some extra…"

She was staring at Gideon's face.

"Towels."

Gideon gave a small laugh and held up his

hands. "No towels here, but she is at the end of the hall if you need me to grab you some."

He was back in his usual work clothes—plaid shirt over a white T-shirt, faded jeans, and his dusty boots. His eyes were a swirl of emotion, hope, sorrow, hesitancy, and combined with tiredness as well.

"What are you doing here? How did you find me?" Margo asked, holding off any emotion.

"You share your location with your sisters, and I used the map option on Mia's phone," Gideon explained.

"I bet she had no trouble giving you that," she said dryly.

"I asked the receptionist for your room number. Told her I was your husband and I had come to join you. Don't blame your sisters. They want you to be happy."

"And you're supposed to do that?" Margo asked.

"Can I come in and we can talk?" Gideon shifted from one foot to the other. "It looks kind of weird, me standing at the door like this, speaking to you. The maid is giving me funny looks."

Margo stepped aside. "I guess, but don't plan on staying. This is my nest."

Gideon chuckled and looked around. "Nest, huh? How many snacks does one person need?"

"Enough for an extended stay." Margo sat on the bed. "What do you want from me, Gideon?"

"To come home." Gideon pulled a chair from the small dinette and sat in front of her. "Margo, I am the biggest fool in the world, and I handled that whole situation wrong. In the process, I hurt you, and you are the last person who should ever be hurt."

"Do you know what hurt me? What cut me to the core?" Margo asked. "When you made me feel like I was on the outside looking in. When you said to me, you're Claire's father and you make the decisions. I thought I was your partner. That we are, were, in this together. You know how much I love her."

Gideon shook his head. "I never wanted you to feel that way. I just got so scared. Grant and Denise have resources I can't even think of. All I saw was a ploy to steal Claire away, their plan B to keep her with them. I acted like a complete jerk to the person I love."

"But do you love me, Gideon?" Margo asked. "Or was I a means to an end? I read how quickly soldiers fall in love and then go directly to marriage. Maybe this is one of those times."

"No, not at all." Gideon cupped her face. "I'm not someone who sees love around every corner. I saw a woman who loved everything with her entire heart and that included me and my daughter. I reacted badly. I was in a place I had come to hate, with people I couldn't trust. I went back to old behaviors that worked for me then. Built a fortress around myself and Claire, and I left you outside—my love, I am so sorry I did that. I can promise you that it will never happen again."

What he was saying sounded good, but when the chips were down, would he react the same way and expect her to overlook it? She couldn't do that because it was her belief that you treated everyone how you would want to be treated.

"Until the next crisis." Margo shook her head. "I can't build hope on sweet words and empty promises."

"They are sweet words but there's nothing empty about these promises." Gideon pulled a brochure from his pocket. "Counseling for veterans and their families. There's a particular program for newly married couples. I'd like to go, if you'd consider it." He handed her the pamphlet. "My counselor for my PTSD said he'd recommend someone for us. It would help to give us a chance to learn about each other and form a strong bond as a couple."

Margo read through the brochure carefully. There were many programs and tools to utilize for both of them, including family activities that would include Claire.

"Are you serious about this?" Margo asked bluntly. She'd had counseling after the trauma of what happened in the accident and believed that it could help.

Gideon nodded. "We can go together to sign up. Margo, I love you and Claire loves you too. Please forgive me and let's try to make this work. A happy future that we all deserve."

Margo looked into his eyes and saw how genuine he was being, how he was speaking from the heart. She released a deep breath and took the plunge. "You hurt me Gideon—down to my very core." She pressed a fist against her chest. "Sometimes I think I love too hard."

"Honey, no." Gideon took her hands and kissed them. "That's what makes you the most incredible woman in the world. You are beautiful inside and out. I won't ever throw away the gift you've given by loving me."

Margo learned forward and pressed her forehead against his. "You gave me a gift as well, loving me, sharing your daughter with me. Let's do the VA counseling and start our family on a solid foundation."

"Starting with love?" Gideon asked and kissed her quick on the lips.

"You'll always have my love." Margo smiled. "I'm making a home for my marine and my daughter."

"How about a walk along the shore for a little bit? Mia said she can pick Claire up."

"Then by all means, lead the way," she said and kissed him fast in return. "Then we can go home."

The walk along the shore was a good one. They talked, and he filled her in on Grant coming to the hotel to make amends.

"I'm so happy he chose to try a new beginning and work with you," Margo said, trying to tuck her braids away from the wind. "Denise needs this. All of you do, to heal."

"Don't." He stopped her from messing with her braids. "You look gorgeous all beach windswept like this."

Gideon leaned down and they shared a kiss, one that chased away her fears and sorrows, and replaced those feelings with love.

"In that case, we should definitely plan a week at the coast before summer is through," she said when he lifted his head, and they began to walk again. "I'm sure Claire would love it."

"That sounds perfect." Gideon's voice held contentment.

Later that day, after the beach and collecting her things, Margo followed Gideon home in her truck. As soon as the door to the inn swung open, chaos ensued. She was hugged by her sisters, then Omar who held Monty.

"I kept him happy and fed—well, all the animals," Omar said with pride in his voice.

"I knew you'd be the best man for the job." Margo hugged him.

"Everything okay now?" Enid asked after kissing her cheek. "The path is clear?"

"We're getting there," Margo said looking over at Gideon. "We've got a plan, and a family that's worth fighting for."

"You did good, Gideon." Micki handed Claire to Margo.

Ryan clapped him on the back. "I'm glad it turned out well, bro."

Gideon gave a huge sigh and a grin. "Me too."

It felt so good to hold the baby, that Margo kept Claire in her arms for a long time. Gideon stepped behind her to wrap his arms around them both. She felt her heart begin to heal.

"With that said, let's get to dinner!" Enid clapped her hands and cheered.

Margo looked at the noisy, laughing ragtag group and loved them all the more. Watching Gideon get Claire into her high chair. And Ryan lending a hand to Enid who was laying out the meal. Omar and Micki arguing about comic book heroes, until Mia jumped in and got everyone seated. This was her family, the man she loved, and her new daughter included. Gideon's eyes landed on her, and he gave her a wink.

This was home.

EPILOGUE

Four Months Later

MARGO CAME BOUNDING down the main stairs of the inn just as Mia came through the front door.

"I have news!" they said simultaneously and grinned at each other.

"What's all the hubbub...bubs?" Micki walked out of the kitchen, wiping her hands.

"We both have exciting news it seems," Margo said and then frowned. "What were you doing in the kitchen?"

"Making cherry preserves from the first batch of fruit from the season," Micki said casually.

They both looked at her in shock.

"What?" she asked in a defensive tone. "Margo Ballad, you are not the only one who can utilize a kitchen."

"Oh, I know—we know, but you've never shown any interest in anything in the kitchen but eating," Mia pointed out. "But hey, good on you for making preserves. We'll have a nice supply for the fall."

"Thank you. I appreciate your trust in my skill." Micki turned. "If you both have news, maybe you should wait until dinner tonight. It's Mom and Dad's first night back since they've decided to stay here for the rest of the year. It's a great time to share good news with the entire family."

"Excellent idea," Margo said. "Tonight, it is! Micki, wait for me. I want to make sure you're not destroying my kitchen."

"I'm not. Go away," her sister called out.

Still, Margo followed and found the kitchen intact. Summer had given way to the fall and while the weather could be warm in the daytime, at night, you noticed the chill of the season coming. Ballad Inn was decked out for Halloween like most of Sardis Woods. With the falling leaves of various colors, Charlotte had turned into another picturesque scene that could be found on a postcard, and in their neighborhood, Ballad Inn was at the center.

She, Gideon and Claire were happy. The counseling sessions at the VA clinic had brought them even closer, and by next spring they would be in their new home in Crawford's pasture. That night, at dinner it was a loud joyous affair with lots of joking and fun stories being told. Rosie and Brian Ballad had got to spoil their grandchildren Omar and Claire just a bit more than their daughters would have liked. They had all gone to the fall festival in Uptown Charlotte.

"Okay, guys!" Mia called out. "Margo and I have news we would like to share."

"Do you now," Rosie Ballad said with a smile. "Let me guess, Mia has a new big accounting client and, Margo, you got a promotion."

"Nope on that for me, Mom," Margo said.

"Ditto," Mia answered. "Margs, you go first."

"No, you go." Margo smiled, her excitement growing.

"No, you…" Mia began.

"Someone, please tell us something," Ryan said around a mouthful of dessert.

Today's dessert was the last of the strawberries from the garden that topped a shortcake with apple crumble in the center. As usual the men in the family, including her father, ate the sweet treat with gusto. It was official. Dessert was their collective weakness.

"I'm pregnant!"

Mia and Margo said the words together, and then stared at each other in shock.

"No way!" Margo said in amazement.

Mia nodded happily. "Yes way!"

Gideon started to cough as the bite of cake he was eating went down the wrong way, and Ryan dropped his fork while staring, mouth agape, at his wife.

Brian Ballad was slapping Gideon on the back while Micki held his arms up. Claire thought it was huge fun; she was squealing and clapping her hands. Omar continued to eat while looking around in interest, and Enid and Rosie began to cry.

"Wh-at?" Gideon wheezed out.

Ryan still hadn't said a word.

"Way to drop a bombshell, sisters. I'm going to be the best aunt ever! Do you hear me? Like ever! All these kids are going to be super spoiled, and not just with love!"

"My family is great," Omar said before tucking more dessert into his mouth and grinning.

Mia came around and tapped Ryan's face. "Hey, talk to me."

"Are you sure?" Ryan asked. "They said…"

"We just had to stop stressing and let nature take its course," Mia said, beaming.

"We went from no kids to…two." Ryan pushed the chair back so quickly to embrace Mia that she gave a surprised laugh. "Is it legal to be this happy?"

Gideon, over his coughing fit, moved slowly to Margo and rested his hand on hers.

She smiled at him. "So, it's happening a little sooner than we'd thought. But baby makes four. Are you happy?"

"Overjoyed," he whispered. "I love you so much."

"I love you too," she said softly as Gideon held her close.

"Well, we're not going anywhere until our second round of grandchildren are here," Rosie said between laughter and tears, gesturing to her husband. "I should learn how to knit."

"I'll teach you." Enid dabbed the tears on her cheeks with her table napkin. "How this family has grown in front of our eyes!"

Margo felt the joy that filled their family home and knew it would only get better from here. Mia and Ryan hugged Omar between them, while Gideon lifted Claire into his arms and Margo looked lovingly at them.

"That leaves only you now, Micki, to find that perfect someone," Margo teased. Mia nodded in agreement.

"Oh, no, you two, do not hex me with your ooey-gooey love juju," Micki warned and quickly stepped back from the group. "I'm way too young and too busy to be settling down."

Margo laughed at her younger sister's wary gaze, knowing that love can find a way when you least expect it.

* * * * *

Look for Micki's story, coming soon from author Kellie A. King and Harlequin Heartwarming!